THE PLAYERS plumbs the hearts and minds of the men who play international tennis for money, fame, and love . . . and the women who follow them . . . And the others, like Mike Wilder.

Cynical star reporter for a prestigious American sports magazine, he's come to Wimbledon to renew an old female acquaintance and cover the matches – and finds himself the target of a woman in love . . . and a murderer on the prowl!

Recent Titles by Gary Brandner from Severn House

THE BOILING POOL
THE BRAIN EATERS
CARRION
TRIBE OF THE DEAD

THE PLAYERS

Gary Brandner

SEVERN
SH
HOUSE

This first hardcover edition published in Great Britain 1997 by
SEVERN HOUSE PUBLISHERS LTD of
9–15 High Street, Sutton, Surrey SM1 1DF.
This first hardcover edition published in the USA 1997 by
SEVERN HOUSE PUBLISHERS INC., of
595 Madison Avenue, New York, NY 10022.

British Library Cataloguing in Publication Data

Brandner, Gary
        The Players
        1.   Wimbledon Tennis Tournament – Fiction
        2.   Tennis players – Attitudes
        3.   Romantic Suspense Novels
        1. Title
        813.5'4 [F]

        ISBN 0-7278-5242-6

Typeset by Palimpsest Book Production Limited,
Polmont, Stirlingshire, Scotland.
Printed and bound in Great Britain by
Hartnolls Ltd, Bodmin, Cornwall.

I

Mike Wilder stood on the flat roof of the Players' Tea Room and gazed around him at the white-lined tennis courts. From his vantage point twenty-five feet above the ground Mike could see most of the sixteen grass courts, empty now where the action would begin in three days in the biggest of all tournaments . . . Wimbledon.

The fussy little man standing next to Mike was an official of the All England Tennis Club, the organisation that ran Wimbledon, and he made no secret of the fact that he was not happy about showing the American journalist round prior to the tournament. He had a hundred other details he should be attending to. However, there was nothing he could do about it. Mike's name and that of his magazine carried enough weight to get him in almost anywhere but Buckingham Palace.

This visit to Wimbledon had been a last-minute idea of Mike's. A message radioed from his transatlantic flight had set it up, and he had come directly here from Heathrow Airport. In addition to the cover story he was doing for *Sportsweek*, Mike would continue to file his syndicated daily column. He thought there might be a thousand words or so in how the arena looked before the battle.

He sniffed derisively at the word 'battle'. Mike's own sport at the University of Missouri had been boxing, and at forty-one he still had the build of a light-heavyweight and a slightly bent nose to go with it. In his personal ranking of sports for toughness, tennis fell somewhere between needlepoint and tag.

The truth was that after twelve years writing about sports, professional and amateur, Mike was having serious doubts as to whether any of them had redeeming social value. In an age when governments toppled, leaders fell, nations starved, and races warred, what excuse was there for grown men to make their living playing games? Closer to home, what excuse was there for a grown man to make his living writing about them?

'What are those flowers they're planting out there?' Mike asked the fussy man, whose name was Landers.

'They're hydrangeas. We have them put in every year for the tournament. They're part of the tradition.'

'I see.' Mike stared without appreciation at the pink and blue flowers. Well, why not? If a football game can associate itself with roses, and a horse race with black-eyed Susans, what was the matter with hydrangeas for a tennis tournament?

Tennis. Mike tried to work up some enthusiasm for the game. There was no denying it had changed dramatically in the past ten or fifteen years. It was a big money sport now like all the rest of them. And the payments were at last above the table, now that the staid old rulers of the game had decided the presence of professionals would not defile their stadiums, and had finally allowed them to play in the hallowed tournaments.

The game itself had changed too. Gone for ever were the patball days with their ritualistic displays of court etiquette. There were still a few of the old-fashioned gentlemen players on the international circuit, but they were usually watching the play from the stands by the quarter-final round. The men who stayed around to collect the big prizes were tough, sun-browned fighters who played the game any way they had to in order to win. Mike had once seen an American player who learned his game on Cleveland playgrounds call his gentle French opponent a name so foul that the Frenchman almost fainted on the court. The American didn't lose another game for the rest of the match.

Wimbledon, of course, retained more decorum than other courts. Here the serious, knowledgeable crowd in the three-tiered stands around the Centre Court would still cry, 'Shame!' at a player who displayed bad manners. But the players were just as tough as anywhere else. They had to be.

Mike scribbled some notes on his spiral pad and said to Mr Landers, 'Where does the name "Wimbledon" come from? I couldn't find it in American reference books.'

6

'I dare say,' Landers sniffed in a tone that conveyed his low opinion of American reference books. 'Wimbledon has been the scene of many an historic battle. Canning and Castlereagh, Tierney and Pitt, Lord Winchelsea against the Duke of Wellington. Ethelbert of Kent fought Ceawlin of the West Saxons here. At that time it was known as Wibbas dune, meaning home of the Saxon, Wibba. Through the years the name has evolved through Wipandune, Wibaldowne, Wymblyton and finally to Wimbledon.'

I'm sorry I asked, Mike thought, but what he said was, 'Interesting. Can we walk down now and take a look at the Centre Court?'

'If you wish,' Landers said coolly, annoyed at having his history lecture dismissed so abruptly.

They walked down through the glassed-in Players' Tea Room where the action for the next two weeks would be as furious as out on the courts. This was where the hustlers, the wheeler dealers, the money men would vie for the players' signatures on deals that would run to six figures for some. Here recruiters for other tournaments, advertising men with endorsement contracts, representatives from sporting goods firms would go after the big names – the winners. What was left over would go to the lesser players for a lesser price. The Players' Tea Room was sometimes called the meat market of international tennis.

A groundsman watched Mike suspiciously as he walked out on to the smooth, hard surface of the Centre Court. The man's scowl implied that he wouldn't put it past the American to wear spikes on his shoes.

The grass was not the velvety green described so enthusiastically by the British press; rather, it was brownish in colour, but the quality of the surface was excellent. At other tennis clubs Mike had seen grass that was a rich shade of emerald, but which tore away in ugly divots under the players' feet.

It was here on the Centre Court, surrounded by the twelve-sided grandstand, that the defending Wimbledon champion, Ron Hopper of Australia, would open the tournament on Monday in his first-round match. And it was here that two weeks later this year's champion would be crowned. Hopper would play all of his matches on one of the three courts that had a grandstand to accommodate the people who wanted to watch the champion. The other players would open on one of the outlying courts. These were separated from one another by paths ten feet wide, lined with benches. It was on these courts that most of the doubles, mixed doubles and women's singles matches would be played. In spite of Billie Jean King, the big attraction at Wimbledon, as at most international tournaments, was the men's singles.

Mike nodded his thanks to the groundsman and walked off the court. The man inspected Mike's footprints, then lifted his eyes in apparent relief that his turf remained intact.

Mike walked out to the car park and said good-bye to Mr Landers, who looked no less relieved than the groundsman at the American's departure. He climbed into the waiting taxi whose driver studied a racing paper while the meter clicked merrily.

'Regency House,' Mike said.

'Right you are,' came the cheery reply.

No wonder he's cheery, Mike thought. This trip will add up to a tidy day's pay for him. Outside, the gathering dusk pulled a curtain across the streets of Greater London. Mike leaned back in the seat and tried to think of something *he* could be cheery about. Paula Teal. He would be seeing Paula tonight. For the first time since his plane took off from Kennedy some ten hours before, Mike Wilder smiled.

2

The man with the knife eased deeper into the shadows. A film of perspiration oiled his face in spite of the chill in the hotel corridor. He wore a loose-fitting camel-hair jacket. One of his hands was tucked inside the lapel, his fingers gripping the hilt of a heavy hunting knife.

From where he stood the man could see the closed doors to the three lifts that carried guests up from the foyer. Opposite him, just before the corridor made a right-angle turn, was room 313. Every little while the man would stop watching the lifts and turn to stare at the door. He waited.

'Your room is 313, Mr Wilder,' the receptionist said. 'I hope you'll enjoy your stay in London.'

'Thanks.' Mike Wilder tried to pump sincerity into his voice, but without much success. He did not like London. As yet he had no reason for not liking the city, but he didn't need one. All he had seen so far was Heathrow Airport, Wimbledon and the inside of his taxi. Nothing specific to dislike, but he would find something. In his mood of general depression there was not a city on earth that would have pleased him.

'You're here for Wimbledon, I expect,' the receptionist said.

'That's right. Are you a tennis fan?'

'I'm afraid not, sir,' the receptionist admitted. He leaned across the desk as though to pass on some slightly scandalous information. 'Actually, I'm rather more keen on rugby league. More of a man's game, it seems to me, than skipping about in shorts and tennis shoes.'

Mike lowered his voice to match that of the other man. 'Actually, I'm inclined to agree with you. But don't tell my editor.'

The truth was that Mike's editor at *Sportsweek* knew all about the writer's low opinion of tennis as a competitive sport. The whole point in sending Mike to cover Wimbledon was to get one of the biting satiric articles for which he was famous. A Wilder piece that hacked up somebody's favourite sport or home town always brought a flood of angry letters to the editor, but never failed to increase news-stand sales.

'I'm a bourbon and hamburger man,' Mike had complained in the New York office when he was handed the assignment. 'Why would you pick me to go all the way across the ocean to sip pink gin and eat strawberries while a bunch of inbred Englishmen applaud politely for a couple of glorified ping-pong players?'

'I see you've already written your lead,' the editor had grinned. 'Look at it as a cultural exchange. We let them have you for a couple of weeks in return for sending us the London 'flu.'

'Funn*ee*.'

Mike had taken the assignment, of course. He made a comfortable living from his column, but these extra commissions were most welcome just now while he was going through a divorce.

'There were two callers for you this afternoon, sir,' the receptionist said. He took a folded sheet of notepaper from the pigeon-hole marked *313* and handed it to Mike.

The message said Paula Teal had phoned, and would he please ring her back. Reading it, Mike's smile returned. It had been a year since he met Paula at a New York publishers' convention. She was there as an editor representing the London office of Worldwide Publications, *Sportsweek*'s parent company. The two of them had spent only a short time together, but there was an immediate mutual attraction and an unspoken promise of good things to come. With Paula here to act as his guide, the London trip might not be a total loss.

'You said there were two calls?' Mike asked the receptionist.

'Yes, sir. The other was a gentleman who left no name or message. He merely asked if you had checked in yet and what your room number was.'

Probably some promoter, Mike thought. He was used to the

wheeler dealers with fistfuls of money and other treats trying to get the name of whatever they were pushing – a brand of golf ball or a ski resort or a jumping-frog tournament – into Mike's column. Those that tried were wised up in a hurry. Nobody bribed Mike Wilder; his column was not for sale. The sharp-shooters might try it once, but never a second time. Mike's icy ridicule in print had sunk more than one promoter's pet project without a trace.

The receptionist touched a bell on the counter, and a smartly uniformed young porter marched forward and took possession of Mike's room key and his two travelling bags. Mike followed the boy to the elevators and into one of the waiting cars, which he reminded himself to call a lift. It was not one of the new push-button models, but operated with a brass handle which the boy cranked back and forth. Like the rest of the hotel, the lift had been re-carpeted and the walls re-surfaced, but the architectural style placed it solidly somewhere in the 1920s. Regency House had about it a feeling of solid respectability without being stuffy. It was a hotel where a man might be comfortable if he did not detest hotels.

As the lift clanked upwards Mike pulled off his black-rimmed glasses and slipped them into the breast pocket of his suit jacket. Although he had worn glasses since high school, Mike had never lost the habit of yanking them off as soon as he was not required to look at something in detail. A stupid vanity, he knew, for a man of forty-one, but he did it anyway. A couple of years back he had tried a pair of tinted aviator-style glasses with gold rims, but decided they made him look like a pimp or a record-company executive. He went back to the old plastic frames, and kept them in his pocket most of the time.

The lift gave a shudder in its ascent, and the porter turned, prepared to reassure his passenger that it always did that, then smiled to himself. This man did not look like the type to be frightened easily. Despite being a two-pack-a-day smoker and a hearty drinker, Mike made it a point of pride that he kept in shape. He would be embarrassed to be caught at it, but Mike spent fifteen minutes every morning doing sit-ups, push-ups, and door-jamb isometrics. There was strength in his face, and a slightly pugnacious look that came from the jutting jaw and the off-centre nose.

'Third floor, sir,' the porter said as they clattered to a stop. 'If you'll follow me, please, your room's just down the corridor.'

Letting the boy lead the way, Mike glanced idly up and down the dim corridor. Much of London was dim these days, a reminder of the late energy crisis. The only other person in the corridor was a man in a camel-hair coat who kept his back turned.

The porter opened up room 313 and trotted round snapping on lights and opening windows. The room was clean and bright, and the furniture had a solid, permanent look to it that was uncommon in hotels.

'Will there be anything else, sir?' the boy asked.

Mike tipped him and said, 'How are chances of getting a bottle of whisky?'

'The chances are quite good, sir. Might I bring you some ice?'

Mike grinned at this recognition of the strange drinking habits of Americans. 'Thanks, some ice would be fine.'

The boy backed out of the room closing the door behind him, and Mike yanked off his tie and dropped into a chair.

It seemed to the man with the knife that the porter was never going to come out of room 313. When he finally did, the man was perspiring heavily. He turned quickly and walked in the other direction until the lift came and swallowed up the boy behind its sliding door.

The American would be alone in the room now. There was no doubt that he was the right one. The man with the knife knew him from his photograph. Oh, how well he knew and hated that square-jawed face with the thatch of brown hair. He had risked enough of a look when they passed in the corridor to be sure he had the right man. The right Mike Wilder. The Mike Wilder who so casually took what belonged to another man. Now it was time for him to pay the ultimate price.

The man drew the knife from the folds of his jacket and ran his thumb across the cruel blade. He held it low, down by his hip, as he had seen knife-fighters do in the cinema. There would be no amateurish hacking, just one straight thrust to the belly and Mike Wilder would be a dead man.

The man with the knife moved towards the door.

3

Round the corner, in room 321 of the Regency House, Tim
Barrett perched on the edge of a settee while his father beamed
at him and his mother fussed round the room putting things
away in drawers and shaking the wrinkles out of clothes as she
hung them up. Tim was a well-built young man with the
healthy good looks of Southern California.

'Tim, you really look great,' his father said for the seventh or
eighth time. 'I mean really great. How do you feel?'

'I feel fine, Dad,' Tim said for the ninth or tenth time. 'Hundred per cent.'

'Your face looks a little thin, dear,' his mother said. 'Are you
eating well?'

'I'm eating fine, Mom.'

'Tennis players are supposed to be thin,' Tim's father put in.
'Who ever saw a fat tennis champion? Right, Tim?'

'Sure, right, Dad,' Tim answered, letting his eyes stray
towards the door. Being alone with his parents, especially his
father, made him acutely uncomfortable. Despite his open-
faced, all-American-boy appearance, Tim was not at ease with
people. The lone exception was his coach, Vic Goukas, who was
father, mother, teacher and confidant. Tim became inarticulate
and evasive in any other personal relationship that was not
divided down the middle by a tennis net. This had given him a
growing reputation for arrogance, which Tim did not try to
deny since it was more acceptable in his world to be arrogant
than to be shy.

That afternoon he had been asked by some of the Australian
players to come along later when they went out to sample
London after dark. Pleased by the unaccustomed invitation,

Tim was anxious to break away from his parents' hotel room. He did not drink himself, but he had always admired the fun-loving Aussies who brought back tales of uproarious adventures as they caroused their way through the cities on the international circuit. Strangely, the oceans of beer they put away never seemed to affect their play.

'It's a shame you can't stay here with us, Timmy,' his mother said. She was a plump, pretty woman with soft brown eyes and a sweet smile.

Tim's father waved away her comment. Jack Barrett, trim and handsome at forty-seven, was an older version of his son. 'Now, Fran, Tim's not a boy any more,' he said. 'He's nineteen. At that age a young man appreciates a little freedom.'

Sure, freedom, Tim thought. Since he had been old enough to look over the top of the net, freedom was just a seven-letter word to Tim Barrett. The game of tennis owned him. When other youngsters of his age were learning the multiplication tables Tim was learning the five basic strokes of the game. When the other boys in his class were discovering girls Tim was training for the Junior Singles. Which he won. It was his father who had steered Tim into tennis. Jack Barrett had been a good club player himself, and had once been ranked in the top twenty by the U.S. Lawn Tennis Association. However, Jack had never really been tournament class. He determined early that his son would make it. Tim would be a champion if Jack had anything to say about it. The boy had the best private coaching available, and his schools were chosen for their tennis facilities rather than scholastic rating. Nominally a freshman at UCLA, Tim had yet to attend a class there. He was given special leave for this year's world tennis tour. Tim was well aware that he had always been given special considerations. But freedom? What was that?

Jack Barrett clapped his big hands together, stood up, and walked over to where Tim was sitting. 'Boy, this is really something, I don't mind telling you. Jack Barrett's son seeded eighth at Wimbledon. You haven't been home to see the office since I had it re-decorated. One wall is nothing but pictures of Tim Barrett, tennis star. A fellow down at the *Times* gets them for me from the wire services. I've had some of them blown up to poster size. You should see the way people react when they find out I'm Tim Barrett's father. It really impresses clients. If you were to get as far as, say, the semi-finals here at Wimbledon people would be knocking the door down to talk tennis and, incidentally, do a little business. Honestly now, what do you think your chances are, son?'

'I think I just might win it all.'

'You mean . . . *win* it?'

Tim's eyes shifted away from his father's gaze. 'Yeah, win it.'

Jack Barrett moved a step closer to his son. 'I mean seriously, Tim. Hell, I know you're good. Nobody knows that better than I do. But maybe you're still a couple of years away?'

'Dad, this is my year. I mean it, I can win it all.'

'But what about Ron Hopper? He's defending champion and top seed. He won the Australian championship, and he's had plenty of rest.'

'The word is he's in pain. Something about a leg. That's the reason he hasn't played since Melbourne. People who ought to know are saying he might not even make the semis.'

'I'll be damned,' Jack Barrett said, a light growing in his eyes. 'I don't wish Hopper any bad luck, but that sure would help our chances. What about that crazy Hungarian? He's given us a lot of trouble.'

'Yuri Zenger? He's tough, and he threw me off-stride in Melbourne, but I know him now. I know his whole bag of tricks. If he can't get you rattled his own game goes to hell. He'll never do that to me again.'

'Brian White? I know you've beaten him often enough, but he *is* number four seed.'

'Brian's the nicest guy on the tour, and you can put his high seeding down to niceness. Oh, he plays well enough, but I can always beat him in the big ones. Brian never wins the big ones.'

Jack Barrett chewed on his trim moustache as he ran the names of the other seeded players across his mind's screen.

'Milo Vasquez?'

'He's playing on his reputation and a big serve. That Latin scowl wins him a lot of points, but the fire isn't there any more.'

Tim's father thought that over, then broke into a big smile and shook his head in a that's-my-boy kind of gesture.

Fran Barrett spoke up, and her son and husband turned towards her in surprise. 'What about this British player, this Alan Doughty? There's been a lot written in the papers about him.'

'Heck, Mom, he's pushing forty. The only reason the papers are giving him so much space is that he's the only Englishman with even an outside chance. One of their own hasn't won at Wimbledon since they wore long white flannels. Alan Doughty's having his last burst of energy like a light bulb just before it burns out.'

'You've changed, Timmy,' his mother said.

'How, Mom?'

'You were always a quiet, modest boy. Confident, yes, sure of yourself, but never boastful. Now you sound so, well, almost cruel.'

Tim reddened in embarrassment. He had become so accustomed to the defensive arrogance he assumed as a shield against the press that he had forgotten to drop the pose here with his parents.

Jack Barrett answered for his son. 'That's not being cruel, Fran, that's telling it like it is. The boy is good and he knows it. And he knows the weaknesses of his opponents. There's nothing wrong with that.'

Fran Barrett relaxed into a smile. 'I suppose I should be used to the way star athletes talk after living around them all these years. Will you be coming home after the tournament, Timmy?'

'Maybe, but just for a few days. I've got to get ready for Forest Hills. I'll be out in California for the Pacific Southwest, anyway.'

Tim's mother walked over and smoothed her son's longish blond hair. 'It will be nice to have you home for a while. The house seems so big and empty with no young people around.'

'Look, I really should go,' Tim said suddenly. 'I promised to meet some people.'

'I wish you could stay and shoot the breeze for a while, son,' his father said.

'Maybe later.'

'That's all right, we understand. You need your rest. Are you sharing a room with Vic Goukas again?'

'What else? The coach gets nervous if I'm out of his sight.'

'Well, he does know his tennis. Maybe your mother and I could come over there one evening?'

'Gee, I'd like that, but it might not be a good idea. You know how Vic gets during a tournament.'

'Yes, of course, we understand.'

Sure you understand. They always understood. Always approved. Tim kissed his mother's cheek, endured a clap on the shoulder from his father, and escaped from the room. If only once in a while they would not be so damned understanding . . . tell him what to do sometimes instead of always letting him decide. No, it was too late for that. That should have happened a long time ago. Tim shook the thought out of his mind and headed for the lifts.

As he rounded the corner Tim almost collided with a man in a camel-hair coat who was standing in front of the door to room 313. The man jumped away with a guilty start.

'Excuse me,' Tim said.

The man stared at him, damp, pale hair pasted to his forehead. He was sweating even in the unheated corridor, and there was something about his eyes that made Tim uneasy. At the lift he turned to look back, but the man was disappearing round the corner.

The man with the knife swore silently through clenched teeth. The boy had seen him, looked closely at his face. The boy would remember him if Mike Wilder died here tonight, and would describe him to the police. The man with the knife would never allow himself to be locked up again. He would just have to bide his time and wait for another opportunity. This chance was gone, but he still had two weeks to act. Mike Wilder would survive this night, but he would not leave London alive.

4

Across the Thames in a flat in Lambeth Alan Doughty and his wife Hazel sat before a small black-and-white television set. Doughty was a tall man with a friendly homely face and curly black hair that he clipped much shorter than was fashionable. His eyes were squinted with sun wrinkles, and his body was so lean there was not an extra pinch of flesh anywhere.

Hazel, a plain woman who turned beautiful when she smiled, was not smiling now. And she was not watching the American police show on the telly. She was studying the deep lines of her husband's face and trying to guess his thoughts.

Alan Doughty's thoughts were far away from the Lambeth flat and the action taking place on the small screen. His thoughts were some seven miles to the south-west on the grounds of the All England Tennis Club in the residential borough of Wimbledon. In his mind Alan was already on one of the outlying courts where he would begin play in the most important tournament of his life. It was the most important tournament because it would be the last.

There would be no crowd of spectators and no reporters watching Alan's opening match, just Hazel and a few friends on the benches. Maybe a few strollers who circulate among the far courts, not having seats in the stands. The real crowds would be at the Centre Court and at courts one and two where the high-seeded players would be toying with the luckless opponents they drew for the first round. Alan was seeded thirteenth this year, the highest ever for him, but he knew nobody really gave him much of a chance. He had got more publicity than he deserved up till now merely because he was British.

His first-round opponent was a Spaniard with a precise base-line game but little else. Alan knew he could beat the Spaniard without extending himself. It was the later matches he would have to work at to win. And he had to win them. This would be his last chance.

The doctor had written the word out for him when Alan had trouble pronouncing it.

Aneurysm.

'What does it mean, Doctor?' Alan had asked.

'Do you ride a bike?'

'Yes.'

'Have you ever had an inner tube with a weak spot that pouched out in a kind of bubble? Well, that's what's happened to one of your large arteries. The wall's become weakened at one point and bulged outwards with the force of the blood pumping through.'

'Is it dangerous?'

'If it ruptures you're a dead man.'

'What can be done about it?'

'Surgery can be performed and a chunk of plastic tubing put in place of the weakened section of the artery.'

'An operation? How soon would I need to have it?'

'Straight away.'

'But next week is Wimbledon.'

'Alan, listen to me. Whether you have the operation or not, you're going to have to forget about competitive tennis.'

'You're not serious?'

'Never more so. In any strenuous activity the body tissues need more oxygen. To supply that need the heart pumps the blood all the faster, putting more of a strain on the arterial walls. Once you've had the operation you'll be able to live a normal enough life and be as active as any thirty-eight-year-old man, but extreme exercise will be out of the question.'

'Doctor, I've been playing tennis since I was fifteen years old. It was tennis that got me out of the mines where my old man died and where my three brothers are living dead now. The game hasn't made me a lot of money, but it's given me a far better life than I could ever have had without it. Just now

I'm playing the best tennis of my life, and for the first time I've got an honest chance at Wimbledon. Have you any idea what winning at Wimbledon could do for me, Doctor?'

'It could kill you, that's what it could do.'

Alan went on as though the doctor hadn't spoken. 'A Wimbledon champion can get a lifetime job with a sporting goods firm, and never have to worry again about the landlord or the greengrocer. And all you have to do is travel about to schools and the like, signing your autograph and showing the kids how to hold a racket. Your company's racket, of course. Doctor, you just don't know what that kind of security could mean to me and Hazel.'

'I understand your situation, Alan, and I do sympathise. But that doesn't change the facts. I can't order you to have an immediate operation. I can only emphasise that if you don't have it, and if you continue to play tennis, you will surely die. Quite possibly at Wimbledon.'

'And if I stop now, what could I do? Go back to the mines? I doubt if they'd even have me now. I have no trade, and no skills except hitting a tennis ball with a racket.'

'Of course, the decision is yours,' said the doctor, 'but if it were me I know what I'd do.'

Alan had looked round the doctor's office, at the richly panelled walls, the leaded windows, the Oriental carpet. 'It's not quite the same thing, is it?'

Now Hazel Doughty reached out and touched her husband lightly on the shoulder. 'Are you all right, love? Would you like me to massage your legs?'

Alan pulled his mind back to the present. He grinned at his wife and said, 'You can if you'd like, woman, but you'll risk driving me into a passion.'

'Go along with you,' she smiled. 'I've lived with you long enough, Alan Doughty, to know there'll be no bedtime frolics until after the tournament when you can relax again. Perhaps you'd fancy a beer. There's a couple of pints left.'

Alan rose and took hold of his wife's hands. He drew her up gently to stand facing him. 'Damn the beer,' he said. 'And damn the tournament. What I want right now is you.' He smiled at her. 'Besides, I'll likely play better than ever afterwards, I shouldn't be surprised.'

Hazel circled his lean body with her arms and pressed close against him. 'I love you, tennis player, do you know that?'

'I suspected as much,' he said. 'Now, are you coming to bed with me or do I have to see what I can pick up down at the local?'

Laughing softly, Hazel walked with her husband into the small, neat bedroom. Alan kept his face turned away so she would not see the tears.

5

Mike Wilder opened the door and stepped out to look up and down the corridor. He thought he had heard someone moving out there, but the passage was empty now, the door of the lift just sliding shut. Mike went back into his room and closed the door. He sat down at the small desk and picked up the telephone. He gave the hotel switchboard operator the number Paula Teal had left. He heard the number being dialled, then the series of rapid pips that signalled a busy line on London telephones.

Mike replaced the phone and doodled on a sheet of Regency House stationery while he waited to ring again. He smiled at himself when he noticed that he had sketched a lopsided valentine heart.

He thought about the gathering in New York a year ago when he had met Paula. As a rule Mike hated conventions – the tasteless dinners, the interminable speeches, the mandatory guest politician. Whenever he could he avoided them like poison ivy. This time, however, Worldwide made it clear to Mike that as the star of their most successful book he was expected to be there. His assignment, frankly, was to court the news dealers, those anonymous people who can make or break a magazine, depending on what kind of display they give it on their stands.

By the final day of the convention Mike was sure he had permanently distorted his face from the constant smiling, and his right hand was bent with candidate's cramp. At an afternoon seminar on postal regulations he decided he could stand it no longer, and chose a moment when no one was looking to slip out of the side door. Paula Teal had picked the same emergency exit, and they nearly bumped into each other on their way out. Mike had seen the pert, auburn-haired English girl earlier at various meetings, but had never really noticed her. Now they felt like co-conspirators.

Mike suggested hiding out at a small, quiet bar he knew on Third Avenue, and Paula happily agreed. They had sipped cocktails and talked easily together long past the end of the seminar, and returned to the convention hotel rather embarrassedly just in time for the evening's closing ceremonies.

The following night, Paula's last in town, they had gone out on an official date – dinner, a show, dancing afterwards. They had talked constantly . . . about writing, about places they'd been to or wanted to go, about old movies, about the ironies of life . . . but little about themselves. Mike was going through the early stages of a divorce at the time, and didn't much want to talk about it. Paula, whose marriage had also ended in divorce, said only that there were emotional scars that had not yet had time to heal.

There came a point in the evening when Mike felt it was time to make the standard pitch for sex.

'Listen, how would you like to see the view of the park from my room?'

'Do you really think it's better than the view from mine?'

'No, but I thought as an opening remark it wasn't too bad.'

'We don't have to play word games, do we, Mike?'

'No, I guess we don't. Maybe I've seen too many old Rock Hudson–Doris Day movies.'

'Let's start again, and this time you be Mike instead of Rock.'

'Okay. Would you like to go to bed with me?'

'I might like to very much, but I'm not going to. Not this time.'

'What is it, am I using the wrong toothpaste?'

'There you go again being light and amusing and utterly false.'

'I'm sorry. Let me put it another way. What's wrong with two people who like each other and have no outside obligations going to bed together?'

'Nothing's wrong with it. Nothing at all. I rather approve of sex, as a matter of fact. It just happens that I've had some rather ugly experiences in that line not very long ago, and I'm still a little bit afraid of it, that's all. I need some time to get over it. Do you mind awfully?'

Mike gave her a mock scowl. 'Hell yes, I mind. What do you think I spent all that money on you for, lady, to shake your hand?'

Paula picked up her cue and sighed dramatically. 'It's just as dear mother told me, you men are after only one thing. Seriously, Mike, am I being awfully stuffy?'

'Sure you are, but that's the way with all you English, isn't it?'

Paula relaxed and laughed with him. 'You have us taped, all right, though I'm surprised you Americans have the time to learn these things what with constantly chewing gum and getting into fist fights with each other.'

The tension was broken for good then, and the evening wound up relaxed and comfortable as Mike walked Paula to the door of her hotel room.

'How about if I write to you?' he said.

'Do you want to?'

'Yes, I do, for some unaccountable reason. I haven't written letters to a girl since I was in high school, but I'd like to write to you. I don't want us to lose track of each other, Paula.'

She had looked up at him for a long moment, her eyes moist and bright. He kissed her. It was a long, warm kiss that promised there would be more to come. Much more. Paula had written the address of her London flat on the back of her business card and pressed it into his hand. She had touched his cheek lightly with her fingertips and disappeared into the room.

Mike smiled now, remembering the coolness of her touch, the elusive flower scent of her rich auburn hair. He had written her half a dozen letters in the past year, and she had answered each of them promptly. Their intimacy had grown steadily from letter to letter, and seeing Paula again had given Mike something to look forward to on this trip to London.

He picked up the telephone and gave her number to the

switchboard operator again. This time he heard the burr-burr signal that meant the other phone was ringing.

'Hello?'

'Paula, this is Mike.'

'Mike, how good to hear your voice. Are you at the hotel?'

'Yes. I just got your message. How soon can we get together?'

'There's been a bit of a hitch about that.'

'Oh?' Mike was surprised at the depth of his disappointment.

'Nothing serious, I'll just be a bit late. They've changed some page layouts on me, and I'm fighting a deadline that will keep me in the office for another hour or so. You ought to know what that's like.'

'Sure. Don't worry about me, I'll just settle in here and try to recover somewhat from the jet lag until you can make it.'

'You'll do nothing of the sort,' Paula said. 'This is your first night in London, and I won't have you wasting any of it sitting around an old hotel room. Now, subject to your approval, I'm sending along a substitute until I'm able to join you.'

'Substitute? What kind of a substitute?'

'Er, well, her name is Christy Noone, and she's rather a knockout. A photographers' model. I suppose I am taking rather a chance on losing you before I even get my innings, but at least I'll know where you are. It was all Christy's idea, actually. She has the flat above mine, and I was telling her how badly I felt about not being able to meet you until later. She suggested that she should stand in for me until I can get there.'

'You said something about all this being subject to my approval.'

Paula laughed deep in her throat. 'You would be the first man, to my knowledge, ever to disapprove of Christy. Unless, that is, you don't like cute little blue-eyed blondes with figures like the early Bardot.'

'My preference is for brown-eyed ladies with hair that smells like flowers,' Mike said, 'but I'll try to make do with the blonde doll until one shows up.'

'Just hold on to that thought, Mike. I should be out of here by ten. I told Christy we'd all meet at Caesar's.'

'What's that?'

'It's a discotheque. Don't worry, Christy knows how to get there.'

'She does, eh? Don't get there too late or I can't answer for my behaviour with your blonde neighbour.'

Paula laughed again. A good laugh, Mike decided. He liked a woman with a good laugh.

'Christy will be there in about an hour. I'll make it as soon as I can, darling. Be strong.'

Mike hung up and grinned at the telephone. He felt like a high school kid going on his first date with the prom queen. Since his split with Lorraine Mike's contacts with women had been of the hello-good-bye type, with the sex perfunctory and non-involving. He was not sorry that he and Paula had not gone to bed last year in New York, but he was damn sure they were going to make it this time. Who could tell, it might even lead to something.

The bell-hop arrived with a bottle of good Glasgow Scotch and a bowl of ice cubes the size of Las Vegas dice. Mike dropped a handful of ice into a glass, filled it with Scotch, and took it into the bathroom to sip at while he soaked away the ache of jet travel.

Fifteen minutes later there was a knock at the door. Mike climbed out of the bath, wrapped a hotel towel around his middle, and padded out through the room.

He opened the door and looked down at a girl with fluffy blonde hair and sparkly eyes. She wore dressy black pants that stretched satiny smooth across her trim rounded hips, and a top of light blue silk with a neckline that plunged towards her navel.

'I'm Christy Noone,' the girl said. She ran her eyes down Mike's body, letting her gaze linger at the towel that was his only covering.

'I seem to be early,' she said, smiling brightly up at him. 'Or did you have something special in mind?'

6

Having sex with Geneva Sundstrum, thought J. J. Kaiser, was like sailing on a golden sea of flesh. Make that a magnificent golden sea, he amended as he plunged into her depths. A magnificent sea of firm, buttery, beautifully apportioned flesh.

Geneva's exquisite, endless legs rode up and crossed behind his shoulders, drawing J.J. deeper into the vortex between her thighs.

'Oh, Lord, honey,' she cried, 'don't stop! Don't ever stop!'

For several more beats J.J. concentrated his will on holding back, then he gave up and let himself whirl down into the wet slippery womanness of her.

They lay on the bed cleaved together, their bodies slick with sweat. Six feet three inches of blonde sumptuous Geneva, and five-feet-six of dark wiry J. J. Kaiser. Gradually their harsh, open-mouth breathing slowed to normal. J.J. eased his arm out from under Geneva's broad, smooth back and stole a look at his wristwatch.

'We'd better get going, we have work to do.'

'Can't we just lay here a while longer?' the big girl asked. Her voice was soft and breathy, almost a whisper; not at all the booming contralto one would expect to issue from those splendid lungs.

J.J. rolled his body off Geneva's and gave her a businesslike slap on the rump ' "Lie here" is what you mean,' he said, 'but laying or lying, we've done enough for one evening. Go take a bath and get yourself all sweet and sexy smelling.'

'Don't I smell sexy now?'

'To me, yes, but the tennis players are the ones we want to pay attention. Put on something to titillate. Maybe that metallic grey number, the one cut down to here that shows off the boobs.'

'If I do, will you bite them?' she teased.

'Later, woman, later. Good Christ, you just took all the starch out of me, or didn't you notice?'

'Mmm, I noticed. Bet I could put some of that starch back in.'

He gave her a shove towards the edge of the bed. 'Up, up, dammit.'

'Oh, all right.' Geneva stood up and stretched to her full luxurious length. She raised her arms in the classic woman's gesture to fluff out her thick blonde hair, and smiled down at J.J. She leaned down to kiss him on the mouth, letting the pale melons of her breasts squash lightly against his chest. She glanced down at his reviving organ and stood up again with a giggle of triumph. Before he could protest, she marched away from him towards the bathroom.

J.J. tried to think up a sarcastic remark to toss after the girl, but he gave it up and smiled instead at her retreating buttocks, round and firm as a matched pair of moons. Damn, if he weren't careful he was going to get hung up on the big broad, and wouldn't that be a fine how-do-you-do.

He swung his legs out of bed and stood up, using a towel he had thoughtfully placed there beforehand to blot the perspiration from his compact body. He walked naked to the far side of the room where one entire corner was filled with new tennis rackets, cans of balls, eye shades, sweat bands, and other equipment associated with the game of tennis. Each item bore the script 'G' that was the trademark of the Gilfillan Sporting Equipment Company, the current employer of J. J. Kaiser.

The reason J.J. was in London for Wimbledon this year was that the Gilfillan 'G' was not nearly the familiar symbol the company officers and stockholders wanted it to be. It had nowhere near the recognition factor of the block 'S' of Spalding or the 'W' of Wilson. It was J.J.'s mission to Gilfillan equipment into the hands and hearts of some of the top-ranked tennis players. Much depended on how well he succeeded – J.J.'s job, for one thing.

It was twenty-seven years ago, at the tender age of twelve, that J.J. Kaiser embarked on his first promotional hustle. He had picked up a box of slightly damaged candy bars at a discount from a burned-out market and carried them from door to door representing himself as being from Father Flanagan's Boys' Town. It took a cold heart indeed to say no to the skinny little kid with the huge sad eyes behind the magnifying lenses. In less than four city blocks his supply of candy was gone and his pockets were heavy with the inflated prices he charged in the name of charity. It was then that J.J. Kaiser had the first vague notions of what his future vocation would be.

Hustling was something he could do better than his bigger, more attractive classmates. Maybe he couldn't make any of the teams, and maybe the popular girls wouldn't go out with him, but J.J. had a quick mind and a quicker tongue to compensate.

Unfortunately, not all of J.J.'s promotional ventures had gone as well as the Boys' Town candy bar caper. In fact, he had hardly done as well in the intervening twenty-seven years. There had been the pyramid-type marketing scheme for an obscure line of health food products. That one almost landed him in jail. Then there was the 'wilderness resort' real estate that turned out to be unreachable except by helicopter. There was the discount travel club that never seemed to get its aeroplane and its passengers together at the same airport on the same date. Finally, there was the Hollywood 'acting school' that held its classes in an empty warehouse. One by one these promotions, none of them quite on the up and up, but none strictly illegal, folded. After that J.J. had done some flackery for the movie studios in California and hired out as a PR consultant to political candidates and a number of shaky sports ventures.

The spectre of final failure was close on his footsteps when J.J. talked his way into a job with Gilfillan by claiming close personal friendship with dozens of athletes who didn't know him from Rumpelstiltskin. It was made clear to J.J. before he left the country that his future with the company depended on how well he did in signing up endorsements of the product at Wimbledon. A good showing at Wimbledon meant a player was newsworthy for at least a year, and the company would be most pleased if whenever the player was photographed he displayed the script 'G' somewhere. One such casual news photo was worth more than a full-page ad in *Sportsweek*.

J.J. leaned down now and retrieved an attaché case from among the stacked tennis rackets. He zipped it open and took out a sheet of paper with the typewritten names of the seeded players. Although he had the list memorised by now, he ran his eye down the names once again.

Ron Hopper, the defending champion and number one seed, could be ruled out. Every product he used or wore or drank or sprayed on his hair was tied up in long-term contracts. That's the way it was with most of the really big names, and it was not going to be easy for Gilfillan, a relative newcomer to athletic equipment, to get a foot in the door.

Tim Barrett, the kid from California, was a hot prospect this year. He was only eighth seed, but he was given a good chance to make the semi-finals. That was the cut-off point for the big-money endorsement contracts. If you finished lower than fourth your name wouldn't sell beer at a teamsters' picnic. J.J. made a mental note to get on the good side of the Barrett kid early. He had the good looks and the crowd appeal to be a blond Mark Spitz, and if he did make the semis the other promoters would swarm down on him like flies on a gumdrop.

The number four seed, Brian White, was always well up in the rankings, but there was little interest in signing him to a contract. He did not have the charisma that the wheeler dealers were looking for. None of this mattered to Brian White, since he was the son of wealthy parents, and had all the money he would ever need. He had never signed up with any of the competing professional groups, and just went amiably along winning his share of the smaller tournaments. They called him the last of the gentleman tennis players. Brian White would never win the big ones because he wasn't hungry enough.

The hungriest player of all a few years back was Milo Vasquez, the Mexican-American from Los Angeles. He had exploded on the tennis scene like an angry Latin skyrocket and won everything worth winning, including Wimbledon. Then three years ago the rocket fizzled out. Nobody could explain what happened to his game, but suddenly it was gone. The trademark scowl was still in place, but without the howitzer serve and the ferocious net game it no longer intimidated opponents. For commercial purposes Vasquez was all washed up. Still, it was always possible he might regain his old form, so J.J. Kaiser resolved to keep an eye on him. Maybe he would drop a few friendly words early on to let the Mex know who his friends were, just in case.

J.J. returned to the name that topped his personal list of prospects: Yuri Zenger. Until very recently players from the Communist countries had stayed well away from any actions that might be construed back home as cosying up to capitalism. A Russian player who was photographed drinking Coca-Cola, say, between sets would have some heavy explaining to do to the beefy 'trainers' who accompanied them everywhere. This year, however, things were loosening up, what with *détente* and all. Furthermore, some of the so-called Iron Curtain countries were looking for little, safe ways to be just a tiny bit independent of the Big Bear. The word was out that Yuri Zenger could be had.

As the number two seed, the Hungarian had a real chance of winning it all. If J.J. could manage to put a Gilfillan racket in his hand, his future at the company would look a lot brighter. Zenger was said to be a bad actor, on and off the courts, but J.J. had dealt with some of the worst. The Hungarian was also rumoured to consider himself quite a cocksman. That's what Geneva Sundstrum was along for.

Not that J.J. liked to think of it in just that way; and he certainly hadn't put it to Geneva in those terms. Just below his consciousness level the word 'pimp' kept trying to push its way to the surface like some malignant toadstool. J.J. fought it back down by reminding himself that this sort of thing had always been an accepted part of his business. Of lots of businesses. Besides, Geneva was being damn well paid for whatever she might be called upon to do. J.J. had seen to that personally.

'Can you come in and scrub my back, honey?' the big girl called from the bathroom, making J.J. start guiltily at his thoughts.

'Be right there,' J.J. called, pulling on his shorts. He walked across the room and opened the bathroom door, letting the steam billow out.

Geneva smiled at him from the bath. Her long legs were drawn up so that her knees rose like rounded volcanic islands above the soapy water. She leaned towards him and made a kiss in the air.

'Cut it out,' J.J. said. 'I thought it was your back you wanted scrubbed.'

'It's all right with me if you want to start somewhere here in front and work your way around.'

'Later,' he said, trying hard not to stare at those tremendous breasts.

Geneva gave a little sigh of resignation and turned her back to him. J.J. lathered up a flannel and began to soap the broad golden back with a circular motion. Geneva made small sounds of pleasure.

It had been a stroke of luck finding the big blonde girl right there at Gilfillan. They had her working as a mail girl, of all things, in the advertising/PR section. Her true function was apparently to keep up the morale of the male employees.

It took all of J.J.'s persuasive powers to convince the company executives how valuable Geneva might be on his mission to Wimbledon. Finally they had agreed to pay expenses for the two of them, but J.J. in an uncharacteristic burst of chivalry had insisted on an additional bonus for Geneva. He had stuck to it even when it meant his own allowance would be cut. Whatever the cost, he thought while kneading the firm muscles at the base of the girl's neck, it was going to be worth it.

'What's the name of the place we're going to tonight, J.J.?' she asked.

'Caesar's.'

'A restaurant?'

'Kind of a discotheque, they tell me.'

'How neat! You've never taken me dancing before.'

'We probably won't have much time for dancing. There's supposed to be a lot of the players hanging out there, and maybe we can spread a little goodwill, if you know what I mean.'

'Sure, I know what you mean, J.J.,' Geneva said without turning round. 'Don't worry about me, I know my job.'

Now what was that supposed to mean, he wondered. Was the broad sending him hidden messages? No, he decided, she's too damn dumb for that. Big and beautiful and good-hearted as all get-out, but face it – dumb.

It had been surprisingly easy to sell her on the London trip. But then J.J. always did have a way with women when he wanted to turn on the charm. That is, it worked with women who didn't examine his motives too closely, or didn't stay with him too long. J. J. Kaiser did not wear well.

He had never married, though he came close to it a couple of times. It was usually with a sense of mutual relief that J.J.'s romances ended. The women he got most deeply involved with were female versions of himself: quick-thinking, fast-talking, sophisticated and hip. For a while they would stimulate each other, but before long it always became a strain.

Geneva Sundstrum was different. Sophistication and deceit were foreign to her. As far as J.J. knew she had never had a smartass thought. Although he was subject to the fabled yearning of small men for large women, Geneva was definitely not the type he would have chosen for personal fun and games. It disturbed him now that an uncommon tenderness seemed to creep inside his emotional shell at times when they were together. That did not fit at all with the plans he had made.

'Okay, sweetheart, you're not going to get any cleaner,' he said, giving her a whack on the lower back.

Geneva stepped out of the bath and turned to face him, a vast expanse of beautifully packaged dripping wet blonde woman. Something caught in J.J.'s throat. He turned away.

'Let's move it,' he said. 'I don't want to miss anybody important.'

7

It took Mike Wilder five full seconds to recover part of his composure while the smiling blonde girl stood in the doorway and let her eyes dance over his towel-wrapped body. When he finally found his voice it came out embarrassingly hoarse.

'Come in. I, uh, just took a shower.'

'So I see.' The girl's bright smile conceded him nothing. She walked past him into the room, her eyes mischievously flicking between his face and the towel around his middle.

'Have a seat somewhere,' Mike said. 'I'll be dressed in a minute.'

Christy Noone dropped on to the settee and stretched her legs out in front of her, crossing them at the ankles. She clasped her hands behind her head, pulling the blouse taut across the small, uptilted breasts. 'I do hope you're going to let me watch,' she said.

'Watch?'

'Watch you dress. A man reveals a lot about himself by the way he puts on his clothes. For instance, which part of your body do you cover up first? Four men out of five simply don't feel easy until they get something on over the family jewels. The old fig-leaf complex, I call it. There are exceptions, though, men who are so proud of the old pump handle that they hate to put it out of sight for even a short time. One man I knew liked to walk about in his shoes, socks, shirt, tie and bare arse. Once he forgot himself and walked me out to the street in front of his house to hail a taxi dressed like that. Luckily it was quite late and there were not many people in the street. One passing lorry driver saw him, though, and bloody nearly ran through a shop window on the other side before he got himself straightened.'

Half-way through Christy's monologue Mike relaxed. Then he began to laugh. When she came to the end of the story he threw back his head and roared, almost dislodging the towel.

When he recovered the power of speech he said, 'I'm afraid I am going to be a disappointment to you. I plan to take my clothes into the bathroom, close the door, and dress myself in privacy.'

'I was afraid you might,' Christy said, not at all abashed. 'So many of you Americans have this thing about modesty. It has to do with your Puritan ancestry, I dare say. I'm certainly glad we got them out of England.'

'It happens that my personal ancestors were potato-eaters from Kilkenny, but I still like to put on my pants in private. How about a drink while you're waiting?'

'I'd love one. Have you got any gin?'

'Sorry, whisky only.'

'Lovely.'

Mike poured a generous shot into a glass. 'There's no soda or anything to mix with it, except water.'

'Why on earth should I want to mix it with anything?' Christy asked seriously.

'Darned if I know,' Mike said, grinning. He handed the glass of straight Scotch to Christy and poured a second for himself, which he carried with his clothes into the bathroom.

He dropped the towel and pulled on his shorts, chuckling as he realised he had just put himself in Christy's four-out-of-five majority that covers up the lower half first. He wondered how she had arrived at her statistics.

'Have you known Paula long?' he called out to her.

'I simply cannot carry on a conversation through a closed door,' came her petulant answer.

'Oh, what the hell,' Mike muttered, and pushed the door open. The girl, still smiling with mischief, moved across the room to a chair where she could see into the bathroom better.

'I see you have the jewels tucked out of sight already,' she said.

36

'You're damn right. I don't want any trucks going through shop windows because of me.'

Christy laughed, a tinkling arpeggio. 'I think I like you. About a year.'

'About a year what?'

'That's how long I've known Paula. That was the question, wasn't it?'

'Oh, yeah. I'd forgotten.'

'How long have *you* known her?'

'Also about a year, but we were only together two days and I haven't seen her since.'

'From the way she talks I thought she knew you quite well.'

'We wrote some letters.'

'Are you in love with Paula?'

'How could I be? I told you we were only together two days.'

'Did you have sex?'

'God, you're inquisitive.'

'How is one to learn things if one doesn't ask questions?'

'Doesn't one ever think that maybe it's none of one's business?'

'Nonsense, of course it's my business. If you and I go to bed together I'll want to know if I should explain anything to Paula.'

'What put that into your head?'

'You mean explaining to Paula?'

'No, I mean about you and I going to bed together.'

'I always wonder about that when I meet an attractive man. Doesn't every woman?'

'I don't know, maybe they do,' Mike admitted. 'But wondering about it and saying it aloud are two different things.'

'I don't see why. It's really quite a natural reaction. I mean as long as both parties are capable physically and psychologically. You are capable, aren't you? I mean, you're not one of those—'

'No, I'm not one of those,' Mike said quickly.

'That's good news, anyway. These days you can never be sure. If you're capable, then what's the problem?'

'I'm inhibited.'

'Oh, well then. That can be overcome.'

'That's a relief,' Mike said dryly. He walked over to the suitcase lying open on the wooden rack and selected a tie. He stood before the dressing-table mirror and worked the tie under the collar of his pale blue shirt.

'Are you married?' Christy asked.

'No. Well, almost no. My divorce will be final in a couple of weeks.'

'What went wrong? With your marriage, I mean.'

'We just got to the point where we didn't like each other very much, and I'm damned if I know why I'm answering your impertinent questions.'

'Do you want me to shut up?'

'No. As a matter of fact, I'm kind of enjoying your impertinence.'

'See, you've lost some of your inhibitions already.'

Mike laughed and shrugged into his jacket. 'We'd better get out of here before I lose the rest of them and attack you, ignoring your pleas for mercy.'

'Who's pleading?'

'Have you no shame, young woman?'

'Absolutely none.'

'Tell me about this place we're going, this Caesar's.'

'Paula chose it mostly because it's so handy, just a short way from here, actually. They always get a lot of sporting types in there. Tonight it should be full of tennis players here for Wimbledon.'

'It's a discotheque sort of thing, I understand.'

'Sort of. Part of it's for dancing, but there's a second bar that's quieter if you'd rather talk than dance.'

'Swinging London, eh?'

'What's left of it. A few years ago it was really exciting, but it's tamed down a lot.'

'Nostalgia time,' Mike said. 'How old are you, Christy?'

'Twenty-one.'

'Uh-huh. And already your best years are behind you.'

'If you talk like that to me you may never get me into bed.'

'Come on,' he growled, holding the door open for her. 'Let's go.'

Christy walked past him into the corridor, letting one of her round little hips brush against the front of his pants. Just in case he had missed it, she turned round and giggled.

Mike couldn't hold the stern expression any longer. He shook his head, grinning, and steered the girl towards the lift.

The man with the knife made little circles on the bar with the wet bottom of his glass. The others in the pub, working men mostly, took no notice of him. The man's mind seethed with fragmented pictures of Mike Wilder doing ugly, obscene things to a woman who did not belong to him. The man pushed the damp yellow hair off his forehead and tried to cleanse his mind of the foul images, but he could not do it. Somewhere at this minute the American might be putting his hands on the woman, reaching up under her skirt, fingering her up there.

He shuddered, and a strangled sound escaped his lips. The other men standing at the bar looked at him curiously. He stared down into his glass.

It was a mistake to have left the hotel, he could see that now. The boy had seen him in the corridor, but he could still have waited down in the foyer until Wilder went out, and then followed him. Perhaps it still was not too late.

He spun away from the bar and ran out of the door, leaving his glass still half full of dark beer. Down Bedford Street he ran — one block, two — heedless of the startled looks from passers-by. Turn the corner into the Strand now. God, what luck, there was Wilder just coming out of the hotel. A woman was with him. Was it . . .? Damn, too far away to tell. The couple got into a taxi and drove off in the other direction. The man stepped from the shadows and ran out into the street to flag down a taxi of his own. He told his driver to follow the other one, and leaned forward to watch the red tail-lights ahead of them. Inside the camel-hair jacket his hand stroked the hilt of the hunting knife.

8

The Australian players moved round so much, leaving the group and coming back, spreading out and reforming, all the time laughing and capering like school children, that it was difficult to tell just how many of them there were. Actually, there were only three of them in the group Tim Barrett had joined, but they seemed twice that number. It was the first time Tim had come along on one of their fabled nights on the town, and the Aussies were making much of the occasion.

'Tim, my lad, I can't tell you how relieved you've made us all by coming out tonight,' said dapper Neal Farady. 'There has been talk going round that you were not a real person at all. The opinion was that your coach, Vic Goukas, winds you up with a key in the morning and sets you out on the tennis court. Then at night he puts you away in a box lined with cotton wool.'

Tim laughed. 'Maybe that idea isn't so far wrong.'

Denny Urso clamped a huge paw on Tim's shoulder. 'Once you've poured a pint or two of the best down your throat, my lad, you'll be surprised at how human you become.'

'Oh no you don't,' Tim said, still laughing. 'I'll have enough to answer to Vic for without coming in with beer on my breath. I know you boys can handle the stuff, but just the thought of it gives me the staggers.'

'Oh dear, oh dear,' moaned little Fred Olney in mock distress. 'What a dreadful curse for a man to carry through life – being unable to drink beer.'

'I'll have to take it up some day,' Tim said, 'but I guarantee it won't be during Wimbledon.'

The players swung up to the front of Caesar's, where an attempt had been made at Romanising the entrance with columns of painted plaster and notices in Latin script. Tim felt warm and alive in the company of the Aussies, a feeling that was only slightly chilled by the thought that he was breaking one of Vic's long-standing rules.

Once inside Caesar's, even the minimal Roman decor was abandoned. The lighting and decorations were strictly psychedelic mod, dating back no further than the 1960s. Just past the entrance was a deep room with a bar running along one wall. Tables no larger than dinner plates covered most of the floor space. Beyond this room was an archway through which could be heard the painfully amplified twang and buzz of electric guitars. Strobe lights in the far room froze the dancers into jerky pantomime. Bodies were everywhere – jammed buttock to buttock at the tables and seemingly moulded into a solid mass on the dance floor.

Tim stopped for a moment to recover from the assault on his senses. The Aussies barrelled on between tables, heading for the bar. They called out and waved to girls as they passed, blowing kisses and reaching out to pat a bottom here or squeeze a breast there. Tim grinned, envying the assurance with which they moved through the crowd. Although he managed to hide it under the mask of fierce competitor, Tim Barrett the golden boy from California was painfully shy everywhere but on a tennis court. He hurried on after the Australians.

Neal and Denny were already surrounded by a cluster of girls who were not quite sure who these rowdy chaps were, but just knew they had to be *somebody*. In recent years the international tennis stars had attracted their own following of eager young girls. Unlike the groupies who attached themselves to rock musicians, the tennis dolls did not follow their heroes from city to city, but there was always a fresh supply at the next stop on the tour.

Fred Olney beckoned Tim to a narrow standing space at the bar. The smallest player on the tour, Fred seldom lasted beyond the early rounds in singles, but in the men's doubles he teamed with Denny Urso to form a duo that was well nigh unbeatable. The Bear and the Flea, as they were called, complemented each other's skills and made up for each other's flaws exactly as a good doubles team is supposed to.

When Tim reached his side, the small Australian already had a glass of dark beer in his hand. He said, 'How do you like it so far, Tim? What'll you have to drink?'

'It's a little overwhelming,' Tim said. 'I'll have a Coke, I guess. I recognise a lot of the players here; does this go on for the whole two weeks?'

'No, this is the last big bash before play starts. Tomorrow everybody goes to Hurlingham, you know, the Sunday afternoon tradition. Then after there's the dinner-party at the Savoy. Not much chance to have fun at either place. A few of the lads go on partying right through the tournament, but most play it pretty straight, at least until they're knocked out of a chance at the prize money.'

'What about Ron Hopper, does he ever come out with your gang?'

Fred's manner changed subtly, and his voice took on a tone of respect when he spoke of the defending Wimbledon champion. 'No, Ron doesn't go in much for hell-raising. He's always been something of a loner. A good bloke, mind you, but a family man, after all, with a wife and kid to think about.'

'I hear he's got a bad leg,' Tim said. 'Is there anything to it?'

The little Aussie's gaze shifted away, and he seemed to withdraw slightly within himself. 'I wouldn't know anything about that,' he said.

Tim understood at once that he had overstepped the bounds. It was one thing for the Australians to take a Yank along with them for a night on the town, but quite another to pass along information that might be used against a countryman. While Tim was embarrassed at having asked questions, he mentally filed away for future reference the knowledge that Ron Hopper very likely *was* in pain. Fred Olney's very evasiveness had confirmed it.

'Look over there,' said Fred, suddenly friendly again. 'There's the madman.'

Tim followed the other's eyes and saw the Hungarian Yuri Zenger seated at a table sipping some foamy concoction from a tall glass. Zenger, with his wiry tangle of black hair and thick, down-curving moustache, was a caricaturist's dream. His eyes peered out like tiny glowing coals from beneath overhanging brows. Zenger was talking, as usual, gesturing expansively with the hand that was not holding the glass. A well-dressed woman in her late forties sat opposite him, hanging on his every word.

'Who's that Yuri's with?' Tim asked.

'Blamed if I know, but you can bet it's not his mum. You can also bet Yuri's not paying for the drinks, if you know what I mean.'

'No kidding.'

Tim watched as the volatile Hungarian reached out and seized the arm of a passing waitress. He held up his empty glass and jiggled it, talking rapidly and angrily. The waitress took the glass and hurried away.

It was ironic, Tim thought, how little he really knew about these men with whom he spent so many hours. He knew them only as opponents. Until recently he'd hardly thought of them as real flesh-and-blood people. He was familiar with their every move and mood when he stood across the net from one of them, but until tonight those others had no existence for Tim outside the tennis court or locker room.

A feminine squeal close behind him spun Tim round in alarm.

A fat girl with a bad complexion was staring at him as though he had just appeared in a puff of smoke. 'You're Tim Barrett!' she exclaimed.

'That's right,' he said, smiling uncertainly.

Several other girls standing nearby had turned to find the cause of the fat girl's outburst. When they heard Tim's name they crowded in close round him.

'Ooh, Timmy, just let me touch you.'

'Isn't he the sweetest thing? I told you he was sweet.'

'Are you going to win at Wimbledon, Timmy? I know you are.'

'Sign your name for me, Timmy. Put it just here on my bra.'

'I've got to dance with him. If he dances with me I know I'll die!'

'Look at the muscles in this beautiful arm!'

'Feel his skin, it's just like a baby's.'

Finding himself closed into a pocket by teenage girls who poked at him and clutched his clothing, Tim began to panic. He had become accustomed to the girl autograph hunters at the courtside who screeched at him and waved for his attention at the end of a match. He never minded signing autographs because not far away there was always the sanctuary of the locker room where the public could not follow. Here there was no escape in sight as the shrill little girls pressed suffocatingly close.

'Here now, here now, what's all this?' boomed Denny Urso, shouldering his way through the giggling girls. 'Out of the goodness of our hearts we bring the Yank along one night to show him a few of the sights, and the first thing you know he's hogging all the girlies for himself. This simply won't do. This won't do at all.' He looped one hairy arm around the waist of a bosomy young redhead. 'Come along, sweet thing, you're about to be taught the Australian boogaloo.'

Denny led the redhead towards the dance floor, and Neal Farady grabbed another girl and followed. The shrieking group that had surrounded Tim dissolved.

Fred Olney moved up beside him. 'You'll get used to them,' he said. 'The thing is to not let them overpower you. If you let them they'll nibble you down to a skeleton like a pack of bloody piranhas.'

'They were a little scary,' Tim admitted.

'They mean no harm. You've just got to kid 'em along, treat 'em like puppy dogs. Spank them when they get out of line. Every now and then you pick out one who strikes your fancy and take her to your room for a bit of slap and tickle. It's the thrill of a young life for the girl, it eases the tournament tension for you, and nobody's committed to anything.'

'It sounds too easy.'

'It is easy, but don't let them fool you. Don't start believing you're the big beautiful star they'll say you are. Today they'll roll on to their backs for you in a minute, but lose out in the early rounds of a few tournaments and they won't know you from a ball boy.'

44

'You seem to know all about it, Fred,' Tim said, smiling at the little Aussie.

Fred Olney grinned back. 'I may not be the star of the tour, but I get my share.'

Denny Urso came lumbering over to join them, waving to the bartender as he approached. 'I must have lost five pounds out on that dance floor,' he said.

'Where's your girl?' Tim asked.

'Red? She's still out there, as far as I know, dancing solo. I doubt she'll notice I'm gone for another two or three numbers. If ever.' Denny's beer arrived, and he took a long, grateful drink, wiping the foam from his upper lips with the back of a hand. 'Say, did either of you notice the bloke who walked in a while ago?'

'Who do you mean?' asked Fred.

'The big one sitting over there now with the little blonde bird.'

'Oh, yes.'

'Know who he is?'

'There is something familiar about him,' said Fred. 'I must have seen his picture somewhere.'

'He's Mike Wilder, the American sportswriter.'

'You don't say. The one who's always bitching and complaining in his column about one thing or another?'

'That's the one. I read in the London papers that he was coming over to cover Wimbledon. What do you say we go and have some fun with him?'

'Right you are. Come along, Tim.'

'You guys go ahead,' Tim said. 'I'm not very good at that sort of thing.'

'Not to worry,' Fred told him, 'all you have to do is watch Denny and me.'

Tim started to decline again when he caught himself looking directly into the intense blue eyes of the girl at the table with Wilder. She smiled, and the sheer female force of her seemed to reach across the room and seize him by the throat.

'All right,' he told the Aussies, but with his eyes still on the girl, 'let's go.'

9

The musical din from Caesar's rolled out across the pavement to the street where Mike Wilder and Christy Noone stepped out of their taxi.

'There should be some special punishment for the man who invented the amplified guitar,' Mike said.

'What would you suggest?' Christy asked.

'Oh, I don't know. Maybe flattening his head slowly in a vice. That's the effect listening to it has on me.'

'How grisly. You come along now, and we're going to enjoy ourselves, you'll see.'

'I'll bet,' Mike grumbled, but he allowed himself to be steered inside by the girl.

Once inside, Christy vanished in the crowd for a moment, then reappeared to announce that she had found them a table. They sat down and Mike ordered drinks – a whisky and water for himself, and a gin and tonic for Christy. The waitress squirmed off between the packed-in customers, and Mike wondered if he would ever see her again.

'I wonder if there's anybody who isn't here tonight,' he said, looking round at the crowd.

'This is where the action is,' Christy said. 'According to Paula we should see lots and lots of tennis players here, which she thought you'd like. Would you?'

'I'm undecided. What about you, Christy, are you a fan?'

'Me? I wouldn't know tennis from tiddly-winks.'

'There are similarities,' Mike said, more to himself than to the girl.

'Is that a friend of yours over there?'

'Where?'

'There by the door. Chap seems to be looking at you.'

Mike turned in his chair to look, but several people rose from their table just then and headed for the dance floor, blocking his line of sight. When it was clear again there was no one looking his way.

'I don't see anybody.'

'He was there a moment ago. At any rate, I thought he was looking over here at you. Blondish chap in an expensive jacket – camel-hair or vicuña.'

'I thought it might be a sportswriter,' Mike said, 'but if he was wearing an expensive coat, forget it.' Something in Christy's description tickled the edge of his mind, but he could not make a connection. Before he could give it more of his attention the waitress surprised him by returning with their drinks.

Mike paid the girl, and as she left three young men approached the table and stood looking at him with expressions of burlesque astonishment.

'Bless me if I don't believe you're right, Denny,' said the smallest of the three. 'We actually have the honour of being in the presence of that world-famous sporting writer bloke from America. The one who hates sports.'

'I told you so,' said the large one. 'It's Mike Wilder himself in the flesh. What do you suppose he's doing in London at this time of year?'

'There must be a golf match somewhere nearby,' the smaller one said.

'Yes, that would explain it. I'm told golf is the only game he can bear to watch without being sick to his stomach.'

The third young man, a shy-seeming blond boy, said nothing, but hung back, keeping his eyes on Christy. Mike, who had done his homework in preparation for the Wimbledon assignment, flipped through his mental card file to place the faces.

'The honour is mine, gentlemen,' he said. 'Unless I am mistaken I'm talking to Fred Olney and Denny Urso, the dynamic doubles duo from Down Under.'

The two Aussies were obviously surprised that Mike recognised them, and they could not conceal their pleasure that the American knew their names.

'That's a point for you, Mr Wilder,' Fred Olney said. 'The truth is we didn't think you'd know a tennis player if you tripped over one.'

'And you might before the evening it out,' Denny added.

'Don't get the idea that I'm a fan,' Mike said. 'That would destroy my image. Why don't you sit down and join us? Your friend too. Tim Barrett, isn't it?'

'Tim Barrett it is,' said Fred, 'but you only get half a point for recognising Timmy. He's had his picture in the paper too many times. And yes, we'd be delighted to join you and, er, the lady.'

'Forgive my bad manners,' Mike said. 'Gentlemen, this is Miss Christy Noone. Christy, these are Olney and Urso from Australia, and Tim Barrett, a countryman of mine.'

'Hi, chums,' said Christy.

'Hullo,' said Denny and Fred in unison.

Tim Barrett cleared his throat. 'We don't want to intrude.'

'Nonsense,' said Fred, 'of course we do. What's more fun than intruding?'

'That's what I always say,' said Christy. 'The more the merrier. Right, Mike?'

'Right. We've been here five minutes, and I was beginning to get lonesome.' Mike ordered a round for the table – beer for the Aussies and a Coke for Tim.

A new blast of sound spilled out from the archway that led to the dance floor.

'Come on, Mike,' Christy said, 'dance with me.'

'To this?'

'Sure, to this. Let it all hang out.'

'I'm afraid it would fall out by itself if I tried to dance what they're doing out there now. When I was a kid they told us too much of that could make a person go blind.'

'What an old fuddy duddy.'

'That's me.'

Christy turned her bright blue gaze on Tim Barrett. 'How about you?' she said. 'Things have come to a pretty pass when a girl has to ask all over the room for somebody to dance with her.'

'I'm not very good at it,' Tim said.

'Hey, I'm available,' said Denny Urso.

'Me too,' said Fred.

Christy gave the two of them a playful look. 'You chaps are *too* available, that's the trouble with you. Come along, Tim, I'll teach you what to do. There's nothing to it.'

'Well . . .' Tim looked uncertainly at Mike.

'Go ahead, Tim,' Mike said, 'but watch yourself in the clinches.'

As the young couple stood up and started towards the pulsating sounds of the music Mike caught the look on the tennis player's face and shook his head. The only word to describe Tim Barrett at that moment was *smitten*.

'Your girlfriend?' Fred Olney asked carefully.

Mike gave him a long look, then delivered a theatrical sigh. 'The first real love of my life. And what happens? Some jock steps in and takes her away from me. Not even a real athlete, mind you, but a *tennis* player.'

The Australians laughed along with Mike, obviously relieved.

'Seriously,' Denny said, 'are you going to write about Wimbledon?'

'That's the plan.'

'What are you going to say?'

'That depends on what happens.'

'You're here a bit early, aren't you?' Fred Olney said. 'Most of the foreign press people don't show up until the second week when the field is narrowed down to the real money players.'

'I don't operate the way most of the press people do,' Mike said. 'I don't pretend to know the game as well as most tennis writers, for one thing. My story will be the players.'

'No kidding. Are you going to write something about Denny and me?'

'Maybe. Do you think you'll do something newsworthy?'

'How about if we played our first match on the Centre Court in the nude?'

Mike laughed. 'You might be able to pull it off at the Los Angeles Tennis Club, but don't you think it's a little avantgarde for Wimbledon?'

The Aussies pretended to consider the idea, then nodded

sagely. Denny said, 'I suppose you're right. It would have been a good show, though.'

'In fact,' Mike said, 'doesn't Wimbledon still insist that the players dress all in white?'

'That they do,' said Fred. 'It's a tough job here for a bloke to get in a plug for his sponsors.'

'How do you mean?'

'In some tournaments there are no restrictions at all. If we wanted to we could wear shirts with *MacGregor Raquettes* stitched on the back. Nobody has actually gone that far, but we're getting closer. Here at Wimbledon they'll let you wear a tiny monogram over the pocket, but that's all. There are ways to get round it, though. Take the monogram on Ron Hopper's shirt. If you look closely, or if the television cameras zoom in on him, you'll see it reads "BP". That doesn't mean Ron's changed his name, it means he has a deal working with British Petroleum.'

'Fascinating,' Mike said.

'Or you can carry a racket cover that spells out Dunlop in big, easy-to-read letters,' Denny said. 'It's not part of your clothing, so the rules don't cover it.'

'And watch how the players take a drink when they change sides of the court,' said Fred. 'A bloke may not care whether he drinks Pepsi-Cola or sea water, but if he's got a deal with Pepsi he'll be bloody sure he holds the label so the gallery and the cameras can't miss it.'

'So you guys are paid to slip in product plugs like that,' Mike said.

'Sure. There's nothing illegal about it, and it's a nice little added income for those of us who don't make a whole lot in prize money.'

'Of course, the higher you're ranked the more they pay you,' said Denny. 'Freddie and I are not in what you'd call your big-money class.'

Mike looked up to see Christy and Tim returning from the dance floor. The girl chattered away gaily while the boy gazed at her like a puppy dog.

'You should try it, Mike,' Christy said. 'You don't know what you're missing.'

'I have a pretty good idea,' he said. Mike found himself a little concerned about Tim Barrett's obvious infatuation with Christy, and not quite sure why he should be. The girl could certainly take care of herself, and as for the boy, maybe he would learn something. Still, Mike could not shake off an uneasy feeling that he was responsible for something that shouldn't happen.

The man with the knife stood outside Caesar's and bit down hard on the knuckle of his right hand. It had been a shock, getting a good look at the girl who was with Mike Wilder. Was it possible he was mistaken about the man? No, that could not be. There was the picture, the letters.

The man's head began to ache. It was just a tiny prick of pain behind his left eye, but he knew it would not go away. The pain would grow until it screamed inside his head like a living thing trying to get out. He had to get to his bed, take his pills. But he could not leave here until he was sure about the man inside.

He slipped into a darkened doorway across the street from Caesar's and huddled there to wait a little longer.

J. J. Kaiser paused just inside the entrance to Caesar's and surveyed the crowd. His attitude was that of a bachelor out on the town looking over the supply of available females. Obviously, however, this was not the case. Geneva Sundstrum, looking her statuesque loveliest, stood beside J.J. with her hand resting lightly on his arm. As they stepped inside, the rhythm of conversation missed a beat as heads turned to look at the big girl, then swivelled back to look again.

J.J. spotted quite a few of the Wimbledon players scattered about the bar and the tables, but they were not the ones who were high on his personal list. Either they were not big enough names or they were known as perennial losers. Or else they were already sewn up contractually by other companies. Australians seemed to be in the majority at Caesar's, but aside from Ron Hopper this was not a vintage year for Australian tennis players.

'Listen to the music, honey,' Geneva said. 'Doesn't it make you feel like dancing?'

'No. Anyway, we're not here to dance, we're here for business, remember.'

'I know, but one little dance wouldn't hurt.'

'Forget it.'

J.J. continued to scan the crowded room. His eyes flicked over a table where two unimportant Australians were sitting, then bounced back. That blond kid with the Aussies, J.J. recognised him from photographs as Tim Barrett. Word was that Barrett never left his room during a tournament. People said his coach sat on him like a mother hen on an egg. This might be a good opportunity to score a few points with the kid.

With Geneva in tow J.J. started towards the table. Half-way there he paused for a moment when he recognised the fourth man sitting there. Mike Wilder, one of the biggest sports-writing names in the business. Normally J.J. would be pleased to have a member of the press on hand, but his last meeting with Mike Wilder had left some unpleasant memories.

The occasion had been the formation of a National Bowling League several years before. The idea was that of a millionaire who made his money in the construction business, and wanted to see his favourite sport go big-time. As the self-made million-aire saw it, teams made up of the nation's best bowlers would represent the major cities, with league schedules and play-offs and championships in various divisions Inevitably, there would be a World Series of Bowling. The millionaire hired J. J. Kaiser to drum up interest in the league among members of the news media. One of J.J.'s first targets was Mike Wilder, and he made the mistake of having a colour television set delivered to the writer's home the day before he dropped round to lay on the bowling-league propaganda.

The result was that the TV set arrived COD back at J.J.'s hotel room, and Wilder wrote an article about the pro-posed National Bowling League that was so full of caustic ridi-cule that the millionaire dropped the whole idea and took up golf.

J.J. was not eager to become involved with Mike Wilder again, but it looked as though there was no avoiding it. What the hell, he was willing to let bygones be bygones.

'Come on,' he said to Geneva, taking her arm.

'Where are we going?'

'Over to that table. The big guy's Mike Wilder, a very im-portant sportswriter. He's an old friend of mine. The good-looking kid is Tim Barrett. He's the one we want to get close to. The other two are Aussies, I think, but they're nobody, so don't bother with them.'

'Who's the girl?' Geneva asked.

For the first time J.J. noticed there was a petite girl sitting between Wilder and Tim Barrett.

'I don't know who she is,' he said. 'Some broad they picked up, probably.' Noting a sudden stiffening in Geneva's posture, he added, 'Don't worry, babe, she'll be as good as invisible when you show up.'

J.J. arranged his face into a genial expression and advanced on the table. 'Well well well,' he said, 'if it isn't Mike Wilder. It's great to see you again. You remember me, don't you?'

The sportswriter squinted up at him for a moment without any sign of recognition. Then he said, 'Yeah, I remember you. J. J. Kaiser, isn't it? Bowling enthusiast and giver of television sets.'

'Oh, yes, well, ha ha, that was quite a mix-up, wasn't it? No hard feelings I hope?'

'Why should there be?'

'Good, good. Listen, Mike, I want you to meet Geneva Sundstrum.'

Geneva put out her hand and leaned forward, bringing conversation to a standstill at all tables within eyeball range.

'Pleased to meet you, Mr Wilder,' she said. 'Is it all right if I call you Mike?'

'Why not?'

While Mike Wilder made introductions all round J.J. produced a couple of chairs and wedged them in at the already crowded table. When he and Geneva were seated he focused his attention on Tim Barrett.

'Listen, Tim, I've been following your career, and as a fellow Californian I want you to know we're all behind you and rooting for you to win the big one.'

'You're from California, Mr . . . er . . .'

'Kaiser. J. J. Kaiser. But call me J.J. Everybody does. Sure I'm from California. I've seen you play there many times.'

'Really? Where?'

Since he had never seen Tim Barrett before in his life, and had no idea where they played tennis in California, J.J. quickly veered away from the subject. 'Geneva here is a big fan of yours too. She was saying to me just this afternoon that she sure hoped she'd get to meet Tim Barrett. Weren't you, Geneva?'

'That's what I said, J.J., I hoped I'd get to meet him.'

Tim Barrett smiled politely, but it was plain he was anxious to return his attention to the other girl, the one Wilder had introduced as Christy Noone. J.J. couldn't imagine what the kid saw in her. The broad couldn't have been any taller than five-two, and had no boobs to speak of. Small arse too, for that matter. Nothing to get hold of. Definitely not the type to interest J. J. Kaiser, but as they said, different strokes for different folks.

'What are you pushing these days, J.J.?' Wilder said, intruding on his thoughts. 'International domino competition?'

'Ha ha, no, I'm out of the sports promotion business. I'm with an athletic equipment firm – Gilfillan. You've probably heard of them.'

'Mmm.'

'We've got a real top-grade product. Everything is quality with capital K, ha ha.' He turned back to Tim Barrett. 'By the way, what kind of a racket are you using these days, Tim?'

Tim turned reluctantly away from Christy Noone. 'Pardon me, what was that?'

'Have you ever tried a Gilfillan racket? A lot of the boys are using them now, and we're getting some really good reports.'

'Thanks, but I've been using a Head for two years, and I'm happy with it.'

'Oh, they're good too,' J.J. agreed hastily. 'Gilfillan makes a complete line of tennis equipment, you know – balls, practice gear, warm-up suits. Like to have you take a look at it if you get the time.'

'I'm sorry, but my coach, Vic Goukas, picks out all my equipment,' Tim said. 'You'd have to talk to him about anything like that.'

J.J. made a mental note of the name. 'Okay, but you think about it, will you, Tim?' He glanced around conspiratorially. 'I'm not really authorised to tell you this, but I know Gilfillan is interested in putting out a Tim Barrett signature racket, and I don't have to tell you about the royalties that go with something like that.'

'You'll still have to talk to Vic,' Tim said.

Christy Noone spoke up. 'I say, are we going to talk business all night or are we going to have some fun?'

'No more business,' Tim said, grinning like a schoolboy.

'Then let's dance, shall we?'

J.J. watched gloomily as the young couple headed for the

dance floor. He hadn't scored many points with the Barrett kid, and Geneva certainly hadn't made much of an impression either. Oh, well, there were other fish to fry.

The two Australians, who had been quietly sitting back with their beer, now joined the conversation.

'Say, how about us, Mr Kaiser?' said Fred Olney.

'We'd dearly love to have our signatures on a racket,' put in Denny Urso.

'We'd even sign a can of balls,' said Fred.

'Or an athletic supporter,' said Denny.

'Maybe we can talk about it later,' J.J. said grumpily.

'Say, maybe Mr Kaiser doesn't recognise us,' said Fred. 'Do you suppose that's possible?'

'Why, I'll bet that's just what happened,' said Denny.

'Allow me to introduce us, Mr Kaiser, this is my little friend Bobby Riggs, and I am William Tilden, better known as Big Bill.'

The Aussies dissolved into laughter, joined by Mike Wilder. Geneva looked questioningly from face to face while J.J. forced out a weak chuckle.

'Quite the kidders, aren't you,' he said. Then, gazing across the room, he spotted a face he recognised on the far side. If you'll excuse us, we've got some people to talk to.' He hoisted Geneva out of her chair and started across the floor.

'What people do we have to talk to, J.J.?' she asked.

'Yuri Zenger. He's at that table by the wall with the old broad.'

'He's the Rumanian, isn't he?'

'Hungarian.'

'Isn't it the same thing?'

'Almost. Remember now, I want you to be nice to him.'

Geneva stopped for a moment between tables. 'How nice do you want me to be, J.J.?'

Now what the hell, he thought.

He said, 'You know, play up to him a little bit. Hint at some goodies to come. Naturally, you deliver nothing before we get him tied to a contract.'

'And after?'

'Look, Geneva, we'll talk about that when the time comes, okay?'

Geneva let a second go by, then she said, 'Okay, J.J. Who's the lady with him?'

'I don't know. A lot of these old society babes like to have the players stay at their homes. The higher ranked the player, the better she looks to her friends. It's a status thing left over from the days when tennis was supposed to be simon-pure amateur.'

'You don't think there's anything else going on?'

'Who cares? Let's go.'

J.J. ploughed towards the table with his hand outstretched in greeting. 'Yuri, Yuri Zenger, I thought I recognised you from across the room. J. J. Kaiser is my name, I'm with Gilfillan Sporting Equipment. It's a real pleasure to meet you.'

Zenger glanced up at J.J., his wiry black eyebrows quirked into a who-the-hell-are-you expression. He made no move to take the proffered hand.

'This is my associate, Geneva Sundstrum,' J.J. went on, shifting gears smoothly. 'She's been dying to meet you. Haven't you, Geneva?'

'That's right,' the big girl said. J.J. was pleased to see she moved slightly to give Zenger a good look at the boobs.

The Hungarian looked her up and down with undisguised interest. He smiled, showing small, very white teeth beneath the drooping moustache. 'Hello,' he said, with only a trace of an Eastern European accent. 'Have you seen me play?'

'Not yet,' Geneva said, 'but I'm looking forward to it. I hear you're very good.'

'Yes, I am,' Zenger said. 'Where are you staying?'

The woman sitting across from Zenger made a point of clearing her throat. She was a carefully preserved fifty, J.J. estimated, with a high-arched nose and pale eyes that didn't want you to get too close.

'This is my friend, Mrs Keith,' Zenger said.

J.J. sized up the situation and saw that Mrs Keith was somewhat more intimately involved with Yuri Zenger than he had thought. Odd that Geneva had sensed it. J.J. also could easily interpret the way Zenger was looking at Geneva.

'We can only sit down for a few minutes,' he said, whisking a pair of chairs into position. 'We're staying at the Regency House, and we'd be glad to have you come up any time, Yuri. I've got some Gilfillan equipment there that I think you'd be interested in seeing, especially our new rackets. I happen to know that the company is considering a Yuri Zenger signature model and I—'

'What room number?' Zenger interrupted. His eyes were still on Geneva.

'I'm in 803,' J.J. answered. 'If you know when you can drop by I'll arrange to—'

'Both? You are both in 803?'

'I'm in 812,' Geneva said.

'Ah.'

J.J. felt an irrational resentment at the way the greasy Hungarian was looking at Geneva. He shook it out of his mind. What the hell, that was the whole idea, wasn't it?

Mrs Keith spoke for the first time. 'Yuri, we really must be going. I promised the Dennisons we'd at least make an appearance at their party.'

'The Dennisons are a pain in the arse,' Zenger said.

'We shan't stay long, dear, but we really mustn't disappoint them.'

J.J. detected an unmistakable tug on the leash in the woman's tone. Yuri Zenger responded with reluctance.

'I will see you later,' he said, keeping his eyes on Geneva's breasts.

'Did I do all right, J.J.?' Geneva asked as Mrs Keith hustled the Hungarian out of the club.

'You did fine, just fine,' J.J. told her. Why, he wondered, wasn't he more elated about it?

'I don't like him, J.J., that Rumanian.'

'Hungarian. I know he's a creep, sweetheart, but if we deal only with nice guys we starve to death.'

'I guess you're right,' Geneva said. 'Is there anybody else here we have to talk to?'

J.J. peered round at the crowd. 'I don't see anybody. I'd like to get with Tim Barrett again, but he's only got eyes for that skinny broad tonight. I wish Milo Vasquez was here, but I'll have to get to him later.'

'If there's nobody else, then can you and me dance?'

'Sure, why not. Come on, baby.'

The big girl and the little man walked through the crowd towards the dance floor, and J. J. Kaiser found himself feeling good because there was no more business to do tonight.

II

After leaving the Fleet Street office of Worldwide Publications Paula Teal hurried to her flat in Chelsea to change her clothes and perform any necessary repairs to her make-up. She wanted to look especially good tonight, though she couldn't have said exactly why.

Mike Wilder was, after all, only one of a number of men who had shown an interest in Paula since her divorce from Eric. And why shouldn't he? Paula was an attractive girl, above average in intelligence, with no serious bad habits. It was not surprising that men desired her company. It just happened that there hadn't been any one particular man since Eric. So what was special about this Mike Wilder?

Maybe it was the way he didn't push things last year in New York. Paula strongly disliked the grope-and-pant school of romance. This was most difficult to explain to men in the liberated 1970s. These days sex was as common as fish and chips, and if you held anything back you were labelled a prude or worse. Paula felt she had sound reasons for holding back, reasons she did not feel called upon to explain. Mike had acted in a remarkably civilised way when she had demurred at sex on their first meeting. He had even made good his promise to write to her.

As her taxi pulled to a stop in front of Caesar's Paula tried to fix in her mind exactly what Mike looked like. What a shame it was that she had lost the picture he'd sent her. Strange the way that happened. She would have to tell Mike about it. Still, she found she had no trouble remembering him. Taller than average, dark brown hair with a touch of grey, nice hazel eyes that looked at you a little out of focus because of his obstinate refusal to wear his glasses. She found the silly point of male vanity rather endearing.

Paula paid off the driver and walked up to the entrance of the discotheque. Solid waves of sound hit her as she pushed open the door, and she wondered if this place had been such a good choice. Perhaps subconsciously she had not wanted too intimate a setting for their reunion. Intimacy, if there was to be any, could come later.

Standing on tiptoe she saw Mike sitting across the packed room at a table with Christy and several young men. Trust Christy Noone to gather men about her.

Paula walked carefully between the tables towards them. Christy was the first to see her, and stretched up an arm to wave. Mike turned and peered myopically in her direction, and Paula smiled to see that he still would not wear his glasses.

Mike stood up when she reached the table, and Paula moved naturally into his arms. The short embrace was a bit more intense than she had been prepared for, and Paula stepped back a little breathless.

'I'm awfully sorry to be so late,' she said.

'I'm glad you're here,' Mike told her. 'You look absolutely terrific.'

'I hope you didn't worry about your gentleman friend, Paula,' Christy said. 'I've been taking excellent care of him, haven't I, Mike?'

'First rate,' Mike said.

'Naturally, I did try to get fresh with him, but he wouldn't have it. He's a man of iron, Paula.'

Mike introduced the young men at the table, who turned out to be tennis players. Two of them were pleasant Australian boys who excused themselves almost at once and went off to join some friends at the bar. The third, an American named Tim Barrett, remained at the table apparently unable to keep his eyes off Christy.

'Come on, Timmy, let's dance and give these people a chance to talk to each other,' Christy said. Tim allowed himself to be taken by the hand and led away towards the dance floor.

Left suddenly alone, a momentary embarrassment overcame Paula and Mike.

'What did you think of Christy?' Paula asked.

'As you said, she's something of a knockout. It looks like she's abandoned me for a tennis player, though.'

'Being faithful to one man is not part of Christy's make-up.'

'As long as I know it wasn't just me.'

'Seriously, Mike, it's so good to see you.'

'You too,' he said. 'You're doing your hair differently.'

'I'm wearing it a bit longer than I was in New York. Do you like it?'

'Love it.'

Mike ordered drinks, and for a time they stopped trying to talk above the din from the dance floor as the amplifiers strained to deliver the last agonising decibel. At a break in the music Christy and Tim Barrett returned to the table flushed with their exertions.

'The music is really super tonight,' Christy said. 'Are you two going to dance?'

'Not I,' said Paula. 'I bruise too easily.'

'The last time I tried one of those dances I spent a week in traction,' Mike said.

'Look, would you mind awfully if Timmy and I left you?' Christy said. 'There are so many places I want to show him.'

'Go ahead,' Mike said. 'We'll try to survive.'

'Good, then, we'll be off.'

The young couple rose together and Tim said, 'Good night, Mike, Paula. Nice to meet you.' With an embarrassed grin he hurried after Christy.

'They make one feel a hundred years old, don't they?' Paula said when she and Mike were alone at the table.

'If so, you are the best-looking hundred-year-old lady I ever saw.'

Paula felt a flush of pleasure creep into her cheeks, and hoped it hadn't sounded as though she were fishing for the compliment.

'You're very kind,' she said.

'Is there any reason why we have to stay here?' Mike asked.

'Not really. Would you like to go somewhere else?'

'Some place a little quieter, maybe, where us elderly folks can talk about the good old days.'

'It's all right with me.'

Mike signalled for the waitress and paid the bill. He led the way through the crowd and back outside where the night air washed over them like a refreshing wave. A taxi moved up along the kerb and stopped in front of them.

'Where to?' Mike asked. 'This is your city, and I put my fate into your hands.'

'We really needn't do all our night-clubbing tonight. If you like, we could go up to my flat.' Paula stopped suddenly, surprised at her own words.

For a moment Mike hesitated, looking at her curiously. 'Do you have a view?'

'I'm afraid not,' Paula said, angry with herself for feeling flustered, 'but it's quiet there and we can talk.'

'It sounds great,' Mike said. He held the door of the taxi for her and they got in. Paula gave the driver her address.

She leaned back in the seat while Mike made small talk that she really didn't hear. She could hardly believe she had actually asked a man up to her flat. It was the first time since her divorce from Eric.

In the first months after their break-up she'd let Eric come up several times. In those days he was still trying to talk her into a reconciliation, but it was obvious to Paula even then that it would never work. As Eric grew steadily more irrational Paula at last forbade him to come again. Since then she had kept her little place as a sanctuary where she could isolate herself from bad news and from business and from men. Now she was bringing Mike Wilder into her private life. Paula hoped she was not making another mistake.

12

Paula Teal's flat was on a quiet, tree-shaded street of sturdy old blocks of flats.

'I'm on the first floor,' she said to Mike when the taxi stopped in front. 'Christy lives just above me.'

They walked together up the short path to the entrance. Paula unlocked the door and started up a flight of stairs just inside.

'I thought you were on the first floor,' Mike said.

'You Americans,' she said in mock exasperation. 'You really need some instruction in the English language. We are now on the ground floor. One flight up is the first floor. After that the second, and so on.'

'I should have remembered that,' Mike said. 'It's like saying petrol for gasoline and crumpets for doughnuts.'

Paula smiled at him. 'I can see we've some work to do on your translation. Come along.'

Paula snapped on the light in her flat and Mike stepped inside and looked round. It was small, furnished in muted colours, and very clean.

'Nice,' he said.

'It's a bit on the quiet side, I suppose, but then that's my nature. It's not much like New York here, is it?'

'Not much. For one thing there's no security guard downstairs. Don't you have crime in London?'

'Oh, I'm afraid we have our share. Not as bad as I hear New York is, but only last month I had a burglary here.'

'What did he take?'

'That's the odd thing, nothing was missing except some of

my personal papers. Including my letters from you, as a matter of fact, and your picture.'

'Now there's a burglar with peculiar tastes,' Mike said, grinning. 'So you kept my letters, did you?'

Paula turned away in sudden embarrassment. 'May I get you a drink?'

'That sounds good.'

'Whisky and water?'

'Fine.'

Why, Paula wondered, did she feel so terribly nervous? Anyone would think she'd never been alone with a man before. Well, the truth of it was there hadn't been all that many.

'Is anything wrong?' Mike asked, following her to the door of the tiny kitchen.

'Wrong? No, of course not. Why?'

'The way you dashed out here like something was after you.'

Paula put down the glasses she had taken from the shelf and walked over to stand before Mike. He put his arms around her and drew her close. He kissed her, and his kiss was blessedly gentle. She liked the warmth of his hands on her back.

She said, 'I was just asking myself what I was so nervous about. I had hoped to be very blasé and sophisticated, but actually it's quite an event for me to have a man in my rooms.'

He grinned down at her. 'It's an event for me too. Now how about mixing those drinks? Do you have a record player?'

'Yes, out in the sitting-room.'

'I'll pick out something seductive while you're pouring the booze.'

Paula felt herself relax as she heard Mike sorting through the records. He really was awfully understanding. Carefully she poured the two drinks – lighter on the whisky for hers. She was not accustomed to drinking much, and she wanted to be clear-headed for whatever was to happen tonight.

When Paula returned to the sitting-room Mike had an album of Cole Porter on the record player. He stood up and smiled as he took the glass from her hand.

'Shall we sit over here?' Paula asked, indicating a settee opposite the record player. Why, she wondered, did everything she said tonight sound so schoolgirlish to her own ears? She so wanted everything to go well. Please, she thought, don't let anything ruin it.

'Have you lived here long?' Mike asked.

'Three years. When I was married we had a house in Belgravia.'

'That's a pretty classy neighbourhood, isn't it?'

'It was costly enough, but Eric could afford it.'

'Your ex?'

'Yes. His father is Sir Oliver Teal. Old family, old money. They have a place out towards Henley – seventeen rooms on about twenty acres. A private lake and all that.'

'Nice cottage.'

'Quite. But I didn't mean to bore you talking about my former husband.'

'I don't mind. I might learn something about you that way.'

'You might at that. It's odd, but I do feel like talking about Eric. I was twenty-two when I married him. Just ten years ago. I thought he was quite the most glamorous, romantic, exciting man I'd ever met. His parents were so upper class, and that estate of theirs . . . well, it was overwhelming for a girl whose father spent his entire career as a civil servant.'

'Pretty exciting, was it?'

'Rather. For the first two years. It was all sailing and riding, with ski-ing in Switzerland and cruises in the Mediterranean, and hardly a quiet moment to catch our breath. Then Eric began to have moody spells. It seems he suffered a head injury in a motor racing accident some years before I met him, and he was subject to periods of deep depression. No one thought of telling me about that before we were married.

'Over the next few years he got worse, his behaviour becoming steadily more bizarre. He would have flashes of violence in which he threatened to attack me, and at other times he would be on the verge of suicide.'

'How long did you stay married to him?' Mike asked. 'And why?'

'Seven years, altogether. He wasn't always bad, you see. There were periods when he was quite his old self, and I always thought, hoped perhaps, that he'd finally recovered. However, it didn't work that way. His rational periods grew shorter and further apart. Finally, after one particularly bad spell I moved out and filed a divorce. Not long after that his parents put him into a private hospital, and that's the last I've seen of Eric. I've always felt that his parents blamed me for Eric's final break-down. At any rate, they haven't spoken or written to me since.'

'It sounds like you're well rid of the whole family.'

'Yes, I can see that now.' Paula shook her head to clear away thoughts of her former husband. 'But look here, I've talked much too much about me. Let's hear some of your secrets for a change.'

'No secrets. I'm an open book. Had an uneventful, well-fed childhood. Graduated from college without distinction. Tried marriage, but wasn't very good at it. Wrote one novel that didn't work either. Now I make a pretty good living writing about men who play games.'

'Don't you like your job, Mike?'

Mike took a long swallow from his glass before he answered. 'I don't want to sound like I'm complaining. I'd a lot rather be writing sports than, say, chopping cotton. Still, sometimes I get the feeling that sportswriters are among the world's utterly dis-pensable creatures. Like tree toads and child actors.'

'I don't know about that, I think tree toads are rather nice.'

'You've got a point. It's just that the whole world could be blowing up and I'll still be asking questions like, "What kind of a pitch did you hit for the home run, Slugger?" Does anybody really care?'

Paula saw that this turn of the conversation was putting Mike into a mood. She suspected he was also a little drunk.

'Was your wife pretty?' she asked, then wondered why the devil she'd said a thing like that.

'Sure she was pretty,' Mike said, returning to a lighter tone. 'Pretty women are the only kind I get involved with. What's that got to do with anything?'

'It just popped out. Woman's curiosity, I suppose.'

Mike carefully set his glass down on the end table and drew Paula into his arms. He kissed her. It started out easy and friendly, but quickly got serious. Paula could feel her body moving against his without any conscious effort.

She disengaged herself from the kiss and leaned back to look into his face. There was no mistaking the hunger in his eyes.

'Oh, Mike,' she said, 'I want you.'

Who said those words? Was that Paula Teal, cool, confident, self-sufficient British working girl? Some foreign person seemed to have taken possession of her body and her tongue. It was not that the emotions were false, she *did* want Mike Wilder. She wanted him physically, and she wanted him now. It was just that Paula Teal would never have spoken or acted so brazenly.

He was kissing her again. She could feel his tongue against her lips. For an instant her nerves tightened, then she yielded and her mouth opened under his. Their tongues met and caressed each other.

His hands moved over her back. Down now, massaging her waist and over her hips. Gently he kneaded the firm flesh of her buttocks through the thin material of her dress. Then his hand was under her dress. Paula shivered as his fingers slid along the nylon length of her inner thigh. He found the soft mound of pubic hair. He touched between her legs, and Paula felt herself grow moist there.

'Oh, yes, Mike. Yes!' she said against his mouth. Her own hands were busy on his body, caressing the firm muscles of his back.

'The bedroom?' he said.

'Yes, it's this way.'

Paula rose and walked towards the bedroom, feeling idiotically clumsy in her movements. Mike followed her. She could not help noticing that he took a last sip from his drink before he stood up.

Once in the bedroom, so feminine and private, Paula's nervousness grew. The bed, with its bedspread turned down so invitingly, seemed like a great naked beast waiting to devour them. Mike remained standing in the doorway, watching her. She gave a little laugh and skinned the dress off over her head.

'Last one in bed's a rotten egg.' Now wasn't that silly. She was thirty-two years old and acting like a giddy schoolgirl. She must get control of herself.

Somehow she got out of all her clothes and slipped into the

bed. How cold the sheets were. It took Mike longer to undress. She wanted to look at him, but she could not. In the darkened room she kept seeing that other shadow of the man coming towards her to do unspeakable things. Things she let him do in the hope it would help him, but he only got worse. She tried to force the thought away from her.

Mike got into bed and moved over next to her. She flinched.

'Hey, it's only me,' he said.

Paula laughed. It sounded shrill and unnatural to her. Mike did not seem to notice. He rolled on to his side and reached across her body to draw her against him. She could feel his sex, hard and erect against her thigh. Mike's hand moved to her breast. His touch was insistent as he squeezed gently and drew his fingertips across the nipple.

She rolled over in bed to face him and searched for his mouth with her own. She kissed him with her eyes shut tight. Kissed him fiercely, hungrily, with her tongue stabbing deep into his mouth. Her lower body moved urgently against him.

Paula willed her mind to shut out all but the physical sensations. She must not think those other thoughts. Not this time. Please, not this time.

Mike's breathing was harsh and hot against her ear. She was acutely aware of the faint rasp of his beard against her cheek. With one hand he gripped her shoulder and eased her over on to her back. Then he was above her, lowering his body on to hers, starting to enter her.

Paula froze.

'No!'

'What? What is it? Did I hurt you?' Mike's words were uneven, broken by his ragged breathing.

'No. Just don't, that's all.'

'Don't?'

'Please.'

For several seconds that were an eternity Mike remained above her, supporting his weight on his elbows. His eyes searched her face. Paula turned her head away so she would not have to look at him.

'Jesus,' he said. He rolled over heavily to lie on his back beside her, but not touching her.

For several minutes they lay like that, in the same bed but miles apart. Slowly Mike's breathing returned to normal. Paula's nerves twitched and snapped like live electric wires. She could feel the man's tension transmitted to her across the mattress. It was up to her to speak. She had to say something, somehow try to alleviate the awful humiliating thing that had happened.

'I suppose it would sound trite to say I'm awfully sorry.'

'Yes, it would.'

'Well, I am sorry. I did want it, Mike. I did want us to ... to ...'

'Sure.'

'Can I do something to help?'

'Let's just forget it, shall we?'

Oh God, she thought, forget it. If only I could. Forget the things that were done to me in the name of love. But she could not.

'I suppose we might as well get up,' she said.

'Right.' Mike swung out of bed and began to dress at once. Paula got out on the other side and put her clothes on again. Neither of them looked at the other.

'Would you like a drink or anything?' Paula asked when they were back in the sitting-room.

'No thanks. I've got to do some work tomorrow, and I want to get an early start.'

'Yes, I see. Well ...'

'Well ...'

As the awkward moment stretched out unbearably there was a knock at the door. Paula hurried to answer it, grateful for any intrusion.

Christy Noone stood in the doorway looking jaunty and fresh. 'Hi, you two,' she said. 'I hope I'm not interrupting anything exciting. But then if I were, you'd not have answered the door, would you?'

'Hello, Christy,' Paula said.

Mike nodded, but said nothing.

Christy looked from one to the other. 'Look, maybe I'll just paddle along to bed. I just thought that if you weren't actively engaged in some sort of fun I'd pop in for a moment.'

'Come in, Christy,' Paula said. 'Mike was . . . about to leave.'

'Was he now?' Christy gave Mike a mischievous grin. 'You're a fast one, aren't you?'

'Can I get you something?' Paula asked.

'Perhaps a cup of coffee for beddie-bye. You're sure I'm not interrupting?'

'Not at all,' Mike said, his tone unconvincingly hearty. 'I've really got to be running along. I'll see you later.' He went out of the door and closed it firmly behind him.

'How was your date?' Paula said, anxious to distract Christy from Mike's hasty departure.

'Simply smashing. We went just everywhere. But Paula, you'll never believe this, when he brought me home Tim just kissed me good night at the door and went away. Imagine, he just went away without even making a pass.'

'Maybe you didn't appeal to him that way,' Paula said.

'Oh yes I did,' Christy laughed. 'He held me so close for the good night kiss that I could tell he was interested. He's a slim lad, but let me tell you he's big enough down where it counts.'

'Then how does it happen you didn't . . . you know?'

Christy giggled behind her hand. 'I believe he simply didn't know how to get on with it and got embarrassed. If he hadn't rushed off so suddenly I'd have bloody well shown him what to do, but he was down the stairs and off before I could grab him.'

'Bad luck,' Paula said. Then as an afterthought, 'Maybe the boy's in love with you.'

'Do you really think so? Gosh, what a lark. I think I'd quite enjoy having a fellow in love with me. D'you think he'll send me flowers and all that? He did ask me to go to Hurlingham with him tomorrow and meet his family. That does sound rather serious.'

Paula's thoughts had wandered, and she tried to pull herself back into the conversation. 'Er, I'm sorry, what did you say?'

Christy sobered and looked closely at her friend. 'What happened between you and the journalist tonight, dear? Nothing good, I'd say, from the look on your face.'

'No, actually we had quite a pleasant evening,' Paula began, then she found she could get no more words out, and she began to cry. She dropped on to the settee and put her head in her hands and sobbed.

Christy, quickly switching roles to that of an older sister, sat down beside Paula and put a comforting arm round her shoulders.

'There we are, Paula,' she said, 'men can be utterly beastly sometimes. Even the nicest ones.'

'No, no,' Paula got out between sobs. 'It wasn't that he did anything I didn't want him to. Oh, God, how I wanted him to. But again I just couldn't do it in bed. It was just like the other times, only this time it was with a man who really mattered to me.'

'Did you tell him about your ex-husband? The things he made you do?'

'No. I couldn't talk about it before we went to bed, and afterwards it would have sounded as if I was making excuses.'

'God, I really did walk in at a bad time, didn't I?'

'It didn't matter any more then. The damage was done and Mike was just looking for an excuse to get out of the door and away.'

'If he cares for you he'll be back.'

'I doubt it. None of the others came back.'

'Maybe this one is different. Would you like me to sit up with you for a bit?'

'No, thanks, I'm all right now. You run along to bed.'

'Very well then,' Christy said doubtfully. 'I'll see you in the morning.'

'Good night, Christy.'

Paula closed the door after the blonde girl and stood for a moment with her back pressed against the panel. She felt completely drained, as if her insides had been wrung out. It had been foolish of her to think she could have a normal relationship with a man again. She had failed consistently ever since Eric. Still, she had so wanted it to be right with Mike Wilder. And for a short time it had seemed to be working out that way.

Mustn't think about it any more. Paula walked to the bathroom, took a sleeping pill, and went to bed.

There were few cars on the road at this hour, and the man with

*the knife drove very fast. His head hurt him badly, but his mind
was clear. He knew now that he had made no mistake about
Mike Wilder. He had seen them together. He would have killed
the bastard tonight, but his growing headache and physical
exhaustion increased the chances of botching the job. He would
go home now, take his medicine, and sleep for several hours.
Early tomorrow he would be refreshed and alert. Then he
would kill Wilder.*

13

The taxi was still some way from Tim Barrett's hotel when he told the driver to stop and let him out. He wanted to walk the rest of the way and let the cool night air wash over him. He also wanted to collect his thoughts before facing his coach, Vic Goukas.

As usual, Vic had chosen a small, quiet hotel for Tim and himself, one well away from the distractions of the city. This year most of the players were staying at the Gloucester, and many of the officials and the press and other followers of the tour were at the Regency House. A few of the top players, mostly the married ones, leased a flat for their stay in London. Others still followed the old practice of 'staying with people', a hangover from the simon-pure amateur days when wealthy tennis fans would make their homes available to the touring players whenever they were in town.

Vic's arrangements for this year were adjoining rooms for Tim and himself at the Beverly Court, a modest hotel in a quiet street in the Kensington area. If the other residents were aware that a star tennis player was living among them, they gave no sign, keeping discreetly to themselves as always.

The light mist that haloed the street lamps did nothing to dampen Tim's spirits as he walked jauntily towards the Beverly Court. In the nineteen-plus years of his life nothing quite like Christy Noone had ever happened to him. Sure, he had dated girls before, but not every often. Vic had not told him in so many words that girls would ruin his tennis game, but he had certainly implied as much. Listening to his coach, Tim had formed a mental picture of a girl tapping his vital juices the way a Vermont farmer tapped a maple tree to let the sap run into a bucket. Tim laughed to himself as he recalled the image.

Other girls Tim had gone out with – all screened by Vic or by Tim's parents – had been shallow-minded teenagers either stupefied into silence or gone all giddy at the idea of being with a genuine tennis star. How different it was with Christy. She was a full-grown woman, and as far as Tim could tell, she liked him solely for himself.

He had felt immensely proud tonight every time he and Christy walked into a different place and he saw the admiring and envious looks from the other men. There at Caesar's Christy could have had about any man she wanted. Tim was delighted and a little mystified that she had chosen him.

The whole evening had been magical. Always shy with girls, Tim had found himself talking freely with Christy about the things that really mattered to him. For her part, Christy never pressed him or made him feel he had to be entertaining. She honestly seemed to enjoy just being with him.

Out of sheer exuberance he gave a little leap into the air, then pulled up sheepishly when a strolling bobby gave him a curious look from across the street. He was acting, Tim told himself, like a goofy teenager involved in his first love affair. Well, what the heck, he *was* a teenager technically, at least for another couple of months.

Sometimes it was hard to remember. It seemed to Tim that he had been an adult from the time he left elementary school and his family had moved for the sole purpose of enrolling him in a junior high school noted for the tennis players it produced. Somewhere along the line his youth had been misplaced.

The one thing about the evening with Christy that bothered Tim a little was the way it ended. Should he have pushed things more, he wondered? Invited himself into her flat? He certainly hadn't wanted to leave her at the time, but he was afraid of being too forward and spoiling the whole thing.

Tim was not greatly experienced, but neither was he a virgin. There had been sex with two different girls. Once cramped into the back seat of a Chevrolet Impala, the other time nervously on the girl's living-room sofa while her parents slept in a rear bedroom. Both times had been vaguely pleasurable, but not the transcendental experience he had been led to expect. Tim tried to imagine how it would be with Christy. Something shared and beautiful and complete. He wanted it to be perfect.

Tim hoped he had done the right thing in not forcing the issue the first night. Sometimes Christy talked as though she were quite experienced sexually, but Tim suspected it was a pose to go along with her swinging Londoner image. Underneath she might be as confused and searching as he was.

As he neared his hotel Tim made an effort to pull his thoughts away from Christy and to concentrate on what he was going to say to Vic Goukas. There was no doubt in his mind that the coach would be waiting for him, expecting an explanation of where Tim had been until so late. Vic did not exactly set a curfew, but he did expect Tim to be in at a reasonable time. And to the coach, 'reasonable' meant any time before midnight.

Tim paused for a moment before the Beverly Court. It was a narrow four-storey building in a street of narrow four-storey buildings. Only a discreet bronze plaque identified it as a hotel. How Vic ever found these hideaways was a mystery to Tim. He drew a deep breath, squared his shoulders and walked in.

A seam of yellow light shone between the bottom of the door and the maroon carpet. Tim used his key and entered. Vic Goukas sat in a straight-backed wooden chair next to a table with a lamp. He held a copy of *Tennis World* before his face in a reading position, but from his attitude it was apparent that he had just snatched up the magazine when he heard Tim's key in the lock.

'Hi, Vic,' Tim said, making it as casual as he could.

'Hi. Have a good time?' Vic said in a rumbling bass. He was a browned leathery man wth a skull-cap of bristly white hair. He had a great prow of a nose and eyes squinted to slits from staring into the sun.

'I had a fine time,' Tim said.

'That's nice. What time is it, anyway? My watch must be running fast.'

'Vic, why don't you just chew me out and get it over with? I don't feel like going through a whole routine tonight.'

Vic dropped the magazine and abandoned all pretence that he had been reading it. He stood and faced his young protégé.

At sixty Vic Goukas was still trim and muscular, his weight the same to the ounce as when he had played in the American Davis Cup teams in the years before World War II.

He said, 'Have you been drinking?'

Tim stiffened. 'No, I haven't. Do you want me to walk a straight line for you?'

'What is it then?' Vic leaned closer and peered at him. 'There's something different about you tonight.'

Tim felt his face grow hot. He wished he could talk to Vic about Christy, about how he felt about her, but he knew he could not make the coach understand what had happened to him tonight.

He said, 'I was out with some of the Australians, that's all. We got fooling around and I lost track of the time.'

'Uh-huh. And which one of the Aussies is wearing lipstick now?'

Tim's hand went to his mouth reflexively, then he dropped it and took a step back to look his coach in the eye. 'All right, I was out with a girl. They tell me that's normal for guys my age. If you're about to give me the usual lecture on the evils of women, forget it. And don't ask me any more questions, because I don't want to talk about it.' He was breathing hard when he finished, surprised by his own outburst.

Vic Goukas was surprised too. He held up his calloused hands in a gesture of peace. 'Hey, all right, Tim, I'm not going to give you any lecture. Especially not about the evils of women. Nobody knows better than me the things a woman can do *for* a man as well as *to* him. After all, I was married to three of them.'

Vic smiled. It was a remarkably appealing smile, almost beautiful in that tough brown face. Tim felt the tension leave him, and he smiled back.

'And believe me,' Vic went on, 'I'd a lot rather see you out with an honest-to-God woman than hanging around the locker room snapping towels like a few of the players we both know. The only thing that concerns me is your tennis game. I don't have to tell you how important concentration is to playing winning tennis, and what I'm worried about is that this girl, whoever she is, will hurt your concentration here at Wimbledon.'

'Vic, this girl can only be good for me,' Tim said. 'You'll get a chance to meet her tomorrow. I asked her to come out to Hurlingham with me.'

The coach rubbed his heavy jaw thoughtfully. 'Do your folks know about her?'

'Not yet, I only met her tonight for the first time. Mom and Dad will meet her tomorrow too.'

'Well, I hope it works out,' Vic said. 'Taking her with you tomorrow is all right, I guess, but once play starts on Monday I hope you'll have your mind strictly on tennis.'

'Sure, Vic,' Tim said quickly. Then to switch the conversation to another topic he said, 'Some guy named Kaiser wanted to talk to me tonight about a deal for a signature racket.'

'Kaiser? Kaiser? I don't think I know the name.'

'He said he was with Gilfillan.'

'Oh, them. The last one of their rackets I tried wasn't fit for backboarding on a playground. What did you tell him?'

'I told him he'd have to talk to you.'

'That's good. I don't want you tied up in any contracts yet. You're a good player, Tim, and you've got the physical equipment to be a great player. When you get a couple of big tournament wins on your record people are going to recognise the fact, and then you'll be able to name your own price for commercial contracts.'

'You know, that's one part of this game I really don't like too much,' Tim said. 'You sign contracts with people promising to wear this and drink that and play their brand of balls. You get your picture taken for magazine ads selling everything from chewing gum to power lawn-mowers. We're getting to be like Indianapolis racing cars with advertising space for rent all over our bodies.'

'Sure, it's commercial as hell,' Vic agreed, 'but the money is a damn sight more honest than when I was playing. We were all "amateurs" then. No prize money, no endorsements, no shaving commercials. Of course, we didn't starve. Some "friend" always took care of our meals and lodging, and somehow envelopes with money inside used to find their way into our lockers. How much money was in your envelope depended on how well you did in the tournament. It wasn't prize money, you understand. We were "amateurs".'

Tim sighed heavily. 'I know it's a fact of life, Vic, and I know that without the extra money from ads and endorsements a lot of the players couldn't afford to stay on the tour. But I still don't like to think about it.'

'Don't think about it,' Vic said. 'That's what I'm here for.' He yawned and stretched his muscular arms. 'Guess I'll hit the hay. You better get some sleep too.'

'I will. Good night, Vic.'

'Good night, Tim.' The coach went out through the door between their rooms and closed it behind him.

Tim went to bed at once, but he lay awake for a long time thinking. Thinking of the laughing blonde girl and the way her body felt when he held her close to kiss her good night.

14

Sunday morning arrived misty and grey, but with a lumines-
cence that promised sunshine later. The man with the knife
cared nothing about the weather. He hesitated before the en-
trance to the Regency House and smoothed his pale hair down
before walking in. He strode across the pillared foyer with a
precise, determined step. The receptionist at the desk looked
up and smiled politely as he approached.

'Yes, sir, may I help you?' he said.

'I believe a friend of mine is registered here. Mr Michael
Wilder.'

'Yes, sir, the American journalist. Shall I ring his room for
you?'

'No, don't do that,' the man said quickly. 'You see, several of
his friends have got up a bit of a surprise for him today. We'll
be waiting across the street, and if you would be so good as to
signal us when he's about to leave the hotel . . .'

The receptionist looked doubtful. 'I really don't know, sir,
whether I should do a thing like that.'

The man drew a wallet from the inside pocket of his jacket
and removed a five-pound note. He smoothed the edges with
thumb and forefinger and laid the note on the counter between
them.

'Your discretion is quite admirable,' he said, 'but I'd appreciate it if you could bend the rules for once. And of course,
no one need ever know.'

The eyes of the receptionist barely flicked over the note lying
on the counter. He said, 'Actually, your friend just rang down
to ask me to arrange a hire car for him. He should be down as
soon as the car arrives.'

'*Thank you,*' the man said shortly, and turned to hurry from the hotel. He left the five-pound note where he had dropped it. It did not stay there long.

This was a lucky break at last, the man thought. Now he would not have to sit for ever in the dreary café across the street drinking coffee until Wilder chose to come out. He hurried round the block to the hotel garage and got into the green Jaguar saloon he had left there a few minutes earlier. He drove back to a spot where he could watch the entrance to the Regency House and waited, the Jag's powerful engine rumbling softly in neutral.

The telephone in Mike Wilder's room jangled as he stroked the last ridge of whiskers from his upper lip. He towelled the lather from his face and walked out of the bathroom to take the call.

'Your car is here, Mr Wilder,' said the receptionist's voice at the other end.

'Thank you, I'll be down in five minutes.'

Mike splashed lotion on his face and dragged a comb through his hair. He felt rotten. All morning he had been replaying in his mind last night's scene with Paula. Now he could see at least a dozen ways he could have handled it better. But as the boys at the race track said, the hindsight system never loses.

Maybe he had just expected too much of Paula. Or too much of him and Paula together. There was no reason for him to assume that because Paula stimulated his mind and attracted him physically, she was going to be great in bed too.

For that matter, how did he know she *wasn't* great in bed? It was time to give the male ego a rest and admit that maybe *he* had done something wrong. It took two to fail just like to took two to succeed. How could he ever forget that wretched period with Lorraine while he was writing his ill-fated novel. He had been close to despair on finding himself impotent both at the typewriter during the day and in bed at night. Then he found out what Lorraine was doing to him.

Yes, it might have helped last night if he had been a little more understanding. He had stomped out of Paula's apartment like some pimply high school kid with his first case of passion cramps.

Mike grimaced at his reflection in the mirror and turned away. He pulled on a soft sports shirt and a jacket and headed for the foyer. He had awakened at dawn this morning after a few hours of fitful sleep. He had hauled out the typewriter and struggled through his column for tomorrow. It was a sarcastic piece based on his encounter last night with J. J. Kaiser, filled with sneering remarks about the growing commercialism of tennis. Mike was not happy with the column when he finished it, but he had sent it off by messenger all the same. You couldn't come up with a literary gem every day.

After that he had been at a loss for something to do. He didn't feel like talking to anybody, and the thought of sitting around the hotel room put his teeth on edge. Then he recalled a brochure he had picked up at the airport that talked about the beauty of the English countryside around London. A drive in the country, he decided, might be just the thing to blow the cobwebs out of his mind. He had called down to the desk and arranged for a hire car to be brought round.

The receptionist looked up as Mike crossed from the lift and had a set of keys and a sheet of paper ready for him when he reached the counter.

'This is it?' Mike asked.

'Yes, sir. All that's required is that you sign the hire agreement. You do have a valid driver's licence in the United States?'

'Yes, I do,' Mike said, scratching his name at the bottom of the form. 'I thought they might send over somebody from the agency to check me out on English driving – keeping to the left and so on.'

'There'll be a folder in the glove box explaining the traffic laws and road signs,' the receptionist said. 'You'll find that you get the hang of it in no time.'

'I hope so. Tell me, what's the best way to get out of London and drive through some restful countryside where there isn't too much traffic?'

'I'd suggest you motor out to Kent, Mr Wilder. If you cross the Thames at Waterloo Bridge, and then take Kennington Road south through Lambeth and Kennington, you can drive

82

east on the A2 motorway into Kent. There are a number of roads with little traffic there that will take you out past some small farms and through an old village or two.'

'That sounds like what I'm looking for.'

'You should find a map in the car. Enjoy yourself.'

'Thanks.' Mike took the keys and walked out in front of the hotel where a small white English Ford awaited him. He slid in behind the wheel, feeling strange and uncomfortable on the right-hand side. He took several minutes to read through the pamphlet on traffic laws and look at the map. When he was ready he started the engine and moved cautiously away from the kerb.

Luckily, there was little traffic at this hour on a Sunday. Mike drove slowly and carefully down the Strand to the turn-off for Waterloo Bridge. As he eased across the bridge and south towards St George's Circus, Mike kept his mind busy thinking, *keep left, keep left, keep left.*

By the time he had passed the warehouses of Southwark and the small, dust-coloured dwellings on the outskirts of the city, Mike was becoming more at ease driving on the opposite side. While this allowed him to relax his grip on the steering wheel and unclench his teeth, it also allowed him to think about other things.

The cars on the A2 were well spaced out, so Mike fell in behind a Morris Minor that was cruising along at a comfortably slow pace. He did not want to think any more about Paula just now, so he let himself think about Lorraine.

At first he had found it flattering when Lorraine had referred to him as a *writer* in her own vocal italics when he thought of himself strictly as a reporter. Later on he put the word in proper perspective when he understood that Lorraine also thought of herself as a *writer*, having taken a number of creative writing classes. The instructors invariably told her she had a rare insight. At Lorraine's insistence, Mike had read some of her early efforts. They were formless, introspective stream-of-consciousness pieces utterly amateurish in conception and execution. Only once did he try honestly to criticise her work. That time Lorraine had gone into a sulk that lasted the better part of a month. She never asked his opinion again, but continued to send her pieces off to 'little' magazines, from which they always returned without comment.

Meanwhile, Lorraine appointed herself Mike's number one critic and literary adviser. It was she, he realised much later, who goaded him into writing a novel in the first place. Her main reason, as far as Mike could tell, was so she could introduce him at parties as 'my husband, the *author*'.

The actual writing of the thing had been sheer torture for Mike. Although he let himself be convinced that he wanted to be a novelist, he grew to hate the damn book. Lorraine's practice of nightly reading aloud what he had written during the day was especially painful. He knew the book was going badly, but he also knew Lorraine's comments were worthless.

It was during this period that their sex life dwindled to an occasional joyless coupling. Lorraine expanded her critical opinions to include his performance in bed. The results were what might have been expected.

Perversely, Mike had felt vindicated when the published novel sank without a ripple. Lorraine never forgave him.

The sound of a horn brought Mike back to the present with a start. While daydreaming he had drifted over towards the right-hand side of the road, and an oncoming lorry had given him a warning blast of the horn. Mike wrenched the steering wheel and veered back to his own side.

Shaken, he turned off at the next opportunity to a narrow road that meandered off between low, gentle hills of green grass speckled with wild flowers.

There was no one ahead of him on the new road, nor to the rear, except for a green car that turned a couple of hundred yards behind him. It seemed to Mike that the same car had followed him for some time, but he gave it no further thought.

The job, that's what he should be thinking about. Tennis. Wimbledon. To do the job they were paying him for he would have to get beneath the surface action. Let the other reporters write about the scores and the turning points of the matches and what Player A's past record is against Player B. People expected more from Mike Wilder. They expected more depth, and they expected a hatchet job.

84

Mike frowned at the thought that he had got where he was because of his reputation as a put-down artist. Somewhere early in his career his enthusiasm for sports had begun to drain away. As his writing became more sarcastic and critical, the number of papers carrying his column had increased. The public loved it when he found boxing brutal, football unimaginative, baseball dull and basketball a haven for glandular cases. At one time or another he had called motor racing bloodthirsty, hunting cruel, fishing stupid, track childish and horse racing a fool's pastime. Once when he tried to say a mildly good word for golf – a game he had just taken up – the papers were flooded with letters accusing him of selling out. Mike Wilder was not supposed to like anything.

A pale sun began to push through the fading cloud layer as the morning drew on. Mike rolled down his window for a breath of the country air. In the rear-view mirror he caught sight of the green car closing on him at a rapid pace.

Nothing unusual about that. Even at home Mike was not a fast driver, and here in England driving a right-hand car on the wrong side of the road he was not going to break any speed limits. He eased over to the left to give the other car, which he now recognised as a Jaguar saloon several years old, plenty of room to pass.

Lately it seemed to Mike that he was no longer writing with the honesty of his younger days. Sometimes he seemed to be doing a parody of himself to please his editors. Like the column he did this morning on J. J. Kaiser. Without mentioning the man by name, Mike had made him out to be a greedy little parasite living on the fringes of sports and contributing nothing. True, Mike had not found much to like about the pushy little man, still, underneath the brashness of the hustler there was a certain vulnerable quality that could be appealing. If he was to write honestly, it was these insights that he must stress, and not take cheap shots like some college humour writer. He would have to start doing better.

Mike glanced in the mirror again, and his hands gripped the wheel convulsively. The Jaguar was right behind him now, and showing no signs of pulling round to pass. The driver wore a cap and wrap-around sun glasses that obscured most of his face, but Mike could see that his lips were drawn back in an ugly grimace.

Even as Mike spotted him, the driver of the Jaguar stamped on the accelerator and the saloon lunged forward to clang solidly into the rear of the little Ford. He let the space between them widen to about three feet, then surged ahead again to thump into the Ford's rear bumper.

'What the hell's the matter with you?' Mike shouted into the blast of air that rushed in through his open window.

Bang! A third time the Jag hit him. The guy must be crazy, Mike thought. He stood on the accelerator, and cursed the lack of response from the little engine. As the Ford gradually picked up speed the Jaguar hung in behind it like a beast of prey.

The road eased into a series of curves among the rounded hillocks, and Mike could not take his attention from the tarmac in front of him long enough to look back at the man driving the Jag. A part of his mind marked the irony of having travelled so many freeways in so many cities only to meet a psychopathic driver on this charming road through the peaceful English countryside.

The larger car was moving up on him again. Mike could coax no more speed out of the Ford. Helplessly he felt the impact as the bumpers clashed again. This time the Jag did not back off, but held contact with the lighter car and accelerated. Mike found himself being pushed at upwards of sixty miles an hour round curves of the narrow English road that suddenly seemed like deadly hairpins. He did not touch the brake for fear the car would slew sideways and roll. With all his strength Mike fought the steering wheel as the little car came closer to breaking loose from the tarmac each time they squealed round a corner.

The two cars roared along at an ever-increasing speed until Mike knew the Ford must flip over at the next corner. Up ahead he could see the road sweep off to the right and vanish behind a clump of alders. He would never make it.

So he did not try to make it. Just before they reached that final curve Mike jammed the accelerator to the floor and prayed for the last reluctant ounce of power from the little engine. A gap of inches opened for a moment between him and the Jag, and instead of trying to wheel round the curve at that deadly speed Mike steered straight ahead.

He shot off the road, through a shallow ditch, and up into the field beyond. The Ford bounced and leaped over hummocks and small boulders. Mike, who had ignored the seat belt as usual, banged his head on the roof, his knees on the steering wheel, and other parts of his body on various protrusions before the car dived hub deep into a marsh and stopped.

Mike sat there for a moment while his head cleared. Then he pushed open the door and staggered out to stand beside the car. His head hurt like fury.

Back on the road, some thirty yards behind him now, the Jaguar had negotiated the curve without trouble and continued on past the alder grove. There the driver brought it to a jolting stop. As Mike watched, the reversing lights blinked on and the Jag came roaring back towards him.

15

Mike stood in the field and watched the green Jaguar as it picked up speed in reverse and raced back down the road towards the point where he had gone off it. He rubbed his head, which ached where he had slammed against the roof of the Ford, and tried to clear his mind for some course of action. As he watched the Jag come, the brake lights suddenly flashed on and the car jolted to a stop. With a grinding clash of gears the driver squealed the tyres and shot forward again. Puzzled, Mike stared after him as the Jag swept on round the curve and out of sight. As the roar of the engine faded Mike became aware that someone was calling to him.

'Hi, there, mister, are you all right?'

Mike turned in the direction of the voice to see a man standing at the roadside holding a bicycle propped against his hip. He wore a blue uniform with a stiff round cap. Spikes of grey hair bristled from under the cap. Gently the man laid his bicycle down and slogged across the marshy field towards Mike.

'Anybody hurt here?' he asked.

'No,' Mike called. Then, feeling his head, he added, 'Not seriously, anyway.' When the man drew abreast of him Mike could see the badge that identified him as a postman.

'Did you see where the other car went? The one who pushed me in here?'

'I didn't see no other car,' the postman said. 'I was just comin' down the lane over there beyond the trees when I hears you go kerwhump into the ditch and out again. "Sounds like trouble," I says to meself, so I pedals on over to see what's took place.'

'Somebody forced me off the road,' Mike said. 'A green Jaguar saloon.'

'You'd be an American, wouldn't yer?' the postman said, eyeing him narrowly.

'Yes, I would,' Mike admitted.

'Sometimes drivin' on English roads can be a bit tricky until you've got the knack.'

'The only thing tricky was the guy in the green Jaguar. He tried to wreck me.'

'Yes, I see. I'd best ride on into the village and get someone to come and pull you out.'

Mike stared morosely at the little Ford, hub-cap deep in the mire. Clearly there was nothing to be gained by further conversation with the postman about the other car. He said, 'How far is the village?'

'Willoughby's just a couple of miles.'

'I'd appreciate it.'

'Glad to be of help,' the postman said. 'I'll get someone back for you in a twinklin'.'

While Mike watched, the postman picked his way back to the road and mounted his bicycle. With a jaunty wave he pedalled off in the direction the Jaguar had gone. Mike sat down on the boot of the little car and tried to get his thoughts to mesh.

Could the driver of the Jaguar have been drunk? Not too likely before noon on a Sunday in the English countryside. And what he had been able to see of the driver's face showed a deadliness of purpose that you wouldn't expect in the face of a drunk. Somebody playing games just for the hell of it? Hardly.

Had Mike been singled out, he asked himself, or was it a random attack by some psychopath behind the wheel? He didn't know anybody in the country who would have a reason to do that to him. He hardly knew anybody, period. Still, the feeling persisted that the green Jaguar had been following him for many miles. He distinctly remembered seeing it turn off the motorway behind him to head up this country road.

Mike ran the various possibilities over in his mind and decided he didn't like any of them. He was still searching for an answer when a breakdown vehicle arrived from Willoughby. In the cab were the driver, the postman and a constable from the village.

While the breakdown vehicle driver hooked a cable to a rear bumper brace on the Ford Mike told the constable what had happened.

'Yes, I see,' the policeman said in much the same tone the postman had used. 'Did you get the number of the other car, by any chance?'

'Well, no, I was too busy trying to keep my own car on the road.'

'You say that after you had run into the meadow the other vehicle began to back towards you?'

'That's right.'

'And even then you did not notice his number?'

Mike ground his teeth. Some hotshot reporter. Always sharp, always alert, always observant of details that might be important.

'No,' he admitted, 'I just didn't think about getting his licence number. Listen, I'm not making this up. There *was* a green Jaguar, and he *did* run me off the road.'

'I have no doubt there was another car, sir,' the constable said earnestly. 'We do get some drivers on our roads out here who lose all respect for speed laws and have no consideration at all for others.'

Mike was convinced there was more to it than some thoughtless driver bullying a smaller car off the road, but the cool response he was getting from the constable showed him the futility of further discussion along that line.

The breakdown vehicle driver secured the cable to his satisfaction and walked back to his vehicle. He started the winch on its rear and the little car bounced readily up out of the marshy ground and rolled easily backwards through the ditch and back up on to the road. The driver walked slowly round the Ford, poking and pulling on it in various places.

'There doesn't seem to be any real damage,' he said to Mike, 'but you might drive it on into the garage and I'll give it a closer going over.'

'Thanks,' Mike said, 'but it's a rented car, and I imagine the rental company will take care of any repairs in their own workshop.'

'Right you are,' said the garage man.

'I would like to use your telephone, though, if you have one.'

'That I do. If you'd care to follow us in, Willoughby's just a short way down the road.'

Mike climbed into the Ford and followed the breakdown vehicle into the village. The little car handled as well as ever, and there seemed to be no after-effects from the bouncing ride into the marsh. Not for the car, anyway, Mike thought, touching the growing lump on his head. But maybe it wasn't a total loss. Maybe the bump had knocked some sense into him.

At the garage in Willoughby Mike dropped the proper coins into the phone box and dialled 01 for London. While the receiver sputtered impatiently in his ear he hauled out his wallet and fished through the cards and scraps of paper for the number he wanted. He dialled the seven digits, then waited while the long burrs, in pairs, told him the other phone was ringing. After the fifth pair of burrs Mike began to worry that no one was at home. Then there was an answer.

'Hello?'

'Hello, Paula, this is Mike.'

'Oh, yes. How are you, Mike?'

'I'm fine. Look, would you consider spending the rest of the day with a jackass?'

'Who are you thinking of?'

'Me. I acted like a juvenile last night. I'm ashamed of myself, and I want to make it up to you.'

'Mike, it wasn't all your fault. Mostly mine, actually. I know what I did to you, and there are reasons for it that I think we should talk about.'

'We can talk about them later. Are you busy this afternoon?'

'Nothing I couldn't postpone.'

'Good. I'm supposed to go out to Hurlingham and soak up atmosphere, and I'd enjoy it a whole lot more if you went with me.'

'Yes, I'd like that,' Paula said.

Mike hung up the receiver feeling years younger than he had

when starting out that morning. Nothing like a girl to cheer a man up. Maybe things would still be all right between him and Paula.

As for the grim race with the Jaguar, he just might be over-dramatising the incident as the postman and the constable seemed to think. Driving back to London he put the whole business out of his mind so he could concentrate on Paula.

16

The Sporting Club of Hurlingham, just outside London, dates back to the rule of Queen Victoria. The main building has windows from floor to ceiling and a gabled roof with sixteen chimney pots. All round the building are beautifully tended green lawns. Lawns for playing tennis, lawns for croquet, lawns for bowling, and lawns just for sitting. Dark red-brown paths intersect the lawns and meander among the giant old copper beeches.

Tim Barrett walked along one of the paths hand in hand with Christy Noone. The sun had come out at about noon, and its diffused light gave the scene a soft-focus eighteenth-century look.

'This place seems to have been here for ever,' Christy said.

'Not quite that long,' Tim said, 'but I guess it's been here for a good many years.'

Christy smoothed her short flowered skirt across her thighs. 'Do you think my dress is all right?'

Tim glanced round at the women who strolled along the paths. Most of them wore big floppy hats and soft-looking dresses in quiet pastels. 'Your dress is perfect,' he said, grinning down at Christy.

'Oh, look over there,' she cried delightedly. 'Those people are playing croquet. I didn't know anyone actually did that any more.'

Tim watched the group of elderly men and women lining up their shots carefully and striking the wooden balls with precision. The solid clack of mallet on ball came clearly across the lawn.

'They're really serious about the game,' Tim said. 'Last year

I watched them play for a while, and you'd have thought the world championship was at stake.'

'How do you know it wasn't?' Christy asked.

'By golly, maybe it was, at that,' Tim said, and they laughed together. Tim thought he had never felt so happy in his life. The one little worry he had was about introducing Christy to his parents. Once that chore was out of the way everything would be perfect.

The young couple strolled past a uniformed band sitting on folding chairs under a grove of trees. The band was playing something with a military sound that evoked the proud old days of the Empire.

'Where are we to meet your parents?' Christy asked.

'We'll catch up with them,' Tim said. 'First I'd like to walk down by the tennis courts, if it's all right with you.'

'Whatever you say, sir.'

Christy hugged Tim's arm against her side and matched her step to his. Tim enjoyed a tingle of pleasure at the envious way other young men looked at him with this exceptionally pretty English girl beside him.

On the tennis courts several of the Wimbledon players were engaged in relaxed doubles with club members. On one of the near courts Vic Goukas, his hickory-brown skin a startling contrast to his tennis whites, was hitting flat, beautiful ground strokes to a white-haired former champion who wore long white flannels in the style of the 1920s. Tim led Christy to the side of the court where they stood and watched the still graceful moves of the older men.

'Who are they?' Christy asked.

'The one on this side is Vic Goukas, my coach. I want you to meet him.'

After a few minutes Vic walked to the unoccupied umpire's chair and picked up a towel to dry his face and neck. He said a few words to the other man and walked over to where Tim stood with Christy.

'Vic, this is Christy Noone,' Tim said. 'She's the girl I told you about.'

Vic draped the towel around his neck and studied Christy for a long moment before he spoke. 'Hello.'

'We were watching you play just now,' Christy said. 'You're quite good.'

'That wasn't playing, that was just hitting the ball back and forth,' Vic said.

'Is there a difference?'

'When you're playing you try to win.'

'I'll bet you could have won if you'd tried.'

Vic gave a short barking laugh. 'I guess I could have, all right. A good sixty-year-old man should always beat a good seventy-year-old man.'

'You're teasing me, aren't you?'

'About what?'

'About being sixty years old. I don't believe you're even fifty yet.'

Vic looked into the girl's eyes for a moment, then laughed his deep rumbling laugh. 'I'll be damned if I don't think I'm beginning to understand what Tim sees in you, girl.'

'You approve then?'

'I didn't say that. I don't know if Tim told you, but the fact is I don't approve at all. It's got nothing to do with you personally, I just don't want to see Tim lose a good shot at the biggest tournament of them all because of some bro – girl.'

'Come on, Vic,' Tim said, 'you'll give Christy the wrong impression.'

'I don't think so,' said the coach. Then to Christy, 'But as you can see, whether or not I approve doesn't carry much weight with the player here.'

Christy smiled at the older man, her eyes alight with mischief. 'I'll do my best not to keep the player here away from his tennis.'

'I'm sure you will,' Vic said dryly. 'Nice to meet you. Tim, your mother and father were looking for you. They were headed for the tent where the food's set up.' He nodded again to Christy and walked back on to the court to resume his tennis.

'I don't think Mr Goukas likes me much,' Christy said.

'Sure he does,' Tim said. 'Vic just doesn't get gushy with people. You made him laugh, and believe me Vic doesn't laugh easily. Tennis is his life, and he's dead serious about it. If he

95

could, I believe he'd have a racket grafted on to the end of my arm.'

'Well, thank goodness he's not a surgeon. Something like that could prove most uncomfortable.'

Tim smiled down at her. 'You can say that again. Let's go meet the folks, if you're ready to get looked over again.'

'I love it. Let's go.'

Tim and his parents caught sight of each other at the same time across one of the broad Hurlingham lawns. Even at that distance Tim could sense a hesitation in his parents' gesture of greeting as they saw Christy.

He took Christy by the hand and they crossed the velvety lawn to where Mr and Mrs Barrett waited. A gaily striped tent was set up there to serve sandwiches, petits fours, strawberries and cream and fruit-cake. Tim rattled through the introduction, watching closely for his parents' reactions.

'It's a pleasure to meet you,' Mrs Barrett said. 'You're not one of the girl players, are you?'

'Oh, heavens, no. I wouldn't even know which end of a racket to hit with.'

'I didn't think you were, with that beautiful complexion of yours. Most of the girls who play get sun wrinkles very young.'

'Ooh, I shouldn't like that at all.'

'Er, do you live in London, Christy?' Jack Barrett asked, sounding unaccountably embarrassed.

'Yes, I do.' Christy cocked her head and looked at him. 'You know, Mr Barrett, I can hardly believe you're Tim's father. You look as though you could be one of the players. I'll bet you do play, don't you?'

'Well, at one time I was pretty fair, I guess you could say. Still, I was never in Tim's class. Nowadays I'm just a week-end hacker.'

'He's just being modest,' said Fran Barrett, smiling fondly at her husband. 'At our club at home he's still the best of his age group.'

'I bet he is,' Christy said. 'And I dare say he could teach a few of the younger men a thing or two.'

Tim was surprised to see a flush creep into his father's face.

'And I can certainly see where Tim gets his good looks,'

Christy went on. 'He has your strong features, Mr Barrett, and definitely your nose. And Mrs Barrett, Tim's eyes are the same lovely colour as yours.'

'What time did you folks get here?' Tim said, thinking Christy was laying it on a little thick.

'Just a little while ago,' his mother said. 'Have you children had anything to eat?'

'I'm not really hungry,' Tim said. 'How about you, Christy?'

'You know me, I can always eat something,' she said, linking one arm through Tim's and one through his father's. 'And I'm certainly not going to miss an opportunity to have tea with two such handsome gentlemen. Would you, Mrs Barrett?'

'No,' said Fran Barrett. 'No, I wouldn't.'

Tim wondered for a moment at a slightly off-key quality to his mother's voice. Then Christy Noone smiled up at him and he forgot about everything else.

17

Alan Doughty stood in the shade of one of Hurlingham's old copper beeches talking earnestly with his friend and manager, a busy, balding man named Paul Quinn. A little distance away Hazel Doughty sat on a bench being careful not to wrinkle the new outfit Alan had insisted she should buy. She smiled to herself as she watched the beautiful, poised women stroll along the paths.

Paul Quinn's eyes widened at something Alan had just said to him. 'What do you mean you're not interested?' Quinn demanded. 'This is a tour with World Championship Tennis I'm talking about. They've got all the top names, and week by week the biggest prize money is won in the WCT matches. I can place you in their Green group, which means you'll do most of your playing in Europe so you'll be closer to home, and now you tell me you're not interested. I don't get it.'

'I'm sorry, Paul,' Alan said, 'but I'm packing it in after Wimbledon. In a year and a half I'll be forty. That's too old for a man to be galloping about a tennis court. I'm already playing boys who could be my sons.'

'All right then, say you only play for one year. You'd still give it up before the old forty mark, and you'd pick up some good money.'

'I just can't do it. I appreciate what you're trying to do for me, Paul, but you should have talked to me about it first. My mind is made up.'

Quinn looked closely into the face of his friend. 'Is there something you're not telling me?'

'What do you mean?' Alan asked quickly.

'It's just that, well, I've known you a long time, and you've never had trouble lookin' me in the eye before.'

Alan laid a hand on his friend's shoulder. 'It's nothing important,' he said. 'Just tournament nerves.'

'Have it your own way,' Quinn said with a shrug of resignation. He drew a battered notebook from his pocket and flipped it open. 'I talked to the Panther Shoe people yesterday. They made me a tentative offer to use you in their adverts. You'll have to show up at department stores now and then, and put in appearances at tennis clinics, but the travelling will be light. Still, I don't know how they'll feel about a contract once they hear you're quitting.'

'I'd rather not sign any contracts until after Wimbledon,' Alan said.

Quinn jammed his hands into his pockets and walked round in a little circle before he went on. 'Alan, let's be honest with ourselves. After Wimbledon all bets are off. At the moment you've got your name in the papers a lot and people know who you are. If you get beaten in one of the early rounds it's all over. You know as well as I do that only the top four finalists get the plums. The rest have to scramble for what's left. I know they've got you seeded this year, but thirteenth isn't very high.'

Alan waited patiently until his friend had finished, then he said, 'Listen, Paul, I'm going to win it.'

'*Win*, did you say?'

'I said win. I mean it, I'm going to win or . . .' Alan broke off in mid-sentence. He had been about to say, *or die in the attempt.*

Quinn opened his mouth to argue, but then he saw the look in his friend's eyes and changed his mind. He said, 'All right, old chum. D'you know something? I'm damned if I don't think you might just pull it off. I tell you this, there'll be one laddie backing you all the way.'

'Thanks, Paul. That means a lot.'

'By the by, what did the doctor tell you?'

'Doctor? What do you know about the doctor?'

'Why, nothing. You told me last week you were going in for a check-up, that's all.'

'Oh, yes. He said I was fine. Just fine.'

'What's this about a doctor?' Hazel Doughty had walked over from her bench to join the men, and had heard only the tail end of their conversation.

'It's nothing, pet,' Alan said, circling an arm about his wife's waist. 'I was just telling Paul the old check-up went swimmingly.'

'You didn't tell me anything about a check-up.'

'It must have slipped my mind. Not important anyway.'

'I see.'

Paul Quinn looked from Alan to Hazel and back again uncertainly. He said, 'I'd best be off now to straighten things out with the Panther people.'

'I'm sorry if you went to a lot of trouble,' Alan said, 'but we'll do a lot better. You'll see.'

'Right. Cheerio for now.'

'What about the Panther people?' Hazel asked as Quinn walked away from them.

'Just business, love. Nothing for you to concern yourself about.'

Hazel Doughty searched her husband's face. She said, 'We never used to have secrets from each other, Alan.'

'Ah, I didn't mean it to sound that way, old girl. I'm just keyed up. Tournament nerves, as I told Paul. We'll have plenty of time to talk after Wimbledon.'

Hazel's worried expression stayed for a moment longer, then she smiled. 'Shall we have some tea and cakes, dear? I see they're serving over at the tent.'

'That's a good idea,' Alan said, taking her arm. 'Let's go.'

Milo Vasquez sat alone with a tiny tea cup clamped in his big brown hand. The tea was hot enough to burn his mouth, but he had drunk two cups and still it had not touched the core of cold deep inside him.

A group of ladies in flowered dresses came down the path as though they meant to speak to him. Milo turned on his blackest scowl and aimed it directly into their eyes. The ladies hesitated in confusion, then changed their direction.

Even in his blazing championship days Milo Vasquez had been the least approachable player on the circuit. Now, since the time of his trouble, he kept to himself more than ever. In the old days when he was winning everything in sight he kept people off simply because he did not like them or trust them. A bunch of phonies with big smiles and loud voices, all the time crowding him, trying to get close to a star. They were the same people who had looked right through him when he was nothing but a young Mexican trying to break into an Anglo game. If the Mexican kid wasn't good enough for them, Milo decided, then they weren't good enough for the champion.

His reason now for keeping people away from him was that he could not spare one shred of his concentration for anything other than playing winning tennis. It wasn't like the old days any more when all the moves were automatic. Then it had been as though the racket moved with a mind of its own to meet the oncoming ball dead centre on the strings. His serve was an awesome weapon, a missile that blurred into a pale streak. If an opponent managed a return, he would find Milo blocking the net like a brick wall.

No more. Every movement he made on the court now had to be calculated in advance and put into action with an agonising effort of will. He was winning again, but now it was hard. It was so hard that Milo Vasquez cried sometimes in the dark of the night.

He gulped down the last of his tea, which had gone cold, and shuddered at the taste. A pattern of brownish dregs remained in the bottom of the cup. People were supposed to be able to tell fortunes from tea leaves. Milo could read nothing in the cup. At least, nothing of the future. The past was there. The past was everywhere. Somehow it was not the glory days that Milo remembered, but the ugly times.

There had been much ugliness in the early years of his life. There was no mother that he remembered, only a father who smelled of stale wine and spent his welfare money with the bookie who drove an ice-cream truck through the neighbourhood. When he lost his bets, which was most of the time, he would drink more wine and beat his son in frustration. When he was fourteen Milo left home and never went back.

Fourteen is considered too old to begin tennis if you want to become a championship player. Milo had no thoughts of championships when he started. He took up the game to have something to do. He did not have the patience to idle around the streets like his friends; his exploding energy needed an outlet. He signed up for a class conducted by the city park department, and with his raw power and determination, he was soon the best in his group. The instructor, a graduate student at UCLA, recognised the boy's natural talent and introduced him to a man named Ybarra, one of the city's best and most expensive private coaches.

Ybarra, bored with teaching wealthy, overweight matrons and film celebrities who wanted to be fashionable, willingly took on the young Mexican boy. Four years later when Ybarra died of a heart attack Milo was on his way to becoming the best player in the world. The coach was one of the good things in Milo's life.

Another good thing was Maria. Slim and dark and shy, with great coffee-coloured eyes that looked at him with love. Maria. His wife.

When Maria and Milo met at a dance they were both sixteen, though he seemed much older and wiser. Milo was working hard at his tennis then, and earning enough to live on from a job Ybarra had found for him. He told Maria he would have little time to spend with her between the tennis and his job. Maria said it did not matter. She gave him all her love, holding back nothing, and they were married.

They were little more than children at the time, and success in the tennis world was still a far-off dream for Milo. Maria's dream was more modest. She wanted only to live in a home. A home like the roomy old house in Boyle Heights where she was born. There she lived for the first ten years of her life, until her father died. There was no insurance, and no way for her mother to keep up the payments on the house. After that the family lived in a succession of apartments on the east side of Los Angeles, each smaller and shabbier than the last.

Now, remembering Maria, Milo made a sound like a moan deep in his chest. Never once in their time together had she spoken to him in anger, though he had deserved it many times. Even on the day he told his wife he no longer wanted her. Maria had simply said she understood, and had even tried to smile at him while tears welled in her dark eyes. How often since that day Milo had wished she had screamed at him, cursed him, thrown something. But he would always hold the memory of her soft, forgiving smile as the tears rolled over her cheeks. It was the last time he saw Maria alive.

'Hello, Milo, how's it going?'

Milo looked up from his empty cup to see Brian White smiling at him. It would be. No one else would walk up unasked and talk to him that way. Brian White – wealthy, friendly, popular – was everything that Milo Vasquez was not. No amount of coaching could have turned Milo into a Brian White. Still, Brian would never be half the tennis player that the Mexican was.

'Hi,' Milo said shortly.

'I watched you warm up the other day,' Brian said. 'You're hitting out again the way you used to.'

'Yeah.' Milo always found it as difficult to accept a compliment as to give one. When he was playing well he didn't need anyone to tell him so.

'I'm just glad we're in different halves of the draw,' Brian said. 'If you play the way you did in Paris, you'd murder me.'

Yes, Milo thought, he would easily defeat Brian White if his game was as sharp as it had been in the French championship tournament. In Paris he had reached into hidden reserves from the past, and with supreme concentration had fought his way to the finals. It was not like the old days when he merely overpowered all comers, but it felt good to win again.

'Look,' Brian said, 'if you don't have other plans for the Savoy tonight, how about coming along with Joan and me. We could all sit together, if you don't mind being with a dull married couple.'

'I'm not going,' Milo said.

'Oh. All right, then.' Brian put out his hand. 'Good luck, Milo.'

Milo shook the proffered hand briefly and watched the lean, clean-cut tennis player walk away.

'Hey, Brian,' he called.

Brian White stopped and turned back.

'Thanks anyway. And good luck.'

Brian smiled and gave him a wave before going on his way.

Milo looked down and saw he was absent-mindedly rubbing his left arm through the soft material of his shirt sleeve. The marks were still there, he knew, along the vein inside the elbow. The deadly tracks of the needle. None of the marks was fresh; Milo hadn't shot up in a year. But the cold was still inside him. The cold that came when Maria died. His eyes narrowed as he looked across to where the defending champion sat.

Ron Hopper of Australia relaxed on the lawn that sloped up and away from the tennis courts and watched championship players of decades past stroke the ball back and forth in a decorous doubles match. Would he be on those courts in years to come, Ron wondered, playing easy, graceful ground strokes while people on the sidelines pointed him out as a former Wimbledon champion? Nobody could be a champion for ever, and Ron Hopper at thirty-five knew his days as a top competitor were numbered. He could retire right now at the top, but he was determined to go down as a champion should – on the courts.

A steady procession of people stopped to speak to him or to ask him to sign an autograph 'for my little boy'. Ron obliged them all, smiling and cordial. From time to time he reached over to pat the hand of his wife, Esther, who was seven months pregnant with their third child.

The kid would have a good life, Ron thought with satisfaction, just as they all would, whether or not he ever played another set of tennis. When he first started making big money out of the game in the mid-1960s Ron had invested wisely both in Australia and in the United States. It had earned him a reputation among the other players of being tight with a dollar, but many of them openly envied his financial security.

When the two of them were alone for a moment Esther leaned towards her husband and rubbed her hand lightly over his thigh. 'How is it, hon?' she asked. 'Any twinges?'

'It's all right, dear. Not even a tickle.'

They referred to a tear in the vastus lateralis, part of the massive quadriceps muscle in Ron's right thigh. The quadriceps controls the extension of the leg.

It happened the week after Ron won the Australian championship at Melbourne. It was not even in a competitive match. Ron was out one afternoon having a friendly hit with one of the younger Aussie players. While charging from the baseline to get a shot that barely dribbled on to his side, Ron felt something tear in his leg. He played out the set feeling only a vague soreness, and went to bed that night confident that it would be gone by morning. In the morning he could not straighten his leg.

Only Ron's doctor and his wife Esther knew the details of his injury. Some of the other Australian players suspected something was wrong when Ron withdrew from the Italian and French championships, but they never mentioned the subject. At Wimbledon the rumour had circulated that Ron was in pain, but no one really knew if it was true, and if true, how serious the injury was.

Ron Hopper knew. He knew that the first time he had to run all out to retrieve a ball the muscle tear would open up again and get larger. It would be all over then. He had no illusions about winning a second Wimbledon this year, but he would go as far as he could in the tournament. It was a matter of pride. He was the champion.

Ron wondered who among this year's entrants would succeed him as Wimbledon champion. Of the 128 men entered for the singles, there were only a handful who had a chance to win. Every year there would be some unknown who would make headlines for a day or two by knocking off a couple of seeded players in the early rounds, but when it came down to the finals on the last Saturday the two men facing each other on the Centre Court would be among the very best in the world.

Ron's attention was drawn to a knot of people moving along one of the paths. At the centre of the group was Yuri Zenger. The Hungarian was getting more attention from the press and public than any other player this year. Colourful, they called him. It was not the word Ron Hopper would have used.

The thought that Yuri Zenger might be the one to replace him brought a frown to Ron's face. Zenger's antics on and off the court offended the Australian's strong sense of tradition and dignity. It might be all right for some American prize-fighter to try to build up the gate by swearing at his opponent and generally behaving like a jackass, but such a thing should not happen in tennis. Ron sighed and turned to smile at his wife. He knew he would have little to say about who would be the next champion.

Yuri Zenger was thoroughly enjoying his position as the centre of attention. He delighted in saying outrageous things, knowing that the reporters would use them tomorrow as leads on their stories. He loved the attention of the public too, especially the women. Yuri was far from handsome in the popular concept, but he had an animal attraction for many women. He was well aware of this attraction, and used it to his advantage often.

Walking at his side with her hand resting possessively on his arm was Mrs Dorothy Keith. Yuri endured the woman's proprietary attitude for a number of reasons. One of them was the slim platinum wristwatch he wore today, a present from the generous Mrs Keith.

Actually, she was not half bad in bed for a woman her age, but then Yuri was not awfully particular. He would go to bed with anything female, the oftener the better. When the time came he would dump Mrs Keith as he had many before her, but not until he had collected a few more of the presents she so enjoyed giving him.

Yuri changed his direction when he spotted Tim Barrett. The young American was standing over by one of the tents with a slim blonde girl and an older couple who had the unmistakable look of proud parents. Yuri had been one of nine children, his father a perpetually tired factory worker, his mother a household drudge with no colour and no personality. Yuri had only contempt for parents.

'Hey, Barrett,' he called when he and his entourage were within earshot, 'sorry to hear about your bad luck.'

Tim Barrett turned away from his conversation with the girl and his parents. 'Hello, Yuri,' he said carefully. 'What bad luck is that?'

'You're in the same half of the draw with me. Too bad.'

'That's right, darn it,' Tim said. 'I don't know whether to default or just kill myself.'

Yuri was thrown a bit off-stride by the American's glib answer. Most of these pampered players from the so-called 'free world' were so used to trading insincere compliments that they became all flustered when you told them straight out you were going to beat them.

'Here's a tip that might help you, Barrett,' he said. 'In Paris I noticed you were dropping the racket head on your backhand. That is probably why you hit so many off the wood.' Yuri knew, as did all good tennis players, that if he could get an opponent thinking about his actions it could cause him to commit errors on shots that should have been automatic.

'Thanks, Yuri,' Tim said, 'I'll keep that in mind. By the way, did you know you've been hurrying your serve? Take it a little slower and I'll bet you cut down on the double faults.'

Damn him, Yuri thought. The boy was starting to play the game. Well, it would be a different matter if they met on the court. For that to happen they would both have to reach the semi-finals, and Yuri wasn't sure the Barrett boy could go that far. If he did it would be no problem. At Melbourne Yuri's constant complaining about calls and other calculated distractions had destroyed Barrett's concentration and allowed Yuri to win a fairly easy match. The same tactics had not worked with Ron Hopper, however. The Australian had many more years experience than Barrett, and Yuri had gone down in the finals in five sets. This time, though, if what he heard was true, Ron Hopper would not be around long.

'I'd like you to meet my parents, Yuri,' Tim said.

'Some other time,' Yuri answered coldly. 'We're in a hurry.' He steered Mrs Keith and the rest of his entourage away, hoping that this bit of rudeness would have its effect on the play of Tim Barrett.

It was Mrs Keith who called his attention to the approach of J. J. Kaiser and Geneva Sundstrum.

'Oh, God,' she said, 'here comes that hideous little man with his glandular freak of a girl-friend who were in Caesar's last night. Let's hurry inside and perhaps we can lose them.'

Yuri turned to look and his eyes focused on the undulating breasts as Geneva strode easily at the side of J. J. Kaiser. He felt a stirring in his crotch. Mrs Keith, though her body was in fairly good shape for an older lady, was no match for the firm golden flesh of the big blonde girl.

He said, 'No, wait a minute. I want to talk to them.' Ignoring the impatient hitch of Mrs Keith's shoulders, Yuri stood and waited for J.J. and Geneva to reach them.

'Whadaya say, Yuri,' bubbled J.J., overflowing with good fellowship. 'Good to see you again. You too, Mrs, uh . . .'

'Keith,' said Mrs Keith icily.

'Right. Say, Yuri, have you given any thought to the little proposition I made you last night?'

'Yes, I think I might be interested.' Although Yuri's answer was directed to J.J., his eyes looked challengingly into those of Geneva Sundstrum.

'That's great, Yuri, just great,' said J.J. 'When can we get together on it?'

'When can I see the equipment?'

'Any time. I've got samples at the hotel.'

'In this lady's room?'

'Uh, yes, that's where I've been keeping the stuff. Geneva's room is bigger than mine, you see, and I—'

'I'll come up on Wednesday after my second-round match and see what you've got.' Yuri made it plain this time that he was speaking to Geneva.

'Oh, Yuri,' said Mrs Keith, 'couldn't you postpone it? I was planning to have several friends in to dinner on Wednesday.'

'Go ahead and have them, you don't need me there,' Yuri said, not taking his eyes from Geneva.

'It doesn't have to be Wednesday,' J.J. put in quickly. 'Any other day this week would be just as good.'

'Wednesday,' Yuri said with finality. To Geneva he said, 'You will be there?'

'I'll be there,' she said.

'Good. I'll see you.' Without waiting for J.J.'s good-bye, he turned his group again and walked away.

18

As Mike Wilder walked with Paula Teal among the lawns of Hurlingham a little of last night's tension was still there. However, Mike thought he could sense a new warmth between them, a growing rapport that had not been there before. By unspoken agreement, neither mentioned the unfortunate bedroom scene. They could talk about that later.

Mike had touched only briefly on his adventure on the road that morning, turning it into a joke about his unfamiliarity with English roads and English drivers. Paula showed a concern for the bump on his head that pleased him and also embarrassed him a little.

Now as he looked round at the well-groomed, well-mannered people who wandered over the lush grounds of the old Sporting Club, Mike decided it was about time he went to work.

As though she had read his mind, Paula said, 'You go ahead and be a reporter. I'm perfectly happy just tagging along and looking at the people.'

'I suppose I should start taking a few notes,' Mike said, 'to justify my salary if nothing else.'

'Look, there's Christy,' Paula said. 'And her young tennis player.'

Following Paula's gaze, Mike saw Christy Noone and Tim Barrett across an expanse of emerald lawn. They were standing with a handsome older couple. Just then Christy looked in their direction and recognised Paula and Mike. She waved enthusiastically, then tugged at Tim's arm, pointing with her free hand. Tim saw them, said a few more words to the older couple, and started across the lawn with Christy.

Mike assumed the man and woman were Tim's parents.

From their heads-together attitude as the young couple walked away from them, he guessed the jury was still out on Christy Noone.

'Hello there, you two,' Christy called when they were within hearing range. 'Did you just get here? We've been having a simply marvellous time, haven't we, Timmy?'

Tim grinned at the petite blonde girl and said hello to Mike and Paula.

'Kind of the lull before the storm, isn't it?' Mike said.

'I guess so,' Tim said. 'It's pleasant enough out here, but I'll be glad when play starts.'

'What court will you be on tomorrow?' Mike asked.

'Number twelve,' Tim said. 'That's somewhere out near the car park.'

'I see you're playing Jan Oesterhouse in the first round,' Mike said. He had looked up the Dutch player and found his record definitely mediocre.

'That's right.'

'Any prediction?'

Tim hesitated before speaking. 'Jan's a good player when he's at the top of his game. His problem is staying in shape. I've only played him once before.'

'How did you do?'

'I won, two and love.'

Mike knew this was the players' verbal shorthand for a victory of 6—2, 6—0. 'Pretty decisive,' he said.

Tim shrugged. 'You can't tell a lot from just one match.'

'Timmy's just being modest,' Christy said, clinging to his arm. 'He's going to win the championship.'

Tim said, 'There's a hundred and twenty-odd other guys who are going to have something to say about that.'

'But isn't it true,' Mike said, 'that about a hundred of them have about as much chance of winning the championship as I would?'

'Maybe,' Tim conceded, 'but I was taught to play every match as though it were the finals.'

Christy's attention began to wander. 'Look, Timmy, at those old people rolling balls across the grass. What are they doing?'

'It's lawn bowling, I think.'

'I've never seen it before. Can we go and watch?'

'Sure.' Tim turned to go with the girl. 'See you later,' he said to Mike and Paula.

'Good luck,' Mike said. 'I'll try to find court number twelve and watch you for a while tomorrow.'

Paula and Mike stood together and watched the younger couple cross the lawn towards the bowlers.

'What are his chances, Mike?' Paula asked.

'Fair, as near as I've been able to dope it out. Tim's probably the best of the younger crop of players, but most people who should know think he's a year or two away from championship level.'

'He seems quite nice.'

'It takes more than being nice to make a winner.'

'Pity.'

Mike slipped his glasses into his breast pocket, and they strolled idly towards the club-house.

'Mike, do you know those people over by that small tent? They've been looking over towards us as though they recognised you.'

Mike squinted in the direction Paula indicated. 'Is that booze those jokers in the white jackets are serving?'

'I believe it is.'

'Then it's a good bet those are fellow sportswriters.' He put his glasses back on for a moment and nodded. 'Just as I thought. Come along and meet some other members of the trade.'

Mike walked Paula over to the small tent where the others were helping themselves to the free liquor and sandwiches. Mike's position as a nationally syndicated columnist and featured writer for *Sportsweek* put him in a higher income bracket than most of the others, and the kidding around took on a noticeably hard edge.

'Gosh, this is quite an event,' said the UPI man, 'having the world famous Mike Wilder show up in person. This might even put Wimbledon on the map.'

'He can't be here for the tennis,' said the *New York Times*. 'Probably has a golfing date with the Prime Minister.'

'Aw, I'll bet he's an expert on tennis just like every other game,' said the AP. 'How about it, Mike?'

'What's so tough about tennis?' Mike said. 'Once you've learned that on the line is in and love stands for nothing, you've got it knocked.'

A rawboned woman writer from one of the tennis magazines pushed her way forward. 'I wonder if you know how to *play* the game,' she said with heavy-handed sarcasm.

'Play? Are you kidding? I was practically born with a tennis racket in my hand.'

The other men laughed good-naturedly at this, but the woman from the tennis magazine snorted contemptuously and moved away.

'You'd better not get Bobbie Jo riled up, Mike,' said the UPI. 'She can probably take you two falls out of three in free-style wrestling.'

'I'll try to stay out of her way,' Mike said.

'You don't have to worry,' the *Times* said with a smirk. 'Bobbie Jo will spend the next two weeks hanging around the locker room. The ladies' locker room, naturally. Or maybe I mean unnaturally.'

'I notice you guys wait until Bobbie Jo is out of earshot before you get off your zingers,' Mike observed.

'We're not idiots,' said the UPI. 'There isn't a man here she couldn't whip.'

There was a stir among the reporters as they caught sight of Yuri Zenger and his company strolling along a nearby path. Mike got the impression that Yuri had timed his passing to catch the attention of as many of the press as possible. The reporters took the bait and hurried over to head him off. The volatile Hungarian was, by unanimous vote, the hottest story at this year's Wimbledon.

Mike and Paula wandered along behind the others.

'I'm not sure I understood all that by-play,' Paula said.

'The boys are great kidders,' Mike told her.

'Were they implying that the woman reporter is a lesbian?'

'That's the rumour,' Mike said. 'I personally don't know of any facts that would confirm it. Sportswriters have a patho-logical dislike of women invading their field, and the whole business could be jealousy. Or maybe it's just that Bobbie Jo does look an awful lot like a man.'

'And what was that about the locker room? Do the women tennis players tend to be a little, well, that way?'

'It's a similar situation. Women athletes, unless they're in some super-graceful sport like gymnastics or figure-skating, are always suspect. Especially to the kind of man who is not quite sure of his own masculinity. Tennis is especially vulnerable to that kind of talk since there have been several well-publicised examples. Involving both men and women, I ought to add. If you ask me, I don't think the sport is any more faggy than a lot of others. There was a good middleweight a few years ago who fought only for the clinches.'

'Now you're pulling my leg.'

'Only a little bit.'

They caught up with the group which had formed a ragged semi-circle facing Yuri Zenger. Mrs Keith was poised a step behind her tennis player, keeping a wary eye on the reporters as though ready to scold if any of them got too close.

'Who's your first opponent, Yuri?' somebody asked.

'What does it matter?' said the Hungarian. 'Whoever it is I will crush him like a cockroach. These early rounds are a bore.'

'What player do you fear most?' asked the AP.

'Fear? I fear no one. Right now I am the best tennis player in the world. The people who make the rankings and the men who run the tournaments do not like me because I break their silly rules. To me it does not matter whether they like me or not. When I am Wimbledon champion the whole world will have to admit that I am the best.'

'What about Ron Hopper?' asked *Sports Illustrated.* 'He's the number one seed, and he beat you out in Melbourne.'

Yuri dismissed the number one seed with a wave of his hand. 'Hopper is a has-been. The only reason he is top seed is because he won here last year. He was lucky in Melbourne. The umpire was against me and I was playing with a fever of 102 or Hopper would not have beaten me. He will never do it again.'

While the other reporters scribbled in their notebooks Mike took Paula's arm and steered her away towards the tennis courts. 'I can take just so much of Yuri Zenger,' he said.

'Is he really as nasty as all that,' Paula asked, 'or is he putting on an act?'

'I'd say he's about two-thirds nasty and one-third act.'

'I hope he loses.'

'Then if he's done nothing else, Yuri's given you a rooting interest in the tournament.'

'I suppose so.'

They started down the grassy slope to the courts.

'Isn't that Alan Doughty?' Paula said. 'Over there signing autographs?'

'Looks like him, from his pictures,' Mike said. 'I wonder who the lady is, standing off to one side and watching him.'

'His wife, I'll bet. She has the look of an English housewife.'

'What look is that?'

'A bit pale from not enough sun, a bit overweight from too many starchy foods, and a slightly pinched expression from worrying about her old man.'

'Let's find out if you're right.'

Mike introduced himself and Paula, and learned that the lady was indeed Hazel Doughty.

'I'm pleased to meet you,' she said, and her smile brought a sudden beauty to her plain features. 'I'm sure Alan will be glad to talk to you as soon as he's finished with the kids. He's always loved kids.'

'Have you any children of your own, Mrs Doughty?' Paula asked.

A brief shadow crossed her face. 'No, we haven't. What with Alan travelling so much with his tennis we thought it'd be best to wait before starting a family.'

'How do you think Alan will do at Wimbledon?' Mike asked.

'Oh, I always feel Alan can win,' she said loyally. 'He's an awfully good player, you know.' A little of the worried look came back. 'Only, this time I wish . . .'

'You wish what, Mrs Doughty?' Mike said. The woman was deeply concerned about something, he saw, and Mike had no hesitation about asking questions. A reporter could not afford the luxury of tact.

Hazel Doughty's smile came back, looking a little forced this time. 'It's nothing,' she said. 'Here comes Alan. He'll be happy to answer your questions.'

When introductions had been made Mike asked the player about his feelings on the eve of Wimbledon.

'I plan to do my best,' he said. 'That's all I can promise. If I do well I hope the world will see it as a victory for England.' He grinned at his words, and the sun wrinkles creased his tanned face. 'That sounds a bit starchy, doesn't it? Still, England could use a victory or two these days.'

'Good luck to you,' Mike said. 'I'll probably be seeing you around over the next two weeks.'

'I only hope I'm around as long as that myself.' Doughty shook Mike's hand and said good-bye to Paula.

Mike wondered about something dark he had glimpsed deep in the eyes of this friendly, homely Englishman. Maybe he was seeing a mystery where none existed.

To Paula he said, 'I think I've seen enough here. Everybody's wearing his own personal meet-the-press mask. How about you?'

'You mean am I wearing a mask?'

'No, smarty, I mean is there anything else you'd like to do here?'

'I'm ready to leave when you are.'

'Let's go then. Uh, Paula . . .'

'What is it, Mike?'

'I know this is kind of late, and I intended to ask you before, but, well, will you go to the Savoy with me tonight? I hate formal dinners, especially when there are going to be speeches, but this one would be a lot more bearable if you'd come along.'

Paula frowned and chewed her lip as though thinking it over. 'Actually, I had several other invitations I was considering. Have you any special inducement to offer?'

'There's the sight of me in a dinner-jacket. Curiosity-seekers have lined up around the block to see that.'

Paula laughed gaily. 'That's done it, it's a date. By a happy coincidence I have a new long dress waiting at home.'

They laughed together then and walked out to the car park. Mike felt a fleeting chill as they reached the hired Ford and he saw the pushed-in rear bumper. The memory of the pursuing Jaguar and the face behind the wheel came back to him.

He saw Paula looking at him curiously, and pushed the thought out of his mind.

19

'Would you like to come inside for a bit?' Paula asked as Mike pulled up in front of her block of flats.

Mike looked doubtful. 'I should go back to the hotel and see if my rented tux got there all right.'

'Please. There's plenty of time, and I do think we ought to talk.'

'Okay.' Mike parked the car and they walked inside and up one flight to Paula's flat. Paula opened the door and they entered the living-room. For a moment they stood there awkwardly without speaking.

'Can I get you a drink?' Paula said.

'No, thanks. Well, maybe a short one.'

Paula went into the kitchen and Mike took a chair, feeling clumsy and not knowing where to put his hands. He lit a cigarette. In a few minutes Paula returned carrying two drinks, handed one to him, and perched on the edge of the settee facing him.

'I want to talk about last night,' she said. 'I want to tell you what happened and why it happened.'

'You don't have to tell me anything,' Mike said.

'Yes, in a way I do. Last night is hanging over us like our own personal cloud. If there's ever going to be anything between you and me, anything important, we have to get rid of that cloud.'

Mike stubbed out his cigarette and resisted the impulse to light another. 'I guess you're right,' he said.

Paula drew a deep breath and began to speak, keeping her eyes directly on Mike, alert for any reaction. 'Last night was not the first time that's happened to me. I tell you this so you won't think it's your fault. Since my divorce from Eric I have been to bed with three other men. Before you. The experience was the same with each of them – I simply could not complete the act, however much I wanted to. I never saw any of them again afterwards. Two of them did phone me again, thinking, perhaps, that I was some sort of challenge to their manhood, but I couldn't bear the thought of seeing them again. I was too humiliated, and besides, they didn't mean that much to me in the first place. With you it's different, Mike. Maybe because of the way we were in New York, and the letters we wrote to each other, but you were . . . you *are* by way of being something special to me. That's why I wanted so much for it to be good with us, and why it was especially bitter for me when I failed again.'

'Paula, you're being too critical of yourself,' Mike said.

'Please don't stop me. I have to get these things said now, or I may never do it. You see, I think there's still hope for you and me. I don't want to let it get away. Mike, I am not a frigid woman. That sounds odd, I suppose, after last night, but really I'm not. I have all the normal, healthy sex urges that every well-adjusted woman does. If anything, I have more of them. And ten years ago I enjoyed sex about as much as the law permits.'

Paula rose and walked across the room to the window. She looked out into the gentle Chelsea afternoon for a minute before she went on.

'My husband and I had a supremely active sex life at first. Then it began to go bad. In a hurry. One day Eric could no longer make love to me. It seems now that it happened in one day, but of course it must have taken longer. I felt awful, as though I had let him down. When I tried to talk to him about it he became furious. I told him I would do anything I could to help him.'

She turned from the window to face Mike. 'That, as things turned out, was a serious mistake. Eric took me at my word, and he began to ask me to do things for him. And to him. And there were things he wanted to do to me. And I tried. I really tried for the sake of whatever it was I thought he and I had together.

'His actions became more and more bizarre until . . .' Paula hugged herself and shuddered as though from a sudden chill.

'Until I felt so utterly debased and degraded that I shrivelled inside when he touched me, even during his more normal periods. You simply wouldn't believe some of the things . . .'

'I might,' Mike said quietly. 'You'd be surprised at some of the stories a reporter gets to hear.'

Paula smiled at him. 'I'm sorry,' she said. 'That sounded rather like "nobody knows the trouble I've seen", didn't it?'

'That's all right,' Mike said. 'Nobody *does* know, but some of us might understand if you give us a chance.'

'I shan't go into clinical detail,' Paula went on, 'but some of the things Eric wanted to do in the bedroom were better suited to the bathroom. Since we've been apart I've read enough books on the subject to know that such deviations are not all that uncommon, but knowing it intellectually and accepting it emotionally are two entirely different things.'

Mike stood up suddenly and walked across the room to take the empty glass from Paula's hand. 'Let me fill this for you,' he said.

'No, please, I've had enough for now.'

'Is there anything more you want to tell me?'

'Just one thing. I want to go to bed with you, Mike. Now.'

'As an experiment?'

'Maybe that's partly it. Mostly it's just that I want you so damn much I ache. I dare say that's a hell of a thing for a woman to confess to a man.'

'That all depends. Are you very sure that's what you want? This isn't just therapy?'

'It's what I want. I mean if . . . if you want it too. I can't make any promises, you know.'

Mike stepped forward and took both of Paula's hands in his own. He said, 'There's just one promise I'm going to insist on.'

'What's that?'

'No more talk.'

Paula pressed her cheek against his chest. 'No more talk,' she said.

They went into the bedroom and undressed. There was not the urgency of the night before, yet the room crackled with suppressed excitement. Soon they lay side by side in Paula's bed under a pale blue sheet. Their bodies touched at several points, but Mike made no move towards her, sensing that this time Paula must be allowed to set the pace.

Gradually Mike could feel the tension leave Paula as her muscles relaxed one by one. Her breathing became deeper and she stirred gently, moving closer to him.

Paula rolled a little to one side and reached over to lay her hand on Mike's bare chest. He turned his head to look at her, but still did not move his body. Paula smiled at him with her eyes, and began to stroke his chest. Very slowly her hand moved lower, across his solar plexus to his flat stomach.

'You had your appendix out,' she said, her voice a husky murmur.

'When I was ten,' he said.

Paula continued to explore his body. Her growing self-assurance was transmitted to Mike through her touch. She traced an ever-diminishing circle around his navel, finishing with a gently probing forefinger.

Although Mike kept his body still, there was no disguising the fact that he was acutely aroused by Paula's caress.

With one swift motion Paula seized the top of the sheet and peeled it down and away from their bodies. With one hand still flat on Mike's stomach she sat up in bed, then moved so she was kneeling above him.

Mike's breathing was harsh in his throat now as he let himself take a long slow look at the nude body of the woman. Her breasts swayed gently with her movement. The soft roundness of her belly curved invitingly into a shadow of reddish-brown hair.

Paula's hand moved again, and Mike gasped aloud and shuddered. She continued to stroke him until he could have borne it no longer. At that precise moment Paula leaned down and placed her lips lightly against his mouth.

'Now, Mike, please.'

He moved at last, not tentatively, but with firm masculine confidence. He found Paula thoroughly ready for him.

The act lasted not more than five minutes. Had it been possible, Mike would have prolonged it, but their passion had built to such a frenzied pitch that there was no holding back from the clinging, shuddering climax.

For a long time afterwards they lay together, their bodies still joined.

Paula was the first to speak.

'May I say that was magnificent?'

'You may.'

'Seriously, darling, do you know what you've done for me?'

'Sssh.'

They lay silently for another long period, Paula making contented woman sounds and Mike feeling like the king of the world. The light that filtered in through the curtains was fading when Paula spoke again.

'If we're going to the Savoy this evening we'd better start thinking about getting ready.'

'I don't want to go to the Savoy.'

'Really?'

'Really.'

'I'm glad. I don't much want to go either.'

'Good. We'll stay right here for ever.'

Paula moved her mouth to his and they kissed with the deep familiarity of lovers. After a while she drew back and said, 'What'll we do if we get hungry?'

'Got anything in the kitchen?'

'Some left-over casserole. I suppose I could warm it up, if that's all right.'

'I love warmed-up casserole.'

'Do you want some?'

'Later.'

'Mmmmm.'

'Much later.'

As Mike lay back drowsy and happy, a not-so-pleasant idea began to edge into his consciousness. It had to do with something Paula had said in the last couple of days about her exhusband. There seemed to be some kind of a connection he should make, but before he could think more about it, Paula's hand started to move over him again. This time Mike let himself respond fully and immediately.

They never did heat up the casserole.

20

It has been said that it is easier to get the Order of the British Empire than a press pass for Wimbledon. Centre Court passes are bestowed, one to each major newspaper and one each to other selected media, by an official of the All England Tennis Club. For these two weeks of early summer this official has Saint Peter-like power to grant or deny entrance to the promised land.

Mike Wilder, holder of one of the coveted passes, gazed round the octagonal, green-roofed grandstand as he had three days earlier when he arrived in England. Today the stands were packed with upwards of ten thousand lucky seat-holders and another three thousand standing spectators who had started queueing up the night before for the privilege of watching the champion play in the opening round.

The upholstered green lawn chairs in the Royal Box were filled with minor nobility. The Queen didn't attend any more, but occasionally a princess would show up and set the crowd astir.

The press section was up behind the glassed-in broadcasters' booth. Mike had put in a token appearance, said his hellos, and slipped away as soon as possible. It was his feeling that sportswriters bunched together tended to quote each other in their stories. As far as the scores and the factual on-court action were concerned, the wire services would carry complete accounts. Mike wanted to be on his own where he could try to get into the heads of the players and those who came to watch them.

The first-round match being played on the Centre Court was utterly devoid of suspense. Ron Hopper, the defending champion, was putting away an awe-struck young Floridian without having to extend himself. Mike left the one-sided contest and walked through the passageway that led to the outlying courts.

The day was sunny and unusually warm for London in June. From all directions could be heard the satisfying *thwock* of racket on ball accompanied by polite bursts of applause from the spectators. The old tennis club was so efficiently laid out that twenty-five thousand people could move freely about with no feeling of being crowded. All the spectators, from the Centre Court on, maintained a traditional decorum and a sense of good manners unique in the sports world.

Mike stopped at one of the stalls set up on the lawn and bought a dish of strawberries in thick Devonshire cream. They were a little rich for his taste, but you simply did not attend Wimbledon and not eat strawberries and cream. They were the local equivalent of hot dogs at a baseball game.

Strolling along the broad paths between the courts, Mike studied the faces of the players. The tension of playing at Wimbledon was as evident on court fifteen as on the Centre Court. Part of the special quality of Wimbledon was, of course, the prize money – more than £120,000 this year. But more important was that the winner at Wimbledon was popularly, if unofficially, recognised as the world champion.

Because of the opening ceremonies, only some forty matches were scheduled for today, all in the men's singles. Tomorrow would be a full day with more than a hundred matches being played as the women's singles began, as well as the men's, women's and mixed doubles.

On one of the peripheral courts Mike spotted Alan Doughty playing an overweight, Latin-looking man. Mike consulted his programme and saw that the other man was a Spaniard, unseeded. Doughty seemed to be having an easy time of it as he angled precise volleys out of the other's reach.

At the sideline Hazel Doughty stood watching her husband. She looked worried. Mike noted that she kept her eyes on Alan rather than following the ball from one end of the court to the other in the accepted manner.

Mike let his thoughts stray for a moment to Paula Teal. He would have liked her to be here with him, but as Paula had pointed out this morning, she was a working girl. She had made breakfast for the two of them and declined his offer of a lift to her office. At that hour of the day, she told him, a bus was a much more efficient mode of transport up Fleet Street than a private car. They had made a date for dinner and kissed in the hallway outside Paula's flat. Mike went away with a good feeling that was still with him.

As Alan Doughty and the Spaniard changed ends of the court Mike walked over to stand next to Hazel.

'Alan seems to be playing well,' he said.

Hazel started, then gave him a smile. 'Oh, hello, Mr Wilder. Yes, I suppose he's playing well enough.'

Something in her voice and in the quickness of her smile struck Mike as off-key. It couldn't be the way the match was going, as the score-board showed Alan had won the first set 6–2 and was serving with a 3–0 lead in the second.

'Do you see something out there that I don't?' he asked.

Hazel turned and looked closely at him, as though to assure herself that he was really interested. 'No, there's nothing wrong with his game,' she said. 'There's something else, though. Some trouble of Alan's that he's not telling me.'

Mike was going to ask her more, but play had started again and Hazel Doughty's attention was completely given over to her husband's match.

Mike wandered off and found an empty spot on a bench. He sat down and scribbled some notes in a spiral pad – quick impressions that he would type out at greater length when he returned to his hotel.

He paused in his writing to wonder again about the curious way the receptionist had acted that morning. When Mike stopped by to pick up his mail the receptionist had smiled in a familiar way and said, 'I trust you and your friends met all right yesterday?'

'What friends?' Mike had asked.

'Why, the gentleman, er, that is, I assumed you were joining friends later.'

Further questioning by Mike brought only increasingly vague responses from the receptionist, who suddenly became very busy elsewhere.

Mike began putting things together. First there was the

anonymous phone caller who had asked for his room number the day he arrived in London. Then the man Christy had seen watching him in the discotheque. Now there was the near-miss yesterday with the murderous Jaguar and the odd evasiveness of the receptionist. Taken singly these events might not mean much, but add them together and throw in a couple of things Paula had told him and it began to form a suspicion in Mike's mind that he didn't much like. He resolved to pursue the matter later, but just now he was distracted by a voice that broke the decorum of tennis manners by shouting his name across a court.

'Mike! Mike Wilder! Over here!'

Peering towards the voice Mike recognised the perky blonde head of Christy Noone. She was sitting on a bench with a group of young men who all seemed to be vying for her attention. Mike gave her a modest wave, but made no move to join the girl and her admirers.

On the court between them Tim Barrett was playing an earnest-looking opponent who kept pushing his horn-rimmed glasses back up on his nose. Tim's attention seemed to be divided between the tennis game and Christy Noone. Behind the umpire's chair sat Vic Goukas. The scowl on the coach's craggy face said plainly that he did not like what was happening on the court.

Mike moved along the path to the court where Milo Vasquez was playing. No wandering of attention here. So intent on his game was the dark-eyed Mexican-American that it seemed he could throw away the racket if he wanted and force the ball over the net by sheer willpower.

A sudden burst of derisive crowd noise that was most un-Wimbledon-like turned heads momentarily away from the quieter matches out on the grounds. The sound seemed to come from court one where the stands held about half as many spectators as the Centre Court. Mike headed in that direction to see what had caused the disturbance.

Yuri Zenger was playing on court one. As Mike approached he saw the Hungarian with his arms spread wide in prayerful appeal to a linesman as he pointed with his toe to a spot well outside the white chalk baseline. The linesman sat impassively as Zenger knelt on the grass and traced a circle with his finger around the spot where he was claiming his opponent's shot had landed. His claim was plainly frivolous, since if he really felt he had a case he would appeal to the umpire, who had the power to change a linesman's call.

The Hungarian continued his pantomime well past the point where it might have been amusing, and the crowd responded with an impatient mutter. Finally he picked up his racket and deliberately served two balls into the far seats for a double fault. A few in the crowd booed this display of contempt.

A glance at the score-board told Mike that Zenger was easily winning the match, and could afford to throw away points if he wanted to. However, the gratuitous humiliation of his opponent did not go down well with the crowd. Sulkily, Zenger turned businesslike and quickly won the next two points and the game.

Mike turned and started out of court one the way he had come. Outside he was stopped by a plump young man with frizzy hair and an uncertain moustache.

'Excuse me, Mr Wilder, I'm Cliff Willits.'

'How are you?' Mike said, wondering who the kid was and whether he was supposed to know him.

'I'm covering the Wimbledon tournament for the *San Francisco Freedom.*'

'*Freedom,* did you say?'

'Yes. We're the new alternative newspaper in the Bay area.'

Oh, yeah, alternative, Mike thought. That was today's word for what used to be called underground or radical. Young Willits had the look, all right. Bright, busy eyes, smirk of superiority.

'Isn't this a little outside your usual coverage?' Mike asked, thinking riots and rock concerts were more the *Freedom*'s sort of thing.

The young man fell into step beside him. 'You're right, of course, but we're not going to give Wimbledon the usual Establishment treatment.'

'I'll bet you're not.'

'I want you to know that I agree with what you've been saying for years, that organised sports are a symbol of all that's rotten in our whole sick society.'

'Have I been saying that?'

'You couldn't come right out with it, naturally, but some of us can read between the lines. You were the only sportswriter anybody read at Berkeley. That's where I graduated.'

'It figures.'

'Your columns about how de-humanising it is for persons to take part in big-money athletics really hit home with us.'

'That's not exactly what I—'

'And the article you did for *Sportsweek* about Little League. Heavy! All those parents trying to force their old restrictive values on their children rather than giving the young people freedom to choose their own paths.'

'I've never liked the idea of adults manipulating kids for reasons of their own, whether it's parental pride or politics.'

'Exactly! It's one more example of how the decadent old force their will on the sensitive young.'

'That's a little stronger than I had in mind.'

Willits plunged ahead, warming to his own rhetoric. 'And the most sickening thing about sports is this whole Western imperialist emphasis on winning. Everybody plays only to win. Beating somebody else is the only thing that counts. Look at the football coaches who are the big Establishment heroes – Vince Lombardi, George Allen, Don Shula. They're nothing but Patton and MacArthur without the uniforms and gold braid. It's the system that counts, and the player means nothing. He's only there to be exploited by the coaches and the fat cat owners.'

Mike stopped walking abruptly, and Cliff Willits nearly stumbled beside him.

'Hold it a minute, Willits. Are you relating articles and columns written by me to these half-ass ideas of yours?'

The young man apparently missed the descriptive adjective, because he went on in the same one-insider-to-another tone. 'I understand that your salary is paid by the Establishment, and you can't come right out and say these things the way we can on the *Freedom*, but you're a good enough writer to get the meaning through.'

'Maybe I'm not such a good writer. You seem to be getting meanings out of my stuff that I never put in.'

'I don't understand.'

'This Establishment you keep talking about; if it's the people who are keeping me employed I can't get all that mad at them.'

'Yes, but—'

'And this exploitation of the players you're worried about. Professional jocks work seven or eight months a year at an average salary of $30,000. Big stars sign contracts for a million and up. The only group that's better paid is rock musicians. If that's exploitation I know a lot of people who'd be glad to stand in line for some.'

Cliff Willits stared at Mike as though he had just heard Joan Baez sing the *Marines' Hymn.* 'But that's measuring everything in dollars. What about the de-humanising emphasis our society puts on winning? They make it a disgrace to lose at anything.'

'This may finish me as a counter-culture hero,' Mike said, 'but I'm going to set you straight on my feelings about winning and losing. First, let me say I agree with you that losing is no disgrace. We've had some pretty good men who were losers. Robert E. Lee for one. Adlai Stevenson for another. They lost, but they were doing their very best to win. Not trying is the disgrace.

'On the other hand, winning is not to be sneered at. You mentioned Patton and MacArthur who are, I presume, bad guys in your philosophy. Maybe they're not my favourite people either, but they were winners, and at the time that was considered a good thing to be, considering the alternative.'

'Okay, so maybe we needed soldiers back then, but sports isn't World War Two.'

'No, it isn't. But it *is* a job. The goal of the job is to win. A professional who does less than his best is cheating.'

'What you're saying is that winning is everything.'

'I'll paraphrase Joe E. Lewis and say I've won some and I've lost some, and I've learned one thing – winning is better.'

Willits swept his arm in a wide arc encompassing all of Wimbledon. 'You can't mean you approve of this silly circus? Here you have young people from fifty nations gathered together not to solve the world's problems but to beat hell out of each other.'

'I'll tell you this, son,' Mike said, softening his tone, 'I'd much rather see them do it with tennis balls on grass courts than with bullets on a battlefield.'

Willits stared at him with bitter reproach, and Mike knew he had just been dropped from the young man's Ten-Most-Admired list. And for what? All his speechifying was not going to have any effect on Cliff Willits's opinions. Only maturity would do that. Maybe.

Still, Mike felt a curious satisfaction in the encounter. In speaking out he had put into words some deep feelings he had never defined. Possibly he had started to clear up some of his own personal doubts.

He became aware suddenly of a change in the tone of the crowd noises. A murmur seemed to roll across the grounds of the All England Tennis Club like a slow-moving wave, and people were moving round uneasily.

An AP photographer whom Mike knew slightly hurried by on the path, shouldering his way through the crowd with his camera cradled protectively against his chest.

'What's going on?' Mike asked him.

'I don't know for sure, but the word is that something funny's happening on the Centre Court.'

Mike turned to say something to Cliff Willits, but the young man had disappeared. Maybe he'd find a more receptive ear somewhere else. Mike grinned after him for a moment, then jogged off towards the Centre Court.

21

The general movement of people in the direction of the Centre Court went unnoticed by Alan Doughty. He was accustomed to having his own matches ignored except by a few friends and relatives. Alan's steady, workmanlike style of play seldom drew many spectators, and today he was beating the Spaniard too easily to be interesting to onlookers. The match was so easy for him, in fact, that it was hard for Alan to keep his mind on the play and off that deadly word the doctor had chalked on the blackboard.

He knew he must not think about the aneurysm and the doctor's awful description of it as being like an inner tube ready to blow out. With that picture in his mind all the skills gained over long years on the tennis court would be worthless.

With no real contest to demand his attention, Alan concentrated on placing his shots in a specific square-foot patch of the court, or splitting the centre line with his first serve. In this way he was able to avoid thinking about the doctor's warning.

When he could, Alan stole a glance at Hazel standing on the sidelines. She seemed to be watching him with more concern than was usual. Was it possible that she suspected what was wrong? How much had she heard of his conversation with Quinn yesterday at Hurlingham? Alan tried to recall how much he had said about the doctor. It wouldn't do at all to have Hazel worried.

Alan won the second set and led the match 6–2, 6–3. During the brief recess he walked over to talk to his wife.

'How am I looking, love?' he asked.

'You're playing beautifully, Alan,' she said. Hazel took the towel from her husband's hands to mop the perspiration from his face. 'How do you feel?'

'Lovely, simply lovely,' he said, wondering why she had asked him a thing like that.

'Don't let yourself get a chill now.'

'No fear. Did I see that American sportswriter fellow stop here a short time ago?'

'Mr Wilder, yes. He seems a decent sort.'

'I suppose so. What did he have to say?'

'Oh, just the usual. You know.'

'Yes.'

It was not like Hazel to be vague in her conversations, and Alan looked closely at his wife. He started to say something more, but the umpire signalled it was time to resume play.

'I'll see you afterwards,' he said.

'Good luck,' Hazel said. 'And Alan, take care.'

Take care? Damn, everything she said was beginning to take on hidden meanings for him. He was unused to keeping secrets from his wife, and he didn't much like it. The sooner Wimbledon was over and he could confide in her, the better.

With these thoughts in his mind Alan lost the next set 4–6 before settling down to win the clincher 6–1.

Tim Barrett had his hands full with the strong-armed New Yorker he had drawn as a first-round opponent. Tim had won the first set 7–5, but dropped the next 4–6, and was struggling in the third with the set score at 6–all.

In spite of trying to ignore them, Tim was acutely aware of the faces watching him from the sidelines. His father and mother sat together on a bench looking uncomfortable. As Tim continued to make errors on shots he normally put away, his father seemed to take it as a personal insult. His mother smiled encouragement as always, but couldn't hide her disappointment at the way he was playing.

Vic Goukas, scowling like a Turk, crouched at the court side as though he wanted to spring out on to the grass and snatch the racket from Tim's hand.

Tim double-faulted away his serve in the next game, and the

New Yorker held his own to win the set 8–6 and go ahead in the match two sets to one.

Between sets Tim stood at the net post and sipped a mixture of tea and honey. Vic Goukas moved in next to him and spoke in a low tight voice. The coach was obviously struggling for control.

'What's the matter with you out there, anyway?' Vic demanded.

Tim was unable to meet the coach's eye. 'This guy's tough,' he said.

'Like hell he's tough. He's got a serve that couldn't break an egg and a backhand like a girl's. Lob him, for Chrissake. Move him back. You're letting him take the net away from you. You should have polished off this beefcake in straight sets, and now you're down 2–1. Get on the stick.'

'All right, Vic, all *right*. I'll get him. Don't worry about it.'

'You won't get anybody if you don't get your mind on the game,' Vic growled. 'You're thinkin' about that girl, aren't you?'

Tim's eyes slid over to the bench opposite the one where his parents sat. Christy Noone sat there surrounded by young men. Punks, Tim thought disgustedly. Not players, certainly. Not even fans, from the way they were ignoring the match. Tim had intended that Christy should sit with his parents, but she had got restless early in the first set and started moving round, picking up admirers the way an ice-cream cart attracts kids.

'Never mind about her,' he told Vic.

'Okay, okay, just get out there and play the kind of tennis you're capable of.'

Tim trotted back out on to the court. His mother smiled at him, and Tim acknowledged her with a bob of his racket. His father, Tim saw, was frowning across at Christy Noone. When Tim looked over there Christy gave him a cheery wave. Tim grinned back, wishing he could be sure about the girl and her feelings for him.

He played unevenly in the fourth set, and had to go to a tie-breaker to win it 9–8. In the deciding set Tim finally began to play according to Vic's instructions. He forced the New Yorker back from the net repeatedly with lobs or passed him down the line. He won it 6–2 to take the match, but no congratulatory smiles awaited him at the sidelines.

'I've seen you play a lot better, Tim,' said his father.

'You look tired, Timmy,' said his mother. 'Have you been getting enough sleep?'

'You were lucky to win it,' said Vic. 'If you don't play any better than that tomorrow we can all go home early.'

Tim agreed with everything they were saying and broke away as soon as he could. He crossed the court to where Christy sat.

'That was simply smashing,' she said when he reached her side. He was pleased to see that her retinue of young men had moved back out of the way in deference to the tennis player.

He said, 'I didn't really play well. Vic thinks I was lucky to win.'

'Nonsense. I never doubted for a minute you'd beat that fellow. He did have a good body, though. Oh, not to my taste, you understand. I prefer my men to be slimmer.'

'Will I see you tonight?' Tim said.

'Let me think now, what had I planned?'

Tim's face fell.

'Of course I'll see you, silly,' she said, patting his cheek. 'Come round at half past seven.'

'I'll be there,' Tim said. He walked quickly towards the locker room before Vic and his parents could catch up with him.

For Milo Vasquez the entire universe was compressed into a green rectangle seventy-eight feet by twenty-seven feet, bordered by white chalk lines and bisected by a net three feet high in the middle, and three feet six inches at the posts. He was winning steadily against the tall, balding man opposite him, but not with the devastating power-game he used to play.

Although Milo had never seen him before, and had already forgotten his name, he burned with hatred for the man across the net. A pale-skinned, freckled part-time player, he had no business returning Milo's best serves with the consistency he had this afternoon.

It was not, of course, quite the same cannonball that Milo

used to blast flat and hard for ten or more aces in a match. The serve had lost just enough of its blazing speed to allow hackers like this bald grasshopper to get it back.

When Milo's power first started to leave him, more than two years ago, he refused to believe it. In his mind he was as good as ever, but on the tennis court he showed the price he paid for the late hours and the liquor and the women.

When he began to lose regularly, all of Milo's frustration came out in anger. With no other target handy, his anger was directed at his wife, Maria. It made him all the more furious when she refused to fight back. On the day he told her to get out, he never thought she would take him seriously, but she did. She walked out of their house and down to the pier at Santa Monica. She walked to the end of the pier and simply stepped off. Two boys fishing nearby saw her go over, but by the time they could reach her down among the pilings, Maria was dead.

That was when Milo started with the pills. Pills to make him forget about Maria and pills to give him back the strength in his arm. For a while the pills seemed to work. Seemed to. Milo thought he was playing better than ever, and could not understand why he continued to lose. His anger boiled constantly, and he lashed out at everyone around him. He lost control of himself to the point where he was no longer invited to the important tournaments. These were the same tournaments the directors had coaxed and pleaded with him to enter when he was a champion.

It was then Milo turned to the needle. He soon dropped out of sight in the tennis world and hit bottom physically and spiritually. Then, with help from nobody, he had begun the long climb back. Now he was in a position to regain the top, be *numero uno* again. He would show them all.

Milo whacked a vicious crosscourt backhand and watched his opponent scramble to reach it. The man barely managed to get wood on the ball, cracking it out of bounds.

'Game, set and match to Vasquez.'

The voice of the umpire surprised Milo. In playing each point with deadly concentration he had lost track of the score. The score-board told him he had won the match 6–2, 6–1, 6–0, but he felt as wrung out physically as though it had been a five-set marathon.

As he dragged himself off the court a voice in his head whispered that he needed something for the ache in his body, something to make him feel better. Milo closed his mind to the whisperer and trudged towards the locker room and a hot bath.

Yuri Zenger was annoyed. The people in the stands were not giving him their full attention. For a while he had held them with his usual bag of tricks – clowning with the ball boys, arguing loudly on line calls, over-dramatising his easy shots. His opponent, a shy boy from Egypt playing in his first Wimbledon, was never in it. Yuri saw at once that he could win as he pleased, so he set about putting on a show for the crowd.

It did not matter to Yuri whether the people liked him or not, just as long as they were aware of him. Today they had been on his side at first, laughing with him when he comically scolded himself for missing a shot, and applauding when he hit a winner. Gradually, though, the people cooled towards him as his antics grew more brash and he deliberately humiliated his young opponent. Yuri didn't care. If these fools wanted to pay their good money to watch him play tennis, he would give them something to remember.

He would give that giant blonde, Geneva or whatever her name was, something to remember too. He grinned at the thought of wallowing around in bed with the woman. There was no end to her.

He would insist that the little man keep out of the picture. That should be easy to accomplish by promising to sign his stupid contract. That seemed to be the price he was asking for the woman. Yuri did not care what he promised, but he had no intention of signing anything.

He wondered if the little man was sleeping with the big woman. No, he decided, it was not possible. There was too much of her and too little of him. Yuri would show her what a full-sized man felt like.

Yuri would have liked to have made it that first night, but there was the little problem of Mrs Keith. He knew she had a surprise present waiting for him at home, and he hadn't wanted to ruin it. Now, though, he figured he had milked the old bag for about all she was going to give. The sessions in bed were becoming a drag too, with the old woman's loose skin and floppy little breasts. It would be good to get next to something firm and young again.

But what the hell was the matter with these people in the stands? They were buzzing among themselves, not paying attention to his match. Idiots! Didn't they know they were seeing the best player in the tournament right now? To hell with them.

Yuri finished off the match in a hurry, not losing a point in the last two games. He gathered up his rackets and stalked off the court leaving the Egyptian boy standing at the net waiting for the traditional handshake.

As he pushed a way through the crowd Yuri caught snatches of excited conversation. Something was happening in Ron Hopper's match, something that had distracted people from Yuri's own performance. As he passed the two policemen guarding the entrance to the men's dressing-room Yuri flipped an obscene gesture in the direction of the Centre Court.

Ron Hopper knew he'd been found out. At first his young opponent had been so overwhelmed at playing his opening match on the Centre Court against the defending champion that Ron had been able to win the first two sets merely by lying back and waiting for the boy to make errors. The tennis-wise Wimbledon crowd had shown some surprise at these tactics, but apparently felt Ron was saving himself for more difficult matches in the later rounds.

Then, leading 4–3 in the third set, he was moving back under a short lob, poised for an overhead smash, when the thigh muscle went. It tore loose with a popping sound that Ron thought must have been heard in the first five rows of the stands.

He gasped at the white-hot flash of pain and mis-hit the easy smash, knocking the ball far out of bounds. A murmur of dismay ran through the crowd, and the umpire leaned forward in his chair, a question forming on his lips. Ron waved quickly that he was all right and the umpire signalled for play to continue.

Ron's young opponent was so surprised by the sudden change in fortune that he didn't take immediate advantage of the champion's injury. By the time the boy realised he was playing a cripple he was too far behind to catch up, and Ron won the match in four sets.

The reporters surrounded him on his way from the court to the dressing-room.

'What happened out there, Ron?'

'Is it your knee?'

'Are you in pain now?'

'Did you consider forfeiting the match?'

'Are you going to drop out of the tournament?'

Ron fought back the waves of pain and answered the questions as calmly as he could.

'It was just a twinge in the leg, fellows. No, it doesn't hurt now. There was never a thought of forfeit, and yes, of course I'll continue in the tournament. Now if you'll excuse me, it was a tough match, I'm hot and sweaty and badly in need of a shower.'

He waved away their further questions with a smile, and forced himself not to limp as he walked through the frosted glass doors into the dressing-room. It was traditional among the Australians that you never admit you're hurt. While some players on the circuit would drop out of a tournament at the first sneeze, an Aussie would play as long as he could stand upright and hold a racket.

Inside the dressing-room there were no questions from the other players. They tactfully kept busy with other things. They saw what had happened, they knew what it meant. Ron Hopper was finished at Wimbledon. This year would see a new champion.

22

Tim Barrett walked up and down several times along the street where Christy Noone lived. His mind was a jumble of confused emotions. He wanted desperately to be with the buoyant blonde girl, yet somewhere a warning sounded faintly. He did not know what to think following their short conversation after his match this afternoon. One moment it would seem that Christy's entire attention was focused on him as someone special, and the next it seemed he was no more to her than any of the other young men who followed her around.

It was possible, Tim decided, that Christy was just as confused as he was. Maybe she was still sorting out her own feelings about him. It seemed the best approach was just to let things work themselves out.

With this resolved, Tim strode into Christy's building filled with joyous anticipation. He climbed the two flights of stairs to her flat and rang the bell.

Christy opened the door and took a step back into the room to give Tim a chance to take in the total effect. She wore a two-piece black velvet outfit that glittered with sequins. The top crisscrossed in front with only two narrow velvet bands covering her small breasts. The bottom was cut well below the navel and clung to her hips and thighs. Below the knees the pants flared out into wide bells over jewelled sandals.

After a moment Tim said, 'Christy, you look absolutely terrific.'

She struck a model's pose. 'I should certainly hope so after I worked on my looks all afternoon.'

She turned and walked away from the door. Tim followed,

unable to keep his eyes off the fluid movements of her trim little buttocks.

'Where are we going tonight?' he said.

Christy turned to face him, her hands pressed flat along her velvety flanks. 'Would you mind awfully if we didn't go out tonight?'

'Not go out?' Tim repeated.

'After all,' she said teasingly, 'I did promise your fierce Mr Goukas that I wouldn't let you do anything that would hurt your tennis.'

'Don't worry about him,' Tim said. 'Vic gets carried away sometimes. I'm the one who decides where I go and what I do away from the tennis court.'

'Of course, if you don't *want* to spend the evening here with me . . .'

'I didn't mean that,' Tim said quickly.

'It's true I'm not the best cook in the world, but I have a pair of frozen dinners heating in the oven for us, and there's not much I can do wrong with them.'

'I love frozen dinners,' Tim said.

'I'm so glad. Then after dinner I have loads of records we can play, and we can dance right here just like in a night club, and then, well, see what happens.'

'That sounds great.'

'Very well then, you just sit down like the man of the house and make yourself comfortable while I make everything ready in the kitchen.'

'Is there anything I can do to help?'

'No, you just stay where you are and don't come in until I tell you.'

Christy went out through a swinging door, and Tim settled into a comfortable armchair feeling like a small boy who'd been invited to make himself at home in a candy store.

After a few minutes Christy pushed the door open and stepped aside with a flourish.

'Dinner is served.'

Tim preceded her into the kitchen. In one corner was a compact dinette set. On the small round table were two blue place mats with matching plates. Christy had transferred the frozen dinners from their aluminium trays to the plates where the potatoes gleamed snowy white, the peas emerald green, and the meat a shiny chocolate brown. A pair of slim candles in the centre of the table provided a soft circle of light.

'Well?' Christy said.

'Beautiful.'

'Do you mean it? I don't often entertain here, and I did so want everything to be nice.'

'I love it.'

'Well then, let's eat, shall we?'

They sat down and Christy watched expectantly while Tim took his first bite. It tasted bland and over-cooked like every frozen dinner in the world.

'Delicious,' he said.

'Really? It isn't overdone or anything?'

'No, it's really good.'

Christy smiled happily. 'I'm so glad you like it.' Suddenly she jumped up from the table and hurried across to the refrigerator. 'I almost forgot,' she said, pulling out a long-necked green bottle, 'I had some wine cooling in the fridge for us. I don't have any proper glasses, so I borrowed a couple from Paula downstairs.' She placed a tulip glass before each of them and poured pale rosé wine into them.

Tim hesitated. He never drank anything with alcohol in it, but if he refused now Christy would think him unsophisticated. He brought the glass to his lips and took a tiny sip. The wine didn't taste at all the way he had expected it to. He didn't like it especially, but at least it didn't make him gag.

Most of the talking during the meal was done by Christy. She chattered happily away about nothing very important, and Tim watched her talk and felt himself growing steadily more relaxed. He enjoyed looking at the little blonde girl across the table. In the gentle light of the candles she was painfully desirable.

Half-way through the dinner Tim was surprised to see that he had emptied his wine glass. Christy quickly refilled it.

'I don't know if I should drink any more,' he said. 'I'm supposed to be in training, you know.'

'One more glass surely couldn't do any harm,' Christy said.

'I'll promise not to tell your Mr Goukas about it if you don't.'

'You can bet I'm not going to tell him,' Tim laughed.

'Besides, how on earth am I going to seduce you tonight if I don't get some wine into you. That's the accepted technique, I understand.'

Tim laughed again. He thought now he was beginning to understand this girl. For all her flippant talk and flirtatious manner, underneath she was a quiet girl who enjoyed spending an evening at home, and wanted to be complimented on her cooking. Possibly the other side of Christy was just a pose to cover the fact that underneath she was as shy as he was.

After dinner they walked together back into the sitting-room, leaving the dishes stacked in the sink. Tim found that the tensions he felt earlier in the evening had drained away. The two glasses of wine might have had something to do with it, but Tim thought it was more the sense of closeness he could feel growing between himself and Christy.

'Let's dance,' she said. 'Do you want to?'

'Fine.'

Christy put a stack of records on the turntable and turned the volume down so the music was just a murmur accented by the throbbing rhythm section. She kicked off her shoes and moved to the centre of the carpeted floor. She held out her arms to Tim, beckoning him towards her.

Feeling a little giddy, Tim pulled off his own shoes and stood up to face her.

'Come closer,' she said. 'This is called touch dancing. It's the latest thing.'

Tim stepped forward and took the girl in his arms. Christy immediately moulded her lithe body against his. He felt himself instantly aroused and was embarrassed for a moment.

'You do like me, don't you, Tim?'

'I like you a lot, Christy.'

She sighed and wrapped her arms around him, sliding her hands along the firm muscles of his back. Their bodies swayed together. They paid no attention to the quiet music.

After a little while Christy put her head back and looked up at him. Tim leaned down to kiss her. Her hand glided up along his spine to the back of his neck. Her fingers wrapped themselves in his hair and she pulled his head down fiercely, smashing his mouth against hers.

When at last they broke apart, both were breathing heavily.

Tim said, 'Christy, I. . .'

'Yes, Tim?' she whispered.

'I want to make love to you.'

'Oh yes,' she said, her breath hot against his neck. 'Yes, please.'

She led him into the bedroom and quickly removed the two pieces of her velvet pants suit, revealing nothing underneath but smooth pale flesh. Tim fumbled with his own clothes while Christy lay back amid a profusion of cushions on the bed and watched him with glowing eyes. As Tim came towards her she held out her arms and ran her tongue slowly round her lips in a way that Tim found unbearably sensual.

Christy looked so slim and vulnerable lying there on the pale sheets that Tim was concerned about hurting her. He eased himself down as gently as he could. However, no sooner had he made contact than Christy gripped him with her arms and with her legs and drew him violently into her.

'Give it to me, Timmy,' she said low next to his ear. 'Give it all to me. Come on, Timmy. Give . . . it . . . to . . . me!'

Tim forgot all about being gentle. He forgot about Vic Goukas. He forgot about tennis and Wimbledon. He forgot about everything except the moaning, writhing girl beneath him who held him tight inside her.

23

His first conscious sensation was a cool softness against his body. His brain went to work sluggishly, sifting through touch memories. Sheets. A bed. Then there was a smell. A faintly sweetish odour with unpleasant associations. Medicine. Sheets, bed, medicine . . . hospital. That was it, he was in hospital.

Cautiously he opened his eyes. Narrow slits at first, then wider. The light in the room was dim, filtered through the curtains drawn across the large window opposite the bed. Something was wrong about the room. It did not fit his picture. The furnishings, the pictures, the carpet . . . they were too rich. They did not belong to the bland, functional hospital room he was prepared for.

He closed his eyes again and tried to remember. Everything was in fragments, like reflections in a shattered mirror. He clearly remembered the start of the race in the little village outside Milan. Then there was the familiar exhilaration of speed and power as the red and white Lotus-Ford snarled through the Italian countryside. He was running well, perfectly, in good position to finish second, or even win. Then, as he steered high preparing to go into a deep curve, something in the front suspension gave way with a metallic bang. Where a second before he and the car and the road had been as one, now he was imprisoned in a wild, murderous piece of machinery.

Up and over the embankment he went, and the Lotus broke free of the earth. Blue sky and green grass and brown dirt whirled before his eyes into a single muddy colour. Then, just before he hit, everything seemed to freeze for a second as when the projector stops at the cinema. The last impression he had was an upside-down signboard advertising Cinzano vermouth. He remembered nothing of the impact that followed.

Very carefully now he moved his limbs. Feet and legs first. They seemed to be all right. Then his hands, finally his arms. Incredibly, nothing seemed to be broken. Or even sore. He felt all over his body. He was wearing pyjamas, not a hospital gown. And there were no bandages anywhere. It was not possible that he could have survived the crash with no injuries. Yet the only thing he could find wrong was a dull ache in his head.

He made an effort to focus his mind. Time and space swirled into changing shapes like paints stirred together. The Lotus racing machine grew into a relatively sedate Jaguar saloon. But that was impossible. He had not bought the Jaguar yet.

And there was a woman. A beautiful young woman with auburn hair that shone with red-gold highlights. Paula. But that could not be. He hadn't even met Paula at the time of the race. He clutched his aching head with both hands and groaned aloud.

'Ah, Mr Eric, I see you're awake.'

He rolled his head on the pillow and saw a grey-haired woman, built square and strong. She wore a crisp white uniform.

'Who are you?' he said, and at the instant he said it the woman's name popped into his head.

'I'm Miss Bellamy,' she said.

'Yes, yes, I know who you are,' he said impatiently. 'What I mean to say is . . . er . . . what day is it?'

'Why, it's Tuesday, Mr Eric. Tuesday morning.'

'Yes, yes, of course.' Stupid woman. 'Is my wife here?'

'I'll ask your mother and father to come in.'

Miss Bellamy withdrew from the room and Eric Teal looked round at the familiar furnishings. It was his own room in his parents' home. How had they got him here from Italy? No, that was wrong. The race, the accident, they happened a long time ago. Years. Where was Paula? She should be here when her husband was hurt.

Sir Oliver Teal and Lady Teal came into the room together. He was tall and erect with bristling grey eyebrows. She was thin and looked worried.

144

'Well, son, how are you feeling?' said Sir Oliver. The heartiness in his voice rang false as lead.

'How should I be feeling?' Eric asked.

His mother placed a cool hand on his brow. 'You seem a bit feverish, dear.'

'Where is Paula?'

His father and mother exchanged a look, and all at once Eric knew that Paula was not there. Paula had left him. What was the matter with his mind that he could not get events into their proper chronological order?

'I suppose you're hungry,' his father said. 'You've eaten nothing for the better part of two days.'

'Two days?' Eric repeated.

'Er, yes. You came home on Sunday about noon feeling quite ill. It was your head bothering you again. We had Dr Ruick out, and he prescribed a sedative. Evidently you had some rather violent dreams, but I'm glad to see you're yourself again.'

Dreams? How much was dreams and how much was real? Where was the dividing line?

'Dr Ruick wanted to take you back to the hospital,' his mother said, 'but we thought—'

'No!' Eric snapped. 'I'm never going back to that hospital. They kept me locked up like some kind of an animal. They put things in my food.'

'Don't worry, Eric,' his father soothed. 'You won't have to go back to any hospital. With Miss Bellamy to help we can take care of you here.'

'What do you mean, take care of me? I'm perfectly all right.'

'Quite so, my boy, I can see that. However, when you came home on Sunday we found you just sitting in your car and, well, frankly you were acting rather queerly.'

Car? Sitting in his car? Eric closed his eyes and again saw the whirling earth and sky and the upside-down Cinzano sign. But was the car a Lotus or was it a Jaguar? And what was that little white Ford doing on the race course? That was very dangerous. Someone could be killed.

'You really shouldn't go off like that without telling us, dear,' his mother said. 'We do worry about you.'

Worry? Why should they worry? He was a grown man. He could take care of himself.

His father smiled down at Eric reassuringly. 'Perhaps in a few days, when you're feeling up to it, a trip to the Continent might not be a bad idea. Austria, or Switzerland if you like. I wouldn't mind a spot of mountaineering. Do us all good.'

Go away? No, that was impossible. There was something he had to do. Something important.

He said, 'I can't go, Father.'

'Well, I didn't mean at this minute, but when you feel well enough to travel.'

'I feel perfectly well, damn it. Why do you all insist on treating me like an invalid? I simply don't want to go to Switzerland, that's all. There is something here I must attend to. Something . . .' Eric's voice trailed off as new pictures formed and dissolved in his mind without ever really taking a firm shape.

Sir Oliver cleared his throat uneasily. 'We'll talk about it later. Is there anything you'd like just now?'

'Nothing, Father.'

'You're feeling better, then?'

'Except for a slight headache.'

'Miss Bellamy?'

The stout nurse crossed to Eric's bedside with a tumbler of water and a red-coated capsule. 'Take this, Mr Eric,' she said.

'What is it?'

'Something to ease your headache.'

Eric swallowed the pill and looked up into the worried faces of his parents.

His father said, 'I'll have luncheon brought up to you, son. Is there anything in particular you'd care for?'

'Anything. It doesn't matter.'

'Perhaps you'd like the television turned on,' said his mother.

'I don't care.'

'Wimbledon will be on shortly.'

'Wimbledon?' The name carried some terrible significance for him. Whatever he had to do was somehow connected with Wimbledon. He must try to remember what it was.

24

The defeat of the defending Wimbledon champion was accomplished on Tuesday afternoon without drama and without suspense. The people crowded into the stands of the Centre Court watched in a kind of sick-room silence as a seventeen-year-old French player named Jean-Pierre Leduc beat Ron Hopper in straight sets, 6–4, 6–2, 6–2.

His loss did not come as a surprise. Word of Hopper's sudden collapse in his first match had spread rapidly, as bad news always does. Hopper had refused to discuss his injury either following the match yesterday or before coming out today. The only visible sign that he was in pain was a wide elastic bandage he wore on his right thigh. On the court, however, he moved like a man in hip-deep water.

When the reporters cornered him after the match he said, 'You fellows shouldn't be wasting your time talking to me. The French lad was the winner out there. He's the one you should be interviewing.'

However, the reporters were not to be put off. 'When did you first hurt your leg, Ron?' asked the UPI. 'Was it in Melbourne? Is that why you didn't play in the Italian and French tournaments?'

'The leg's all right,' Hopper told them. 'A bit of a muscle-pull is all.'

'But it slowed you down, didn't it?'

'The way young Leduc played out there today he could have beaten anybody. Give him credit.'

'What are your plans now?'

'Take a little rest, do a little fishing. Then we'll see.'

'Was the loss today a big disappointment to you?'

The group abruptly fell quiet, and all eyes turned on the *New York Times* reporter who had asked the inane question. A flush rose from Ron Hopper's neck to his freckled forehead as he regarded the young man. Mike Wilder, standing a little apart from the others, thought for a moment that the red-haired Australian was going to lose his temper.

However, when he spoke Hopper's voice was as controlled and courteous as ever. 'Yes,' he said, 'it is a very great disappointment to lose. It always is. A man who tells you it doesn't hurt to lose is either a liar or he's not a professional.'

For a moment there was silence, then the moment passed and all the reporters were asking questions at once. Ron Hopper raised his hands for their attention.

'Gentlemen, I'll have to ask you to excuse me now. I really must go in and towel off. Thank you all very much.'

With a wave and a smile last year's champion turned and walked away towards the dressing-room, a narrow-shouldered man, shorter than average, with muscles like twisted wire rope. He walked without even a faint suggestion of a limp. The watching reporters could only guess at what that effort cost him.

'If you ask me, he's played his last match anywhere,' said the AP.

'Why should he care?' said Reuters. 'I hear he's got enough squirrelled away to live well for the rest of his life without ever lifting a racket again.'

'It makes you wonder why he even went this far,' remarked CBS. 'He could have gone in the tank yesterday and not risked hurting the leg any worse. I know I would have.'

A pipe-smoking man from the *Melbourne Tribune* spoke up. 'There's the difference between Ron Hopper and you, old chap. He's a champion.'

Yes, thought Mike Wilder, he *is* a champion. Mike had seen the purplish streak of broken blood vessels that had spread down his leg below the bandage by the time Hopper had finished taking his beating. Twice the umpire had asked him if he wanted the allowable five minutes rest for an injury, but the Aussie just shook his head and motioned for play to continue. Mike thought ruefully about some of the opinions he had expressed in print about 'sissy' tennis players. It seemed he owed some apologies.

A stroll round the other courts and a check of the score-boards told Mike that the defeat of Ron Hopper was the only real story on this second day of Wimbledon. All the other seeded players in the men's singles were winning as expected. The only one having trouble was Milo Vasquez. The angry Mexican seemed to die a little these days every time he took to the court. Still, he somehow beat his second-round opponent in four sets.

Tim Barrett, looking a little peaked, won in straight sets, yet managed to look bad doing it. Mike noted that Christy Noone was not at Tim's court today and wondered why.

Nearby, Alan Doughty, playing his usual steady, un-spectacular game, won his match before a bare handful of spectators. As before, he was closely watched by his wife Hazel.

Fred Olney, the diminutive Australian, lost his match to Brian White and pretended impatience with big Denny Urso who won to stay in the competition. It was most selfish of Denny, Fred complained, to cut into their practice time for the doubles this way.

Mike wandered over to the courts where a few of the first-round women's matches were under way. Tomorrow the entire grounds would be given over to the women and the beginning of doubles play. Mike watched a couple of thick-legged girls swat baseline strokes back and forth at each other for a while. He decided the action was faster in the lawn bowling at Hurlingham. Women's athletics had never been a favourite subject for Mike, and rather than criticise and risk the wrath of Women's Lib, he merely ignored it.

As he started away a tall, Scandinavian-looking blonde on one of the courts knelt to tie a shoelace. The movement was so gracefully feminine that Mike smiled with pleasure. At that moment the girl looked up and saw him. She returned his smile, showing square, even teeth that gleamed white against her tanned skin. No game, Mike decided, that attracts girls like that one can be all bad.

With little that was newsworthy happening on the courts, Mike strolled up to the Players' Tea Room to see how things went in the market-place. There was no lull in the action here. The babble of voices and clash of dishes made a constant din in the place. Everywhere players, players' agents, tournament directors and hustlers of all kinds bargained unceasingly. As Mike moved through the crowd he picked up bits and snatches of conversations.

'*I do need some shoes, but the Adidas man is supposed to come round tomorrow afternoon.*'

'*Forget about him. I'll have half a dozen pairs of ours at your room in the morning. Any colours you like.*'

'*We'd really like to have you come to Mexico City. The weather is beautiful there in the fall. Naturally we'll take care of the air fare, and you'll have a really nice hotel room . . .*'

'*All you have to do is take one swig out of the bottle during the television interview. Fake it if you want to, just make sure the label is turned towards the camera . . .*'

'*I know you're signed up with MacGregor, but that's only in the States and in Europe, right? Now, when you're playing in Cairo . . .*'

'*Believe me, La Costa is* the *club in California now, they've got Segura there as pro, you know . . .*'

Mike spotted J. J. Kaiser at a table talking fast and earnestly to Yuri Zenger, who had clowned his way through a second easy match. Between them sat Geneva Sundstrum looking like some great golden goddess.

Mike had seen enough of Wimbledon for this day. He left the grounds and drove his hired Ford back to the Regency House. Back in his room, he uncased his typewriter, rolled in a virginal sheet of paper, and began his column for the day:

A while back somebody wrote a piece about how tennis players rated right along with hairdressers and chorus boys for toughness. The guy wrote that tennis was a snob's game played in bored silence by a couple of creampuffs with Roman numerals after their names. He said tennis players were as inbred as the Hapsburgs and the game had more cry-babies than a maternity ward. Today the guy who wrote all that stuff had some second thoughts. He watched a display of courage today like nothing he had seen since a heavyweight with no chance to win went the last nine rounds of a fight at the Garden with a broken hand. Only this wasn't any prize-fighter today. This was a tennis player. A champion.

Three hours later the column was written and sent off. Mike showered, changed his clothes, and left to pick up Paula at her flat.

'Where are we dining?' Paula asked as they walked out together.

'I reserved a table at a place called The Mirabelle. I hear it's pretty good.'

'Pretty good? The Mirabelle is known for having the best of everything. And comparable prices.'

'Tut tut, my girl, we need not concern ourselves with price.'

'Spoken like the holder of a fat expense account.'

'You are so right.'

They ordered dinners of lobster, which were superb. The service was excellent, and the wines from the best French vineyards.

When they finished eating, Mike lit a cigarette and rolled the cognac around in the bottom of the balloon glass. Paula watched him thoughtfully.

'Is there something you want to say to me?' she asked.

'God, am I that transparent?'

'Let's say you're not inscrutable.'

'As a matter of fact, I'm curious about something, but I didn't know how to bring it up gracefully.'

'Why not just blurt it out?'

'Why not?' He tried to make it casual, but didn't feel he was pulling it off. 'I got to wondering about your ex-husband, Eric Teal.'

'Oh?'

'Did you say something about him being a sports car driver?'

Paula looked at him curiously, but her answer was calm. 'He did some racing before I knew him. Grand Prix cars, the big ones. People tell me he was quite good at it. I wouldn't know, I never followed the sport.'

'He didn't race any more after you were married?'

'No. He gave it up after his accident. He still liked to fool around with sports cars and so on, but nothing competitive.'

'And you don't know where he is now?'

'I haven't heard a word since his parents put him in hospital. Why are you interested, Mike?'

For just a moment Mike considered telling her the truth – that he suspected Eric Teal had been at the wheel of the green Jaguar that engaged him in the deadly chase on Sunday morning. He rejected the notion as soon as it occurred to him. It was very possible he was mistaken, and it would be better to check it out himself without involving Paula.

He said, 'No reason. Just making after-dinner conversation.'

Paula searched his face, but she didn't ask him any more. 'Would you mind awfully if we talked about something else?'

He grinned at her. 'I wouldn't mind a bit. What say we talk about you and me for a while?'

'Lovely idea.'

The mood lightened then, and they talked comfortably about Wimbledon and about Paula's job and about their plans for the next week and a half. At the same time a part of Mike's mind was trying to recall something Paula had said in an earlier conversation – something to do with where her former in-laws lived. 'A place out near Henley,' that was it. He resolved that tomorrow he would pay a visit to the Teal family estate.

25

The little Ford hummed smoothly westward out of London past Heathrow Airport towards the town of Henley. Wednesday had dawned grey and gloomy with a light mist hanging in the air. Tough luck, Mike thought, for the lady tennis players, who were having their first full day at Wimbledon. They would likely find some way to blame male chauvinism for the weather too.

Getting directions to the country house of Sir Oliver Teal had not been difficult. Since his over-talkativeness with Mr Wilder's 'friend' on Sunday morning, the receptionist at the Regency House had leaned over backwards to be helpful. He had found out the exact location of the Teal estate and marked it on the map for Mike.

Driving on the left was beginning to feel almost natural to Mike by now. It was remarkable, he thought, how adaptable the human machine can be. He still glanced regularly in the rear-view mirror, but so far no menacing green Jaguar had appeared.

Mike had stopped at the London bureau of Worldwide Publications earlier this morning to do some research on the Teal family. Sir Oliver had been knighted in the early days of World War Two in recognition of the conversion of his chemical plants to the war effort. Lady Teal, the former Ann Prentice, was a woman of poise and no special talents who came from good English stock. Their only offspring, son Eric, was something of a playboy, having been involved with racing cars and show girls and the like. After his accident in Italy, there was no further mention of him until his marriage to Paula. Subsequently he had dropped out of the news. Too bad, Mike thought, that he hadn't dropped off the world.

Mike was careful in seeking out the information to keep his inquiries secret from Paula. With things developing so well between them, he thought it would be best just now to keep his suspicions about her ex-husband to himself.

He turned off the M4 at the secondary road marked on his map. He drove on through fenced farmlands that had a leaden, dismal look under the heavy grey clouds.

The Teals' house came into view as the Ford crested a low hill. It was a handsome structure of red brick and flint with a profusion of chimneys and ivy spreading over the walls. Out behind the house Mike could see a wide garage and a long low building that looked like a stable.

Mike parked on the broad drive in front of the house and walked up to the entrance. The door was blackened oak with a heavy iron knocker in the shape of a horse's head. He raised the knocker and let it fall. After a short wait, the door was opened by a smooth-faced man with the self-possessed attitude of a good English butler.

'Yes, sir?'

'My name is Michael Wilder. I'd like to see Mr and Mrs Teal.'

'Sir Oliver and Lady Teal are in the garden,' the butler said, gently correcting Mike's form of reference. 'May I tell them the nature of your business?'

'It's about their son, Eric.'

'Very good, sir. Will you wait inside, please?' The butler's expression remained bland at the mention of Eric's name.

Mike stepped into a high-ceilinged entrance hall with a tiled floor and dark oil paintings on the walls. The butler went out towards the rear of the house.

After about three minutes a tall, grey-haired man came in. He wore the kind of 'gardening' clothes you saw in the pages of magazines like *Country Life*. Very rural, in a gentlemanly way, but definitely not for getting down in the dirt.

He put out his hand and Mike took it. His grip was firm, but the man's pale eyes were wary.

'I'm Oliver Teal,' he said.

'How do you do. Mike Wilder.'

'I understand you know my son.'

'Not exactly. I know his former wife.'

'Oh?' There was a perceptible chilling in Sir Oliver's tone.

'We both work for Worldwide Publications. She here in London and I in New York.'

'I see.'

Mike waited, but apparently Sir Oliver was not going to volunteer any information.

'May I ask where your son is now?'

Before Sir Oliver could answer, a slim woman with sharp, clean features came in. She walked over and stood beside him, presenting a united front.

'This is my wife, Lady Teal,' Sir Oliver said. Then, to the woman, 'This gentleman is inquiring about Eric. It seems he is a friend of the Sadler woman.'

The tone of this reference to Paula by her maiden name told Mike as much as he needed to know about the Teals' feelings towards their former daughter-in-law.

Lady Teal said, 'What is it you want to know about our son, Mr . . . er . . .'

'Wilder. First of all, I'm trying to find out where he is.'

'I presume you know that Eric has been ill,' said Teal.

Mike decided he would get nowhere carrying on with the polite chitchat. He said, 'I heard he was in a hospital for psychiatric care.'

'Eric was under treatment for a nervous condition,' his mother corrected firmly.

'Whatever it was, I am told that he had spells of violence.'

'Perhaps you had better state your business with us more explicitly,' said Sir Oliver.

Mike considered briefly how blunt he ought to be with these people. Maybe he could shock them into giving him some information through total frankness.

He said, 'I have reason to believe that your son, for what reasons I don't know, followed me round London on Saturday night, and that on Sunday he tried to run me off the road with his car.'

'That's preposterous!' said Sir Oliver.

'Not to me, it isn't.'

'What conceivable reason could my son have for following you, not to mention doing you an injury?'

'That's something he would have to answer. I think it has to do with Paula, his ex-wife. Her flat was broken into, and several of my letters to her were stolen along with a picture I'd sent her. From what I've heard of your son's past behaviour, he could have psychotic feelings of jealousy towards me.'

Lady Teal spoke up. 'I can assure you, Mr Wilder, Eric has no psychotic tendencies of any kind, especially concerning that woman or any of her friends. What is more, my son has been in the south of France for the past two months, and is not expected to return until August.'

Sir Oliver looked quickly at her and away again, but not before Mike had caught the questioning glance that passed from husband to wife.

'Is there anything else you wished to discuss?' Teal asked pointedly.

'Does your son own a car?'

'Of course.'

'What kind?'

'I don't see—' Lady Teal began.

'Eric's car is a Bentley,' her husband said firmly. 'A silver-grey Bentley. Last year's model.'

'I see,' Mike said, thinking that he was indeed beginning to.

'Then I hope we've been able to clear the matter up for you.'

'Thanks, you've been a big help.' Mike headed for the door where the butler materialised, holding it open for him. He walked back out to the Ford and heard the big oak door boom shut behind him.

He waited for a moment beside the car to see if anyone would appear at one of the front windows. When no one did he walked quickly round the side of the house to the back where he had seen the garage when he drove in. It had a set of heavy doors that were fastened in the centre with a hasp and padlock. Mike worked his fingers into the crack between the doors, trying to pry them far enough apart to see inside.

'Lookin' for somethin'?'

Mike spun round at the sound of the voice to see a powerfully built man in real gardener's clothes standing some five yards behind him. The man carried a long-handled hoe loosely in one hand, not quite menacingly, but in such a way that it could be quickly brought into use as a weapon.

'I just wondered what was inside,' Mike said, trying a disarming smile.

'It's a garage,' the man said, not smiling back.

'So I see. Well, I guess I'll be on my way.'

The man with the hoe stayed where he was, but his eyes followed Mike all the way back to the front of the house. As Mike drove away he imagined he could still feel eyes watching him. Not until he was over the low hill and out of sight of the house did he relax and begin to think about what to do next.

He could call in the police, of course, but Mike rejected that idea immediately. He had no real evidence to back up his suspicions, and if it came down to his word against that of Sir Oliver and Lady Teal, he had no doubt whom the local constabulary would believe. All he could do was stay on his guard from now on.

Maybe his visit out here today would do some good. At least the Teals were aware now of Mike's suspicions about their son, and they might keep a closer watch on him. He felt these were essentially honest people despite the fact that they had lied to him about Eric.

The gardener's interruption had kept Mike from getting a good clear look inside the garage, but he had seen all he had to – the rear end of a dark green Jaguar saloon.

26

Yuri Zenger perched on one of Mrs Keith's tapestry-covered eighteenth-century wing chairs and held the telephone receiver pressed to his ear. He drummed his fingers on the chair arm as the hotel switchboard made connections and he heard the phone buzz on the other end.

A jaunty voice crackled through the instrument. 'J. J. Kaiser speaking.'

'This is Zenger.'

'Yuri baby, good to hear you. I loved your match yesterday. You were terrific, just terrific.'

'Yeah. Listen, I can't come up to your hotel tonight like we planned.'

'You can't?'

Yuri could visualise the little man's face sagging with disappointment as he saw a big contract starting to slip away.

He said, 'There's something else I have to do, so how about making it this afternoon instead?'

'This afternoon? You mean right away?'

'Sure. Unless you're busy with something else.'

'No, no, this afternoon will be fine. Come on over.'

'Everything will be ready?'

'I have the contracts all drawn up.'

'I mean everything else.'

'Geneva will be here. Room 812.'

Yuri hung up for a moment, then quickly dialled another number and ordered a taxi.

That had been easy enough. Not that Yuri had ever doubted J. J. Kaiser would be more than ready to oblige him. The little fool would do anything to get Yuri Zenger's name on a contract tying in with his cheap line of equipment. Not that Yuri had any intention of signing his name to anything, but J. J. Kaiser didn't have to know that. At least not until after Yuri had enjoyed the full-blown charms of Geneva Sundstrum. The sheer size of the woman would make bedding her an adventure.

It had been Yuri's original intention to spend a leisurely evening walloping round on the big blonde's mattress, and to hell with Mrs Keith's dinner party. That was before Mrs Keith mentioned that one of the dinner guests was to be Lyle Coombes.

Coombes was currently the hottest of the young international set of movie directors. Not only were his films loved by the critics, they made money, so Coombes was never wanting for backers. What concerned Yuri Zenger was Coombes' reputation as a star-maker. He had already made celebrities of a French barmaid and an American truck driver, neither of whom had had five minutes of previous acting experience. Yuri Zenger's consuming ambition was to be a world-famous film star.

After he had won Wimbledon – as he had no doubt he would – there would be no higher prize for him to win in tennis. True, there was money to be made in tennis, but he could make just as much and more in films. Tournament tennis was hard work and Yuri would like to take things easier. Along with the money, he wanted the special kind of fame that comes only to film stars. And the women. Not just the young and under-developed tennis groupies that were so easily available now, but real women – actresses, models, dancers. The thought made Yuri's mouth water.

And the man who could do all this for him was Lyle Coombes. When he learned that the director was a friend of Mrs Keith, Yuri postponed his plans for dumping the lady. Using her friendship, plus his own powerful personality and arresting looks, Yuri was sure he would be Lyle Coombes' next star. For that reason he had agreed to attend the dinner party tonight, cutting his time with Geneva back to an afternoon quickie.

Now he paced back and forth on Mrs Keith's Oriental rug, wishing the taxi would hurry up. Unspent energy had built up in him like an electrical charge. His first two opponents at Wimbledon had offered little challenge, and he had won both matches without losing a set. When the victories came so easily he could not even enjoy upsetting the other player or arguing with the officials.

The tennis court was not the only arena in which Yuri was not getting enough action. Mrs Keith, although she was eager enough once they were alone in bed, had no feeling for sex techniques beyond the basic missionary position. This grew tedious fast for a man like Yuri who delighted in some of the more exotic forms of coupling. Maybe he could indulge himself with Geneva Sundstrum. He smiled at the vision of ripe golden flesh pressing in on him from all sides.

The erotic day-dream snapped off as Mrs Keith entered the room. She said, 'I hope you were able to reach that Mr Kaiser about cancelling your appointment tonight.'

'I made it for this afternoon instead,' Yuri said.

'Dear, I do wish you didn't have to go out today,' she said. 'I'd be so disappointed if you're late for dinner.'

'I won't be late for dinner,' Yuri said. 'This is business. I have to do these things when I have the time.'

'Why couldn't you have the man come over here?'

'Because he has all his equipment at his hotel, and that's what our business is about.'

'I suppose Mr Kaiser's over-sized lady friend is at the hotel too?'

Yuri shot a quick look at Mrs Keith, wondering if she suspected the real business he planned to transact at the Regency House. Normally he would have told the old crow it was none of her damn business. He hated it when they got possessive. However, he had to stay friendly with the woman, at least until he had gained an entrée with Lyle Coombes. Once he had achieved that he would no longer need the old bag and he could tell her to fuck off.

He said, 'I don't know where the woman is staying. Who cares anyway?'

'Are you sure you don't want Charles to drive you?' Mrs Keith asked. 'He could wait in the car and bring you back here when you've finished.'

'No, riding with a chauffeur makes me nervous. Besides, I've already called a taxi.' Damn her meddling anyway.

'I'm only trying to save you trouble.'

Now she's going into her little-girl-with-hurt-feelings act, Yuri thought. What a relief it would be once he was rid of her for good.

The doorbell chimed and a maid entered shortly to announce that there was a taxi outside. Yuri brushed Mrs Keith's powdered cheek with his lips and hurried out of the door.

He told the driver to take him to the Regency House and settled back against the cushions to anticipate the feast of flesh to come.

In room 812 of the Regency House J. J. Kaiser filled a small sponge bag with his toilet articles from the bathroom.

'I wonder if I ought to take my clothes out of the closet?' he said.

Geneva Sundstrum stood over by the window watching him. 'I don't think you need to worry about that. The guy's not going to go poking through the closet. And what if he does? He must know you and me aren't brother and sister.'

'You're probably right,' J. J. said. 'I just thought we ought to keep up appearances.' Why the hell, he wondered, was he so frigging nervous? Running around like the father of the bride. Jeez.

'What time did you say he was coming up?'

'Any minute now. I'd better get out of here.'

'What's the rush? He'll call from the lobby first, won't he?'

'Yeah, yeah, that's right. Have you got everything straight now?'

'Sure. First I show him the equipment. The rackets and stuff, I mean. Then I bring out the contract. He signs, then, well . . . you know.'

'Yeah, yeah. I'll make it up to you, Geneva, when we get home. I'll see that you get a nice bonus.'

'Make what up to me? I'm just doing the job you brought me along for, aren't I?'

J.J. looked deep into those wide, guileless eyes and wondered if he had detected a faint note of irony in the breathy, little-girl voice. Nah, she was too dumb. That was what he had to keep in the front of his mind – she was just a big dumb blonde.

'You're doing a fine job,' he said.

The telephone bell shrilled, and J.J. leaped as though he'd been stuck with a needle. He nodded to Geneva, who picked up the instrument.

She spoke briefly into the phone, then covered the mouthpiece and looked over at J.J.

'It's him.'

'Tell him to come up,' said J.J. in a stage whisper.

Geneva passed on the message and hung up the phone.

J.J. took a last look round the room and tucked the sponge bag under one arm. He said, 'I guess I'd better split now.'

'I guess so.'

'Call me after . . . after he leaves.'

'Okay.'

'I'll be in 803.'

'I know.'

J.J. stood awkwardly in the doorway for a moment with Geneva towering over him. He knew the girl expected him to kiss her good-bye, but under the circumstances he couldn't bring himself to do it. He had an idiotic impulse to wish her good luck, which he quickly suppressed.

'Well, I'll see you.'

He walked away down the corridor. There was no sound of a door closing behind him, so he knew Geneva was still standing there watching him. With an effort he refrained from looking back, and kept his pace steady and casual until he was out of sight round a corner. There he leaned against the wall for a moment and drew in a deep breath. He did not feel good at all. Must be coming down with something. This damn London weather was doing it, most likely.

He set off again for 803, a small room in the back of the building, next to the old-fashioned fire escape. He had taken the room mostly for appearances' sake on the expense report that would go to the home office. This would be the first time he had been inside.

He walked into the room, slammed the door, and tossed the

bag of shaving tools on to the bureau. He looked round at the plain, dull furniture with distaste. Jeez, he was tired of hotel rooms. He had seen far too many of them in his thirty-nine years. He dropped into a chair and tried not to think about what was going to happen in room 812.

Yuri's excitement grew with every step he took from the lift down the corridor to room 812. Visions of the naked Geneva that he had conjured up during the taxi drive churned in his mind. He checked the numbers until he found the right door, and rapped twice.

Geneva answered his knock promptly. She wore a satiny white pants suit that clung lovingly to her full, firm breasts and her round womanly hips.

'Won't you come in?' she said.

'Try and keep me out.'

Yuri entered, and Geneva closed the door after him. His eyes roved round the room, coming to rest on the bed, freshly made with the bedspread peeled back invitingly.

'All the things are over here,' Geneva said, moving towards the other side of the room.

'Things?'

'The tennis rackets and balls and stuff like that. You want to look at it, don't you?'

'Sure, later. Come here.'

'But don't you at least want to see what we have? Before you sign a contract, I mean.'

'I can see what I want from here.'

Geneva crossed to the desk and picked up a thick envelope. 'Here's the contract,' she said, 'all ready for signing.'

'How convenient.'

She spoke as though reciting a memorised speech. 'It gives us the exclusive right to use your name in ads. You agree to use our equipment in tournaments, and Gilfillan will produce a Yuri Zenger autographed racket to your specifications.'

'Why are you stalling me?'

'Stalling?'

'That's what I said. I came here to go to bed with you, both of us know that. I don't give a shit about your tennis rackets or any of that other crap. You be good to me, and maybe I'll sign your contract. Now how about it?'

'I think we ought to talk about business first.'

'Then to hell with it. Tell your little friend he'd better find himself another player. Yuri Zenger is not interested.' He started for the door, confident that she would call him back. These people would not just let him walk away.

'Wait.'

He turned to face her. 'Well?'

'You will sign the contract afterwards?'

'We'll talk about it. After.'

Geneva put the envelope back on the desk and moved to the centre of the room. She stood submissively, arms hanging loose at her sides.

Yuri walked back into the room and stopped just in front of her. At five foot eleven he was not a small man, and he found it a new and exciting experience to have to look up into the eyes of a woman. What a conquest this was going to be.

He reached round and ran his hands down her back to the yielding mounds of her buttocks. He kneaded the firm flesh and pulled her against him so she could feel his erection.

'Do you like that?' he said.

'Mmmmm.'

'Come to bed now. I will show you what a real lover can do.'

They started towards the bed. Yuri's eyes feasted on Geneva's huge breasts. From the way they moved when she walked, he knew the woman was not wearing anything under the white satin. God, what beautiful things they were. He ached to put his hands on them. His mouth.

The telephone rang.

'Don't answer it,' he said.

'I have to.'

'Why do you have to?'

'It's the kind of person I am, that's all. I can't let a telephone ring. It drives me crazy if I don't know who's calling.'

'Jesus Christ, go ahead then.'

Yuri released his grip on Geneva's arm and sat on the edge of the bed muttering to himself as she walked back to answer the phone.

164

'If it's that sonofabitching little friend of yours, tell him to—'

Geneva held up her hand for silence as she spoke into the instrument. She listened for several seconds, then turned to Yuri. 'It's for you.'

'That's impossible. Nobody knows I'm here.'

'It's some lady.'

Yuri groaned aloud and pushed himself off the bed. Mrs Keith. This time the old bag had gone too far. He snatched the phone out of Geneva's hand and barked into the mouthpiece.

'What is it?'

'Hello, Yuri,' said the calm, cultured voice of Mrs Keith. 'I hope I'm not interrupting your business meeting.'

'You are.'

'I'm sorry, dear, but I just had a call from Lyle Coombes, and I thought you would want to know.'

Yuri swallowed the angry words that were on his tongue. 'What did he call about?'

'He won't be able to come to dinner tonight. He has to make arrangements to leave for Paris in the morning.'

'Not coming? Well, God damn it—'

'So I invited him to tea instead.'

'Tea?'

'Yes. He'll be here shortly. I know how anxious you are to meet Lyle, and I thought that since this could be your last opportunity, you might want to cut short your business and come back here.'

Yuri glanced over at Geneva. The big blonde was standing a few feet away, watching him without expression. Damn, he wanted to get into that. The old biddy had him by the short hair this time, though. No piece of ass in the world was worth losing his chance to get next to Lyle Coombes.

'I'll be there,' he said, and hung up the phone immediately so he wouldn't have to talk to the old bitch any longer.

'Is something wrong?' Geneva asked.

'I have to leave.'

'Oh?'

Yuri could not be sure whether the tone of her voice reflected disappointment or relief. To hell with her. The woman's feelings were not important.

He said, 'We won't be doing any business this time. Next time we'll start all over. And take the telephone off the hook.'

'Do you want to take the contract with you?'

'Don't be stupid. You know what it takes to get my name on that contract.'

'I was just asking.'

With a snort of annoyance Yuri stalked over and yanked open the door. 'I'll be back,' he snapped, and marched into the corridor.

J. J. Kaiser read for the third or fourth time the same paragraph in a paperback novel he had purchased in the foyer. It was no use, he could not get his mind to focus on the written words.

He flipped the book aside and got up from the chair. He walked into the bathroom, poured a glass of water, took a swallow, and dumped the rest into the basin. He blew his nose on a Kleenex and flushed the tissue down the toilet.

A funny-looking little fink peered out at him from the mirror. 'What are you moping around like this for?' the little fink said. 'Everything's going just the way you planned, isn't it?'

'Yeah, yeah, only . . .' J.J. began.

'What do you mean, *only*? Yuri Zenger's getting his ashes hauled, you're getting his name on a contract, and Gilfillan is getting their first bona fide tennis star. Everybody's happy, right?'

'Aren't you forgetting somebody?'

'The big broad?'

'Sure, Geneva. She's the one who's doing the most for this whole deal.'

'So what? She's getting paid for it. And it's not like you're sacrificing a virgin or something. The broad may be dumb, but she's been around the block.'

'Shut up!' J.J. hit the little fink in the face with a damp towel and walked back to stare out of the window at a brick wall a few feet away.

He picked up the paperback novel, riffled the pages, dropped it again. Maybe he should go and get a magazine. Something with a lot of pictures that would more readily distract him. No, Geneva might call when he was out, and he didn't want to miss her.

A soft knock at the door sent J.J. straight up in the air. Jeez, he was getting goosey about sudden noises. It was probably a maid or something. He walked over and opened the door.

'Hello, J.J.'

Geneva Sundstrum stood in the doorway looking so painfully beautiful at that moment that J.J. wanted to wrap his arms around her and sob.

He said, 'What are you doing here?'

'He's gone.'

'Zenger? Gone? Already?'

'Five minutes ago.'

'Did he . . . Did you . . .?'

'He didn't. I didn't. We didn't.'

J.J. moved aside to let the big girl enter the room. He closed the door behind her.

'What went wrong?'

'He got a phone call. I think it was from that old lady he's living with. I don't know what she said, but it made him hustle out of there in a hurry.'

'That idiot at the desk must have put the call through to your room. What about the contract?'

'He wouldn't even look at the contract until after, and we never even got started.'

J.J. raised and dropped his arms in a dramatic gesture of defeat. 'Well, that's that. I guess we can kiss Yuri Zenger goodbye.'

'We don't have to.'

'What do you mean?'

'He said he'd be back to finish the business.'

'Did he say when?'

'No. I got the feeling that I'm supposed to stay ready for him.'

J.J. frowned thoughtfully, chewing on his moustache. 'Well, that's something,' he said. 'At least we haven't lost him altogether.'

'I did the best I could.'

'You did fine, babe, just fine. Look, are you hungry? We could go out for a bite. Maybe take in a flick. What the hell, the afternoon's shot anyway, we might as well relax.'

'I'm not hungry, J.J. And I don't want to go to a movie. Listen, honey, you don't have to feel guilty or anything. I understand.'

'Guilty? What guilty? Who's got anything to feel guilty about?'

'I just thought maybe—'

'Well, think again, babe. I've been hustling too many years to start getting the guilts now. Jeez!'

Geneva was silent for a moment, then she said, 'J.J.'

'What?'

'There's a freshly-made bed in my room, all turned back and ready. It's a shame not to use it.'

'Uh, yeah, yeah. I'd really like to, you know I would, babe, but there are some phone calls I ought to make. It may take quite a while. Why don't you go on back to the room and watch TV or something. I'll be up later.'

'Couldn't you make your calls from the room? I'd be as quiet as a mouse.'

'There's, uh, some people I've got to go see too. I'll get back to you later, okay?'

'Sure, J.J. Okay.'

The girl couldn't hide the hurt in her eyes as she turned and walked out of the room. J.J. kicked the door when she was gone, sending a stab of pain up his leg. He kicked it again.

This was really too much, he thought. Turning down a romp in the hay with the most magnificent piece of woman-flesh he'd ever had. Jeez!

When he was sure that Geneva had had enough time to get back to room 812, J.J. left the smaller room and headed for the lift. He would go down to the bar and start belting down the booze. J.J. well knew that he was no drinker, and it shouldn't take many to put him in a stupor. Then he could stagger up to Geneva's room, give her some story about getting drunk with an old buddy, and pass out. It would save a lot of explaining. Both to Geneva and to himself.

27

Yuri could feel the beginnings of an ache in his crotch when the taxi dropped him off in front of Mrs Keith's town house in the super-fashionable residential section of Belgravia. He had got just close enough to Geneva to stir his blood, and being called away had left him badly frustrated.

When the maid ushered him into the sitting-room, Mrs Keith was already having tea. Seated next to her on the sofa was a languid young man with glossy hair and soft, pouty lips. He sat with his knees pressed together as he carried on an animated conversation.

As Yuri entered the room Mrs Keith looked up and smiled. 'Ah, Yuri, there you are. Lyle dear, this is the young man I told you about.'

Lyle Coombes turned from his conversation, and for a moment his eyes stabbed intently into Yuri's. Yuri knew the look. He had seen it in the hungry faces of the men who waited hopefully outside the locker rooms, peering into the eyes of one player after another, looking for the special answer.

Apparently Coombes did not find the answer he wanted, for his eyes grew vague and guarded again. He extended his hand, allowing Yuri a brief grasp of four fingers. 'Charmed,' he said.

'Do take a seat and join us, Yuri,' said Mrs Keith. 'Lyle has just been telling me the most deliciously funny story about some of our mutual acquaintances.'

Yuri piled several of the dainty sandwiches on to a plate and took a cup of tea. He sat down glumly in a chair opposite Mrs Keith and the movie director, keeping a politely interested expression on his face as Coombes continued his anecdote, accompanying himself with gestures and flourishes. Yuri pleaded silently for him to get to the point.

'And *so*, my dear,' Coombes finally wound up, 'if you can *imag*ine, the poor woman was left *stand*ing there without a *word* to say. Let me tell you, it was simply *mar*vellous.'

'Oh, Lyle,' gushed Mrs Keith, 'you do have the most delightful way of telling a story. It must be your cinematic background.'

Yuri cleared his throat loudly, and the other two looked over at him.

'I've always enjoyed your films, Mr Coombes,' he said, thinking even as the words left his mouth how inane they sounded.

'Really?' said the director. 'Which one of them did you like the best?'

Yuri squirmed in his chair. He had never seen one of Coombes' pictures. Didn't even know any of the titles. He was desperately afraid of offending this man who had the power to make him a star.

He said, 'It's difficult to pick one, I enjoyed them all so much.' Inwardly Yuri cringed at the words, which sounded as though they were spoken by somebody else.

'How nice,' the director said coolly. He turned away once more and resumed his conversation with Mrs Keith. 'Dorothy dear, have you seen the show at the Hayward Gallery? It's that new Spanish boy ... oh, dear, what *is* his name? Anyway, his work is absolutely *charming*. Far more subtlety than one usually finds in the Spaniards.'

'I haven't seen it,' said Mrs Keith, 'but I shall by all means make it a point to go if you really recommend it.'

'Oh, I *do*. I do in*deed*.'

Yuri clattered his tea cup and saucer down on the antique table beside him.

'Yuri, dear boy, you simply must forgive us for ignoring you,' said Mrs Keith. 'It's just that whenever Lyle and I get together we fly off into our own special world.' To Coombes she said, 'Yuri is a tennis player.'

'Is that so? Do you know Kurt von Rotke? I believe he was involved with tennis for a time. De*light*ful boy.'

'I don't know him,' Yuri said.

'Pity.'

'I don't intend always to be a tennis player,' Yuri blurted.

'Oh? You have ambitions along another line?'

'People have often told me I should be in the movies.'

'*Have* they?'

'I have a good face for photographing, people say.'

'I see.'

'But I hear that getting into movies is very difficult.'

'Yes, it is. Perhaps we might talk about that.'

'I would like to very much.'

'It will have to be some other time, I'm afraid,' Coombes said, rising. 'I really must be going now. Dorothy, it was just super seeing you again. Let's be in touch soon.'

'The pleasure was mine, Lyle,' said Mrs Keith. 'And next time you hear about a special showing at the Hayward, be sure and tell me first, you naughty boy, or I'll be furious with you.'

'Ta ta, then. Nice to meet you, Zenger.' The director tossed a cashmere coat over his shoulders and sailed out of the door.

Yuri could feel the anger rising inside him like black smoke. He held himself in check until the maid had left the room, then he stalked over to face Mrs Keith.

'What the hell was the idea of that?'

'Yuri darling, I don't understand.'

'I was supposed to meet Coombes so we could talk about him getting me into pictures. Instead, I have to sit here and listen to a lot of fag talk about people I never heard of and somebody's crappy paintings.'

'But, Yuri, Lyle did say he would talk to you about a possible film career. He's an extremely busy man, you know.'

'So am I a busy man. Talk to me when? Two weeks from now I'm supposed to be in Belgium for the clay court championships.'

Mrs Keith smoothed the front of her black taffeta dress. She said, 'He'll be back from Paris in a few days. I'm sure I can arrange to bring you two together again.'

'I hope to hell you can. I come all the way back here and only get to say half a dozen words to the sonofabitch before he is giving me "Ta ta, Zenger, I must be off".'

'Poor dear,' said Mrs Keith. 'Were you able to complete your business with Mr Kaiser?'

'No.'

'I'm awfully sorry about that, but then, if you become a film star you won't have to deal with people like that, will you? Was that the huge blonde woman who answered the phone when I called?'

'What? Oh, yes, I think that was her.'

'What was the woman doing there? I thought your business was with Mr Kaiser.'

'She works for the guy, for God's sake. Why shouldn't she be there?'

'Quite right. Well, I don't suppose there's time for you to go back there now. Not before the dinner party.'

Yuri ground his teeth. The old hag had him dancing on strings like a puppet. He would have loved to smash his fist into her smug, twice-lifted face, but as long as she held out Lyle Coombes as a possible reward, he could not afford to displease her.

He said, 'It's all right. I'll go back and finish the business another time.'

'There's a good boy.' Then looping a finger around one of the buttons on his shirt, she said in a low, seductive tone, 'As long as there is still some time before we have to start preparing for the guests, why don't you and I tiptoe upstairs—'

For a moment he considered turning her down. It would be fair payment for the dirty trick she had played on him. But as long as she could still be useful he would have to pay his dues. Besides, he was feeling horny from his close call with Geneva, and doing it with the old lady was still better than jacking off.

'Sure,' he said. 'Why not?'

28

Hazel Doughty sat in the doctor's waiting-room feeling vaguely ashamed for being in good health while the other people who sat there in the plastic chairs and thumbed through copies of old magazines probably had serious things wrong with them.

It also bothered Hazel that she had lied to Alan about coming here. He had slept late this morning, it being Wednesday, and no Wimbledon action in the men's singles. After luncheon she had left him reading the sporting papers and gone out, saying she wanted to do a spot of shopping. She would find ways to make it up to him, if only the doctor would put her fears at rest.

Ever since his check-up two weeks ago Alan had been acting queerly. Hazel waited for her husband to tell her about it, and when he didn't she began to suspect something serious was wrong. Last night she had seen him taking medicine that she knew had not been in the house before. When she asked about it Alan put her off with a quick answer about the medicine being something the doctor had given him to quiet his nerves. You can't stay married to a man seventeen years and not know when he's keeping something from you. Alan Doughty had never had a nervous day in his life. It was then that Hazel had made the decision to come down here and speak to Alan's doctor.

The brisk receptionist slid open the glass panel that separated her from the people in the waiting-room. 'Mrs Doughty?'

'Yes?' Hazel rose from her chair uncertainly.

'The doctor will see you now.'

Hazel made her way past the waiting people, all of whom,

she felt, could tell there was nothing wrong with her and probably resented her taking up the doctor's time. She passed through a door and walked down a passage that smelled sharply of medicine. The doctor sat at a desk in an office-like room at the end of the passage.

'Yes, Mrs Doughty,' he said, 'what can I do for you?'

'My husband was in to see you not long ago.'

'Yes, he was.'

'I – I wonder if you might tell me whatever it was you told Alan then?'

'He didn't tell you?'

'No.'

'And you have tried to speak to him about it?'

'Yes, that is, not really. Alan's not keen on talking about it.'

'Under the circumstances, I'm not certain it would be proper for me to give you any information about my examination. These things are, after all, confidential between doctor and patient.'

'He may be your patient, doctor, but he's my husband.'

'Yes, I see. I suppose that does alter the situation. How much, exactly, has Mr Doughty told you?'

'Nothing, actually, just that he saw you for a check-up and that all was well.'

'And you have reason to believe otherwise?'

'It's the way he acts, really. He won't look me straight in the eye when I ask him how he feels. Then last night I saw him taking some medicine that he said was for his nerves, but I'm sure that's not true.'

The doctor walked over and closed the office door, and then sat down again. He stared thoughtfully at the floor for a long moment before answering.

'I see in the papers that your husband won his second match at Wimbledon yesterday.'

'Yes, he did. Alan seems to be playing better than ever, yet I'm sure there's something wrong.'

'Yes, Mrs Doughty, you're right. It would have been far better if your husband had lost in the first round.'

Hazel's breath caught in her throat. 'Why do you say that?'

'Actually, my advice to him was not to play at Wimbledon at all.'

'But he's made up his mind that this is to be his last tournament.'

'Yes,' the doctor said grimly, 'one way or another.'

'Please tell me what it is.'

'Your husband is suffering from an aneurysm, Mrs Doughty. That is a weakening of the wall in one of the major arteries.'

'Is that quite serious?'

'Quite serious. He needs surgery to correct the condition, and the sooner the better.'

'And what about playing tennis?'

'In his condition it is as dangerous as playing Russian roulette. If the arterial wall should rupture due to the increased amount of blood pumped by the heart during exercise . . .' The doctor shook his head, leaving the sentence unfinished.

'You told Alan all this?'

'I did.'

'What did he say?'

'He said the importance of playing at Wimbledon this year outweighed the danger.'

'You've got to stop him,' Hazel said.

'I'm sorry, Mrs Doughty, all I can do is give your husband my professional opinion and my advice. I did that in the strongest of terms. I cannot otherwise prevent him from taking chances with his life, if that is what he wants to do.'

'You did your best, I'm sure,' Hazel said, 'but there must be some way.'

'If you have any influence with your husband, I'd suggest you use it now to get him off the tennis court. His life may very well depend on it.'

Hazel nodded her understanding. 'Thank you, doctor.' She clutched her bag tightly to her, and walked straight out through the waiting-room, not looking at the people sitting there.

Once out in the street she took a hanky from her bag and blew her nose. I am not going to cry, she told herself. I will not be seen weeping in public. She straightened her posture and walked a little way to the bus stop where she took her place at the end of the queue.

Back at the flat in Lambeth Hazel blew her nose again and examined her face in a tiny mirror before she walked in. She found Alan sitting in the kitchen with a pot of tea on the table before him and a stack of new tennis rackets on the floor beside his chair. He had unwrapped the grip from one of the rackets and was shaving wood from the handle with a kitchen knife.

'Hello, pet,' he said. 'You're back from shopping early. Where are your parcels?'

'I – I couldn't find just what I wanted.'

'Too bad, dear. Not to worry, though, you can go on a real spree after Wimbledon, eh?'

He set the knife aside and began carefully re-wrapping the grip on the racket. When it was fully wound he tested it for feel. He stood up and swung the racket through a slow-motion backhand arc.

'Not quite right,' he said, and sat down to begin unwrapping the grip once more.

'Alan.'

'Yes?'

'I didn't go shopping today as I told you.'

'Oh?'

'I went to see the doctor.'

'You're not ill?' he asked quickly.

'It was your doctor I went to see.'

Alan watched her without saying anything.

'He told me you shouldn't be playing tennis. He told me why.'

Alan put aside the racket he was working on and stood up. He took Hazel into his arms and held her close.

'The doctor's an old worry bug, love. You mustn't let him upset you. You've seen me playing the last two days. Did you see anything wrong?'

'He said you should have an operation.'

'Doctors always say a bloke should have an operation. That's where they make their money. Anyhow, there'll be plenty of time for that after Wimbledon. You just leave these things to me, dear.'

Hazel pulled free and stepped back so she could look into his face. 'Please don't treat me like a child, Alan,' she said. 'You're my husband and I love you. What happens to you is quite rightly my concern, and I won't have you killing yourself on the tennis court.'

For a moment Alan regarded her levelly, then he said, 'You're quite right, Hazel. I was wrong not to tell you about it at once. I've never been able to keep anything from you anyway. I should have known better. As the doctor told you, it's rather a serious thing I've got, but once I've had the operation and they stick a patch on the old artery I'll be almost as good as new.'

'You're doing it again,' Hazel said. 'You're making light of the thing as though it's something I can't understand. I was at Southampton with you four years ago when Aubrey Cooper had a heart attack and fell dead on the court. I saw it, Alan, I was close enough to see the look on his face. I don't want to see you fall out there.'

'Believe me, I don't want that either,' Alan said in a serious tone. 'It may seem to you that I'm being frivolous and foolhardy about this, but you should know me better than that. This is the one chance we'll ever have, you and me, to live out our lives comfortably. To me it's worth the gamble.'

'Alan, it's your *life* you're risking,' Hazel said, angry with herself because she could not keep her voice from breaking. 'Nothing is worth that.'

'What would you have me do, drop out now after having played the first two rounds?'

'Yes,' she said. 'If you love me you'll do it.'

'That's not fair, Hazel. I love you more than I could ever put into words, you know that. There is nothing I wouldn't do to make you happy. But you're asking me to quit. I've never quitted in my life. You wouldn't want me to start now, would you?'

'At least you'd be alive,' she cried.

Man and wife stood facing each other for several seconds, and Hazel watched the play of conflicting emotions across Alan's long, homely face. She ran forward and threw her arms round him, pressing her face against the front of his shirt.

'I'm sorry, Alan,' she said. 'You have to do what you think is right. I'm just so afraid of losing you.'

'Nobody'll be lost, dear, you'll see. I'll have five more matches, then it'll be over.'

'That's five matches if you go to the finals.'

'You don't doubt that I will, do you?'

Hazel used the sleeve of his shirt to wipe the tears from her cheeks. She looked up at her husband and smiled. 'No, Alan, I don't doubt it. Not for a minute.'

'That's my girl.' He gave her a last squeeze, then returned to the racket he had been working on. He finished unwrapping the grip and took up the knife to shave a little more of the handle.

'I don't know why,' he said, 'but they never build quite the right feel into these things.'

Hazel watched him bent over his whittling, as intent as a little boy. Her instinct cried out to her to plead with him not to play again. She knew he would do it for her too, but it would be at the cost of his pride. She would have him then, but he would be less than the man he was. She loved him too much to do that to him.

With a sense of betrayal, Hazel gave a silent prayer that tomorrow he would lose.

29

Once the excitement of the opening round of play is past there is a lull at Wimbledon, at least from the point of view of the average newsman. This lasts until the first Saturday when the number of players still in the tournament has been cut down to a manageable sixteen.

Wimbledon continues to draw daily capacity crowds, of course, and there is plenty of drama in the second- and third-round matches being played on the sixteen grass courts. However, these matches receive only superficial coverage outside the London area. The interest of the foreign press picks up only when there is an upset – a seeded player knocked out of the tournament by an underdog.

So far, upsets had been rare at this year's Wimbledon. Apart from the defeat of Ron Hopper by young Jean-Pierre Leduc, the tournament was going strictly according to form. Mike Wilder and the other reporters filled their daily dispatches with features and human-interest angles not directly related to the on-court action.

Mike adjusted his days to a comfortable pattern – work in the early morning at his hotel room, Wimbledon in the afternoon, and Paula in the evenings. Once they had broken through the initial barrier, an intimacy had grown between Paula and Mike that made it seem they had known each other for years. Mike found himself thinking in terms of 'we' for the first time since his marriage started to go wrong. In the back of his mind he began to wonder how he would feel about leaving England and Paula when the tournament was over.

Very much in the front of Mike's mind were thoughts about Paula's ex-husband, Eric Teal. Since his visit to the Teal estate on Wednesday, Mike had been on guard. He watched continually to see if he was being followed, and he took special note of any occurrence that seemed out of the ordinary. However, in the next two days there were no followers and no suspicious happenings, and Mike began to think that Eric Teal was off his back. Maybe the parents, reluctant as they were to discuss it, had got the message and were keeping a closer watch on their son. Mike hoped so, but he would not relax so far as to be an easy target again.

For his working day Mike liked to get out to Wimbledon early and stand outside with the crowds to watch the players arrive. They drove up in cars provided by the All England Tennis Club to pick them up wherever they were staying and transport them to the grounds in style. Rolls Royces, Mercedes, Humbers bearing pennants in the mauve and green of Wimbledon drove down from London with the players sitting in the back, royalty for a fortnight. It was one of the touches that made Wimbledon unique.

Not all the players chose to accept the club's offer of luxurious transport. One such was Alan Doughty. He preferred to make the daily drive from his flat in Lambeth in his four-year-old Rover. As the son of a coal miner he was uncomfortable, he told reporters, sitting in the back seat of a Rolls. The drive through the streets and byways of Greater London calmed his mind, Alan said, putting him in a proper mood to play tennis. There was a certain amount of risk involved because, according to the tournament rules, if a player is ten minutes late his opponent wins in a walk-over. So far, Alan had always been on time.

The Englishman continued to play well, although he had to go to five sets to get past his third-round opponent, with the fifth set going all the way to 14–12 before he won it with a series of sharp strokes. At Wimbledon a tie-breaker is used if a set goes to 8–all, except for the deciding set, which must be won by two games, no matter how long it takes. Also, they continue to require the best-of-five-set matches for all rounds in the men's play, while many other tournaments have gone to two-out-of-three, at least in the early rounds. There was the usual grumbling from the players about these physically taxing rules, but Wimbledon was not ready for such a big break with tradition.

The sophisticated calm of Wimbledon was ruffled slightly by something that happened during Alan Doughty's marathon fifth set. He was playing on court two, with the bleacher stands on either side, when he slipped while running to reach a cross-court shot and fell to the ground. To the spectators it appeared an ordinary sort of tumble, but Hazel Doughty, sitting in the first row of the stands, gave a little cry and ran out on to the court as though to assist her husband. This was an open breach of tennis etiquette, and brought a murmur of disapproval from the crowd. Alan had bounced to his feet and waved his wife off before she reached him, but Hazel, obviously upset, had left the court in tears. Alan looked after her for a moment, then continued to play, eventually winning the match. He hurried to the locker room afterwards giving up his usual relaxed interview with the reporters.

In his brief acquaintance with Alan and Hazel Doughty Mike had grown to like both of them. Seeing Hazel's emotional reaction to her husband's fall and Alan's grim expression as he watched her flee made Mike wonder what the trouble was between these plain, likeable people.

The British tennis fans, while they cheered sentimentally for 'our Alan', didn't really believe he had a chance. His steady, almost error-free game was too lacking in drama to attract large crowds, and everyone assumed that when the seeded players started meeting each other Alan would be one of the first to drop out. They would be sorry to see him go, but they could all be proud that he'd done as well as he had.

One player nobody would be sorry to see lose was Yuri Zenger. The public's dislike of the volatile Hungarian was unusually emotional for a Wimbledon crowd. As though he were inspired by the vocal animosity of the people, Yuri's behaviour grew steadily worse, stopping just short of grounds for disqualification. He berated officials, screamed at ball boys, slammed balls into the seats, insulted reporters and intimidated his opponents. Through it all he continued to play superlative tennis. By Friday it began to look as though Wimbledon might soon have its most unpopular champion ever.

Mike discussed the situation with Vic Goukas while the coach waited for Tim Barrett to come on to the court for his third-round match.

'What makes a guy like Zenger tick, anyway?' Mike asked. 'He's surely a good enough player to win without all the b.s.'

'That's what passes for colour, today,' Vic said. 'But it doesn't work with Zenger. He's not colourful, just nasty. In the old days we had players who were colourful – Tilden, Budge, Perry, Bobby Riggs. Pancho Segura is still making people laugh on the Grand Masters circuit. These people weren't clowns, you understand, they were first-rate tennis players, but they didn't mind having a little fun with the game. Or take Gonzales. He had a temper that could scorch the grass, but when he got mad he did it with style, not like some crybaby schoolboy.'

'Why do you think the colour's gone out of the game today?' Mike asked.

'That's easy – money. In 1968 when the amateur tournaments opened up to professionals the really big money came in. That's when the game turned dead serious. When you're playing for the kind of prize-money they put up today you play to win and to hell with entertaining the gallery.

'I'm not knocking it, you understand. When I was in the game a top player could put away ten, maybe twelve thousand dollars in a good year. A lot of us would wind up at the end of a year with nothing. We'd exist from day to day on hand-outs from the tournament people and rich fans. Now there's players earning well into six figures, counting their outside deals. You've got to expect them to be businessmen as well as athletes.'

'What about Tim Barrett?' Mike asked, shifting the subject back to the game. 'What do you think his chances are of becoming a great one?'

Vic's eyes ranged out over the court. 'Tim can be as good as he wants to be. He's got a few things to learn yet, but he's young. He's got the talent to stay in the top half dozen for a long time if he doesn't . . .'

'If he doesn't what?'

'If he doesn't fuck it up.'

Tim came out on to the court then to begin his warm-up, and Vic's attention was completely given over to the young player.

While Alan Doughty, Yuri Zenger, and Tim Barrett received varying coverage in the media, Milo Vasquez was in a position to become the hottest item at Wimbledon. All that held him back was his failure to co-operate with reporters, who love a come-back story almost as much as they do a Cinderella story.

Unlike Zenger, Milo did not insult the newsmen, he merely brushed them off, giving the briefest possible answers to their questions in the post-match interviews. He pleaded exhaustion, and from the strung-out look of the Mexican after one of his super-intense matches, reporters agreed that he did look as if he were on the verge of collapse.

Whatever Milo did away from the courts he kept to himself. After a match he dressed and left the grounds immediately, saying as little as possible to anyone. He was a no-show at all off-court functions attended by the other players. There was a look in his eyes that made Mike uneasy watching from the court side, but he couldn't have said exactly why.

To give some balance to his coverage Mike wandered over on Friday to watch some of the women's singles matches which were now in full swing. After years of playing for peanuts, the girls were finally receiving prize-money more in line with what the men were getting. This was all right with Mike, but he had to conclude that after watching the top men play, the women's game looked like backyard patball.

He found there was a general hostility to sportswriters among the women players. Now that they were closer to financial equality, they felt their space on the sports page should increase proportionately. Mike did not agree, and he made the mistake of arguing the matter with one of the top American players. To strengthen her side of the debate she offered at one point to haul off and deck him. Mike prudently backed away from further discussion, not wanting to test his reflexes against the woman's roundhouse right.

Moving away from the potential violence, Mike gave some thought to writing a column on what it feels like to stand on the hallowed grass courts of Wimbledon with a professional tennis player hitting balls across the net at you. To put his idea into action he had a talk with one of the club officials and the head groundsman. Then he went looking for Fred Olney.

The pixyish Australian had been eliminated, as expected, in the early rounds of the singles. He now pretended disgust with his doubles partner, Denny Urso, for winning his first three matches and staying in the competition.

'It's high time,' Fred complained, 'that Denny quit mucking about with the prima donnas and put his mind to what really matters at this tournament – the doubles.' It was evident, however, from his smile that the little Aussie was brimming with pride in his friend's unexpected success.

Mike sympathised with him about his partner's crass selfishness, then brought up his idea.

'So you want to have a hit, do you?' Fred said, his eyes twinkling with merriment.

'Just a few balls,' Mike said, 'nothing strenuous. I've got an okay to use court fourteen for half an hour at six o'clock.'

'What do you say to a little wager to make it interestin'?'

'Not a chance. I haven't had a tennis racket in my hand since I was in high school, and then it was only because the girl I was going around with played and she conned me into it. I spent about an hour chasing the ball, and that was the end of my tennis. Tell you what I will do, though, you name the pub, and tomorrow night your beer is on me.'

'All I can drink?'

'Sure, I'm a sport.'

'You're on,' said Fred. 'I'll meet you on the court at six.'

Mike scrounged a pair of gym shorts and raggedy tennis shoes, and wore a plain white T-shirt. He arrived at the court a few minutes early and stood around feeling foolish as he waited for Fred.

The Aussie showed up at six on the dot wearing a set of crisp new whites. He looked Mike up and down critically. 'As a sportswriter you may be a winner, but you're a sorry excuse for a tennis player.'

'Okay, okay,' Mike said, grinning, 'let's get on with it.'

Fred selected a racket from the three he had brought along

and handed it to Mike. 'This is a Ron Hopper autograph model. How does it feel?'

Mike took hold of the racket and swung it. 'What am I supposed to feel for?'

'Try the grip. This one is four and a half inches around. You may find it a bit small. Some of the larger blokes use a four and seven-eighths.'

Mike curled his fingers around the leather grip. 'I doubt if I could tell the difference,' he said. 'How much does it weigh?'

'That one's thirteen ounces, just about average. It's strung at sixty pounds tension, also average.'

'What, exactly, does sixty pounds tension mean?'

'It's as though each string is as tight as if it was tied to the ceiling with a sixty-pound weight at the other end. There was an Italian here a few years ago who strung his racket at thirty pounds. The ball used to disappear into that thing as though it was a butterfly net. His forehand floated at you like a soap bubble.'

Mike took a tentative swipe with the racket. 'I guess I'm as ready as I'm going to be. You want to serve me a couple first? Then just bang a few ground strokes over. Enough to give me the feeling.'

'Is that the way you're going to hold the racket?' Fred asked.

'Something wrong with it?'

'It's a lovely grip if you intend to pound nails with the thing. On the other hand, if you want to hit a tennis ball with it, I'd suggest a small adjustment.' He gave the racket a quarter of a turn in Mike's hand, and repositioned his thumb. 'There we are, all ready to go. I'll keep everything to your forehand so you won't have to change the grip.'

'Thanks,' Mike said dryly. He took up a position a couple of feet behind the baseline, roughly copying the bent-knees stance he had seen the players in as they waited to receive service. The first thing he noticed was how much larger the court looked from down here. Watching from up in the stands, the neat green rectangles seemed scarcely bigger than the average suburban front lawn. At ground level, facing another man across the net, the court seemed to expand to football-field proportions.

'Ready?' Fred called from the opposite end.

'Let 'er come,' Mike said.

Fred Olney was not noted for the strength of his serve. Indeed, from Mike's previous vantage point on the sidelines it had seemed a soft ball that no one should have much trouble returning. Tennis was one of those sports, like golf or pocket-billiards, that the average man secretly feels he could master on a professional level with a few months' intensive practice. Some such thought was in Mike Wilder's mind as little Fred Olney tossed up a ball for his first serve.

The Aussie arched his back and swung. Racket met ball with a resounding *thwack*. Something small and pale streaked across the net, raised chalk at the service line, and thumped against the canvas backstop before Mike could move out of his crouch.

'Come on, wise guy,' he yelled, 'ease up. That thing sizzled as it went by me.'

'Sorry, old cock,' the Aussie said, grinning. 'I'll slow the next one down for you.'

'I'll appreciate it,' Mike said.

On the next serve Fred appeared to swing in slow motion, with a mere whisper as the racket stroked the ball. It floated into the air and over the net, giving Mike plenty of time to get into a position where he would have a good whack at it. The ball hit the grass six feet in front of him and slightly to the right. Perfect. Mike swung the racket and hit nothing but air as the spinning ball bit into the grass and ricocheted off at a crazy angle. Mike could only shake his head as Fred Olney doubled up in laughter.

While a small group of onlookers sniggered the little Aussie hit Mike another half dozen serves of varying speeds. Of these, Mike managed to get his racket on a total of one, pounding the ball straight down at his feet.

The results with ground strokes were much the same. Mike would bounce the ball once and sock it across the net, then watch helplessly as it came blazing back, humming with top-spin, impossible for him to hit. Well before the half hour was up Mike was dripping with sweat and gasping for breath.

'Freddy,' he said between gasps, 'you look like you could use a rest.'

The little Aussie came round the net laughing. 'Not as easy a game as you thought, is it, old cock?'

'You can say that again,' Mike admitted. His mind was already choosing the words he would use to describe the helpless feeling of the average man having tennis balls fired at him by a professional player. And a pro who seldom survived the early rounds in singles at that. His column might give second thoughts to a few armchair athletes who figured they were only a few lessons away from Forest Hills.

'Have you anywhere to shower?' Fred asked.

'No, I'll just towel off and drive back to my hotel.'

'I wish I could get you into the players' dressing-room, but they're awfully stuffy about that.'

'So I hear,' Mike said. 'I'd give a lot to get in there on a tournament day just to watch and listen. Be great material.'

Fred looked thoughtful. 'You say you'd give a lot, eh? How about including a few of my mates in the free beer offer if I get you safely into the locker room tomorrow?'

'I'm probably crazy offering to set up brew for the whole Australian tennis team, but if you get me into the locker room it's a deal.'

'There's just a chance we might pull it off. One of our old blokes was supposed to play in the seniors division, but he's had to cancel it. Came down with bloody pneumonia. I might be able to get his pass for you. I hope you'll get some proper togs, though, and not that bloody underwear you've got on.'

'It's worth a try,' Mike said. 'And whether we make it or not, the invitation for you and your buddies stands.'

Mike left Fred Olney at the players' dressing-room and walked out and around the Centre Court stadium, heading for the car park. A knot of brightly dressed girls in their early teens waited by the gate where the cars picked up the players to take them back to their hotels. One of the girls in particular stood out. She could not have been older than fifteen, but her chest would have been the envy of many a topless dancer. Mike had seen her on the opening day wearing a T-shirt that stretched across her abundant bosom and bore the legend: *Timmy's For Me!* Today the T-shirt had been replaced by another that read simply: *Jean-Pierre*. Each half of the hyphenated name bulged forwards over a boob.

Ah, the inconstancy of youth, thought Mike. He wrapped the towel closer around his neck and continued out to the car.

30

Tim Barrett, too, had seen his former adoring fans switch their attentions to Jean-Pierre Leduc. Suddenly, nearing twenty, Tim felt quite old compared to the seventeen-year-old French player.

For Tim the defection of the teenyboppers was not a cause for great concern. Jean-Pierre would be more the type for that sort of thing. The dark-haired boy with his long-lashed Bambi eyes and flirtatious smile gave the little girls the kind of response they wanted. Tim had always been embarrassed by their giggling hero-worship, and unnerved by their childish attempts at seductiveness. He was happy enough just playing his game and being left alone.

Still, the experience gave him a glimpse of how fleeting fame could be. The crowd that loved you on Monday could ignore you by Friday. It would be nice, Tim thought, to have someone who cared for him as a person, not as a tennis player. Somebody who would love him and stand by him even when his competitive days were past. Tim did not want to wind up alone like Vic Goukas.

This line of thinking brought him round to Christy Noone. Being with her made him feel like a whole flesh-and-blood person, and not merely an appendage to a tennis racket. He had hoped to spend this Friday evening with Christy, but she begged off, saying she had long-standing plans to see her brother who had come up from Brighton for just the one day and she simply could not disappoint him. Tim was not happy about it, but felt better when Christy promised that for the rest of Wimbledon she was his alone.

The change in plans left him free to spend this evening with his parents, something he had not done since they arrived in London a week ago. Tim was not looking forward to it, but it would make his mother happy.

He took a taxi from the modest hotel in Kensington where he and Vic stayed to the Regency House. When he arrived at his parents' room on the third floor dinner for three was already laid. Vic Goukas had been invited to join them, but the coach declined.

Jack Barrett met his son at the door and gripped his hand, pulling him inside and thumping his shoulder heartily. Tim's mother hugged him and told him he looked thin. His father phoned for room service to bring up the food, and the three of them stood round feeling strangely ill at ease.

'Isn't this elegant,' Fran Barrett said. 'This is the first time I've ever had dinner served in a hotel room. I wish I could cook for us, but I guess this is the next best thing.'

'I was all for going out to a restaurant,' Jack said, 'but your mother wanted to stay here. She thought it would be nice to have just the family together at least once while we're over here.'

Tim nodded, pretending not to notice the reproach in his father's tone.

'We're having roast beef,' his mother said. 'They had some fancier things on the menu, but I know you've always been a meat and potatoes eater like your father.'

'Roast beef will be fine,' Tim said.

There was a discreet knock at the door, and a waiter came in wheeling a trolley on which were covered dishes of various sizes. The waiter served the food on to the plates and went out.

Tim and his parents sat down and began to eat. The food was a little overcooked, but still tasty.

'Well, I guess tomorrow the real action starts, eh, Tim?' Jack Barrett said. 'Just the sixteen best players left.'

Oh-oh, Tim thought. Here comes one more expert opinion on what's wrong with my game. He said, 'That's right, Dad.'

'What do you think your own chances are from here on?' Jack asked casually.

'I've got as good a shot as anybody.'

'That doesn't sound as confident as the way you were talking a week ago.'

'Maybe I've grown up a little since a week ago.'

'Have some more gravy on your potatoes, Tim,' said Fran Barrett, trying as she always did to head off a potential clash between her husband and her son.

'Are you all right physically?' Jack asked.

'I'm fine.'

'I've been watching your play closely this week, son, and to put it bluntly, you're lucky to still be in the tournament.'

'They've all three been tough matches,' Tim said, keeping his eyes on his plate.

'That's what I'm talking about, they shouldn't have been that tough. You normally beat players of that quality ten times out of ten, and from here on you start meeting the good ones. You've got to get your game together.'

'I know what I have to do, Dad. I'll be all right.' Tim wanted to scream at the old man to stop it for God's sake. From his opening match on Monday this was all he'd been getting from Vic, from reporters and from people he didn't know from Adam. *What's wrong with your game, Tim?* What made people feel they had the right, the duty even, to criticise him? They seemed to look at him as a tennis-playing machine whose flaws, if any, could be corrected by some simple mechanical adjustment.

Christy Noone was the exception. She thought it was fun that he played tennis for a living, but she would probably think it was fun if he sold ties. What was more, it didn't seem to matter to Christy whether he won a match easily or just squeaked through. It probably wouldn't even matter a lot to Christy if he lost.

Even as the thought flashed through Tim's mind he rejected it. Losing was something you never allowed yourself to think about. This was what Tim had been taught as far back as he could remember. If you think about losing you *will* lose, and the world is made for winners.

'It's your concentration,' his father was saying. 'You haven't got your mind on what you're doing out there. You've played the game long enough to know you can't afford to be day-dreaming out on the court, Tim. Not if you expect to win.'

All right, all right, so it was his concentration. Tim didn't need his father or his coach or anybody else to tell him that. For the first time in his life there were other things on his mind when he played tennis. To be precise, just one other thing – Christy Noone.

She was something new in his limited experience with girls, and Tim did not know how to take her. At first it was all frivolous fun, but after they had made love in her flat on Monday night Tim had thought there would be a marked change in their relationship. For his part Tim felt a new deep tenderness for the girl. He was even ready to call it love. Christy, however, acted as though nothing had happened. She was the same laughing, irrepressible fun-time girl as always. She had brushed aside all Tim's attempts to talk seriously about the two of them.

Now there was this business about going out with her brother tonight. If there *was* a brother. Tim forced the suspicion out of his mind. Even if it was true, he ought to have gained precedence over a brother.

'It's clear to me that the girl is just not good for you.'

Tim started at the sound of his father's voice, and realised he had missed some of what he'd been saying.

'What do you mean by that, Dad?'

'I don't want to sound like an old-fashioned heavy father, but I know what I'm seeing out there on the court. The trouble with your game is that you're too wrapped up with that girl, that Christy Noone.'

'Is there anything wrong with me liking a girl?' Tim said, making an effort to keep his voice level.

'Can't we wait until after we've had dessert to talk?' his mother said.

'No, Fran, it's best that we get this out in the open now,' Jack Barrett said.

Tim laid his knife and fork across the plate and met his father's gaze.

'Son, this girl just isn't the kind you should be seeing right now.'

'Oh? What kind of a girl is she, Dad?'

'Now hold on, Tim, I'm not accusing the girl of anything. She's probably great at a party, but this isn't a partying time of your life. She's flighty, she's frivolous and she probably hasn't a thought in her head deeper than what to wear tomorrow.'

'What if I told you I was going to marry Christy?' Tim said.

He sat back and watched the reaction. For a long moment his father and mother sat frozen in their chairs as though paralysed by the news.

'You can't mean it,' Jack Barrett said finally.

Tim let them sit there staring at him for several more seconds. Then he said, 'I hadn't really thought about it until just now, but maybe it's not such a bad idea. I like her a lot, and she likes me. Keep that in mind if you're going to say anything else about her.'

'I'm sure your father didn't mean to sound harsh,' said Fran Barrett. 'The girl did seem quite nice in her way. And, Timmy, you know that anyone you choose will be welcomed into our family.'

Jack Barrett said, 'All I mean is that you ought to wait until after Wimbledon to have your, er, relaxation. Keep your mind on the game in the meantime.'

'Dad, I'm not a kid any more, and I wish you wouldn't treat me like one.'

'Sometimes you act like a kid, dammit.'

Father and son locked eyes over the table. Jack Barrett was the first to look away. In a quieter voice he said, 'I'm only thinking of you, son.'

Like hell you are, Tim thought. You're thinking of the trophy room in your office and how impressed the clients will be if you can add the Wimbledon Cup.

He said, 'It's getting late. I'd better go.'

'It's only eight, Timmy,' his mother said. 'Couldn't you stay a little longer?'

'He needs to get his sleep, Fran,' Jack Barrett said. 'Tomorrow's a big day.'

Tim said hurried good-byes to his parents and as quickly as he could got out of the room and out of the hotel and down in the street where he could breathe again. This was the first time he had stood his ground in an argument with his father. The fact gave him no satisfaction. He wished he could talk freely and openly to his parents, tell them about the turmoil in his mind over his feelings for Christy Noone. But somehow they had never learned to talk together. The only subject they ever discussed comfortably was tennis. Now it seemed they couldn't even do that.

Tim waved away a taxi that pulled up at the kerb. It was too early to go back to his room. And he didn't feel like talking to Vic Goukas, that would just be more analysis of his tennis game.

On an impulse he found a public telephone and dialled Christy's number. No answer. Well, what did he expect? Damn her brother, anyway. Why couldn't he have stayed in Brighton at least another two weeks?

The streets were crowded with Friday night merrymakers. Tim wished he knew where the Australian players had gone tonight. He could enjoy himself with the Aussies and not be expected to contribute much to the conversation. However, finding them was out of the question. Every night they started at a different pub. They might stay at the first until closing time, or they might go rollicking off into the night hitting one pub after another, depending on their mood.

There was no one else Tim wanted to be with. After walking aimlessly for a while he bought a ticket for a cinema showing a pair of American movies. He went inside and sat down alone in the dark. A hell of a way, he thought, for a recent teenage idol to spend Friday night.

31

Jack and Fran Barrett did not speak for a long while after Tim had left their room at the Regency House. While his wife bustled aimlessly about the room, Jack slumped into a chair and wondered why the hell he couldn't talk to his son.

Why was it, he asked himself, that he always sounded like a pompous jackass when he talked to Tim? He knew what he felt and what he wanted to say, but the words wouldn't come out right. He had never had that trouble with anyone else, only with his son. Among his business associates and his friends at the club, Jack Barrett was known as a friendly, articulate man. He envied other fathers who could sit down and talk freely with their sons, even joke with them.

Fran Barrett was busy at the little table, stacking the dinner dishes.

'You don't have to do that,' Jack said, more sharply than he intended. 'Just pick up the phone and call room service.'

'I know,' Fran said. 'It's just habit.' She went on straightening up the table.

Several more minutes passed during which neither of them spoke. Finally Jack said, 'Do you want to tell me what's bothering you?'

'What do you mean, Jack?'

'All that clattering around with the plates.'

'I suppose I'm just disappointed about the way the evening went. I was looking forward to the three of us having a nice dinner together.'

'I'm disappointed too. It's not my fault that Tim got upset and walked out.'

'I've never seen you two clash like that before.'

'I don't know what I could have done to prevent it.'

'You might have picked a subject to talk about that was less touchy.'

'Less touchy than tennis?'

'There *are* other things.'

'Not during Wimbledon, there aren't. Fran, our son has a chance to win the biggest tournament of them all. As his father, don't I have a responsibility to keep him from throwing it away?'

'Is that what he's doing?'

'That's the way it looks to me.'

'You can't play the matches for him, Jack. Tim is an experienced player. I'm sure he knows how important Wimbledon is.'

'I wonder.'

They dropped the subject then, leaving many things unsaid as they always did. After a while they went to bed.

Jack Barrett lay for a long time with his hands clasped behind his head, staring up at the ceiling in the dark bedroom. It was true, as Fran said, that he could not play the matches for his son, but there must be some way he could help. Talking to the boy was not going to do any good; he would have to take some kind of action. Abruptly, Jack made his decision. Tomorrow he would go to see the girl who was the cause of Tim's problems. Now that he had a plan of sorts, he could relax.

Jack reached out tentatively towards his wife. He laid his hand on the curve of her hip. Fran stirred as though in her sleep, but did not respond. He withdrew his hand. Most of the time Fran Barrett was a compliant, easy-going woman, but sometimes when they had a near-quarrel like tonight's she would withdraw from him for a day or so. In the early years of their marriage this had been a cause of considerable irritation to Jack. However, he had come to accept it as a small flaw in an otherwise superior wife and companion. He rolled over on his side and went to sleep.

On Saturday morning Jack was up early. At home in California it was his habit to rise with the sun and jog two miles every day

196

before breakfast, and he found it impossible, no matter where he was, to sleep late.

Fran eyed him sleepily from the comfort of the bed. 'What are you doing up already, Jack? Are you getting dressed?'

'I'm going out for a walk. I don't feel like I've been getting enough exercise this week. You go ahead and sleep in. We'll have a late breakfast when I get back, then go on out to Wimbledon.'

Fran rolled over and made muffled sounds of assent into the pillow. Jack leaned down and kissed the back of her neck. He pulled on a suede jacket over a brown turtleneck pullover and left the hotel.

The morning air was fresh and damp, and there were few people in the streets yet. Jack walked down the Strand until he found a tobacconist whose shop was open. There he consulted the London directory at a public telephone. He found Christy Noone's number and checked her address on a pocket-size street map of the city. He saw that the street she lived in in Chelsea was too far away to walk, so he went back outside and hailed a taxi.

On the drive through London Jack felt a growing tingle of excitement. It was, he told himself, a natural reaction to the fact that he was at last doing something, taking positive action.

He had not yet decided exactly what he would say to Christy when he got there. All he had was a vague notion about persuading the girl to go easy on Tim's emotions during the tournament. Last night when the idea had come to him, it had seemed simple and logical. Now he was beginning to have doubts. He certainly didn't want to seem like some heavy-handed parent. It was best, he decided, not to plan his approach in advance. He would wait and see how the encounter with the girl went, then play it by ear.

The taxi pulled up in front of a block of flats in Chelsea, and Jack paid the driver and got out. For a moment he stood on the pavement, settling himself into a calm, dignified mood. He was surprised to see that his palms were sweating. He wiped them on a clean handkerchief and walked into the building.

He found Christy's name on the board and climbed the two flights of stairs to her flat. He gave the door a business-like three knocks and waited. There was no response. No sounds of movement from within.

Jack felt a disappointment that was out of all proportion to the situation. He explained this to himself as a natural frustration over being unable to put his plan to work. He knocked once more before starting back down the stairs.

'Just a minute!' a girl's voice called from inside. 'I'm coming.'

It was nearer three minutes, but at last Christy Noone opened the door. She wore a pair of nylon pyjamas that were cut off at the legs and arms. Her hair was disarrayed from being in bed, but her eyes were wide awake. She seemed unaware that the top three buttons of the pyjama top were open.

'Why, Mr Barrett, hello,' she said.

Jack Barrett's calm, dignified pose evaporated like mist before the sun. He had not prepared himself for a girl in cut-off nylon pyjamas who didn't even seem surprised to see him.

He said, 'I, uh, seem to have got you out of bed. Maybe I should come back another time.'

'As long as I'm up now, why don't you come in?'

Christy stepped to one side and Jack walked into the flat.

'What can I do for you, Mr Barrett?' she said. A spark of mischief glowed in her eyes.

Jack gazed around the sitting-room. Magazines, articles of clothing and various bits of feminine paraphernalia lay everywhere in disorder. Still, there was something appealing in the very untidiness of the room.

'I thought you and I should have a talk,' he said.

Christy sat down on the sofa and curled her legs under her. She made no move to close the pyjama top.

'What did you want to talk about?' she said.

Jack removed a fashion magazine from the seat of a straight-backed chair and sat down gingerly.

'It's about Tim,' he said, and found he had to clear his throat.

'Tim's an awfully nice lad.' Christy smiled brightly and waited for him to go on.

Jack Barrett drew a deep breath and pondered how he should begin. He decided to plunge right in. 'I wonder if you know how important the Wimbledon tournament is to Tim?'

'He's awfully keen on it, I know that much.'

'Yes, he is. He also has a chance to win it. The trouble is that the way he's playing now, he won't make it as far as the quarter-finals.'

'Why ever not? Tim's won every time so far, hasn't he?'

'So far, but the way that he's won his early matches is not encouraging. The boy's not concentrating the way he has to in order to play winning tennis.'

'I think I see,' Christy said. 'You're afraid that Tim's mind is on me rather than on his tennis. Is that it?'

'In a nutshell, yes, that's about it.'

'I see. Tell me, just what is it that you want me to do?'

'This sounds a little foolish, but I'm not sure exactly what you *can* do. When I came up here the whole thing seemed like a good idea, but now I'm embarrassed to find I really have nothing to say.'

'Perhaps I can help. Were you by any chance going to ask me not to see Tim again?'

'No. I may be out of the square generation, but I know better than that. I think what I had in mind was something like asking that you and Tim not get too, well, involved until after Wimbledon.'

'Have you talked to Tim about it?'

'I tried, but frankly it didn't go very well. He walked out on me.'

Christy leaned forward slightly. 'Mr Barrett, if when you say *involved*, you mean what I think you do, there's something you ought to know. We already have.'

'You're not engaged or anything?'

'Certainly not. What's between Tim and me is strictly fun and games. At least, that's the way it is as far as I'm concerned.'

'I have a feeling Tim might think that it's something more serious.'

'I'm sorry if he does, but that's his problem.'

'Yes, I suppose it is.'

Jack caught himself staring at the open buttons on the girl's pyjamas. He clapped his hands on his knees, stood up, and made a move towards the door.

'I'd better be going,' he said.

Christy rose from the sofa and walked over to stand in front of him, placing herself between him and the door.

She said, 'Mr Barrett, I promise I won't do anything that will harm Tim's chances at Wimbledon if I can possibly help it. Not seeing him is out of the question, though, as I do enjoy his company, and I've already promised to be at his match this afternoon.'

Jack shifted uncomfortably. He was acutely aware of the girl's firm young body, covered only by the thin material of her pyjamas.

'Thank you, Christy,' he said. 'I appreciate your help. I hope you won't tell Tim I was up here.'

'Not if you don't want me to.'

'I don't think he'd understand. On second thoughts, maybe he *would* understand. Either way it would cause more problems.'

'I won't tell him.'

'I'll be going then.'

Christy made no move to get out of his way. 'Mr Barrett, you aren't going to leave without telling me the real reason you came?'

'Real reason?'

'I saw the way you looked at me the other day out at Hurlingham. You liked me.'

'Well, sure, but . . .'

'More than liked me. A woman can tell when a man's thinking *those* thoughts. I don't mind saying I was thinking the same thing about you. You're a very good-looking man.'

Jack Barrett stood with his mouth open, but he couldn't think what to say. He was in turn shocked, flattered, amused and tempted. However, he was too flustered to identify any of these feelings.

'Don't be embarrassed,' Christy said. 'This is a perfectly natural, healthy way for a man and woman to feel about each other.'

'Who said I'm feeling *any* way?'

'Aren't you?'

'I must be dreaming this conversation,' Jack said, turning away to break the eye contact.

Christy moved round behind the sofa and stood with her hands resting on its back. 'Why?' she said. 'Is it because I'm skipping all the silly prattle people go through before they finally get round to what they really want?'

'Which is . . .?'

'Sex, of course. People waste so much time playing word games. Like do we say, "Let's make love," or "Let's go to bed," or simply "Let's fuck"?'

In spite of his intention to be stern, Jack felt a grin tugging at the corners of his mouth. He heard himself say, 'Which one do you like?'

'It depends on who I'm with. Usually, I'm a "fuck" person, but some fellows get all sick and nervous when you use the word. They have trouble with parts of the body too. For some reason they blush like crazy if you talk about their "cock" or "prick". I don't know what else in the world you'd call it. I've never been able to say "penis" without feeling terribly clinical.'

'I have to ask,' Jack said, interested in spite of himself, 'why it's necessary to call it anything at all?'

'One could simply point at it, I suppose,' Christy said, 'but that wouldn't do in the dark, would it?'

Jack relaxed now and laughed aloud. 'I guess I've never really thought about it. My generation didn't do much talking. At least not during.'

'A lot of fellows are still like that. Regular clams. Others chatter away the whole time. Give you sort of a running description of what they're doing. It can be rather exciting.'

'Do you really get around that much, Christy?' Jack asked more seriously.

'Not really. I'm a load of bluff, you know. Oh, I do my share of the old slap and tickle, but I have a habit of exaggerating.'

'I kind of thought so.'

'So are we going to?'

'Going to what?'

'Make love. Go to bed. Fuck.'

'Good God, you mean it, don't you!'

'Of course I do.'

'Christy, I'm—'

'I hope you're not going to tell me you're old enough to be my father.'

'As a matter of fact, I was.'

'What difference does that make? As long as you're not too old to—'

'Hold it!' Jack interrupted, raising his hands in a *Stop* gesture. 'Before this goes any further I want you to know I'm very flattered by your suggestion and, yes, tempted to take you up on it. But it's not going to happen.'

'Why not, for heaven's sake?'

'There are other people involved.'

'Nonsense, there's just you and me. Who else?'

'There's Tim, for one.'

'Yes, I suppose you're right about that,' Christy admitted reluctantly.

'And there's my wife, whom I happen to love very much. And who *does* understand me.'

'Would she mind awfully?' Christy said.

'*Mind?!* You bet she'd mind. She's not *that* understanding.'

'Ah well, nothing ventured, and all that.'

She smiled winningly at Jack, and he grinned back. He crossed to the door and started to go out.

'Good-bye, Christy.'

'Good-bye, Mr Barrett. I presume I'll see you at Wimbledon this afternoon?'

'I presume.'

'And don't worry about Tim. He just might be tougher than you give him credit for.'

'He might, at that,' Jack said, and walked out of the girl's flat and back down the stairs.

When he was back out in the street, the sense of unreality returned to Jack Barrett. Had he really been standing there in the flat of a pyjama-clad girl of twenty-one calmly discussing the possibility of their going to bed together? He shook his head and smiled, wondering whether he was a virtuous fellow for walking away, or a damn fool.

He walked a little way to the King's Road where he flagged down a taxi. On the drive back to the Regency House he tried to sort out his thoughts. In her feather-headed, earthy-wise way, Christy Noone might just have taught him a valuable lesson this morning. At least he knew now that Tim would have to win or lose his own matches, on the tennis court and elsewhere. Also, Jack would have to stop making a career of being Tim Barrett's father.

32

The first Saturday of the fortnight marks the half-way point in the Wimbledon tennis tournament. Out of 128 young men who began play the previous Monday in the men's singles, sixteen were still in the running for the championship on Saturday morning. By now the pretenders were out of it – the players who were too weak or too slow or who didn't want to win badly enough. A few of the good ones were gone too – those who were not in good physical condition or took their opponents too lightly or eased up too soon in a one-sided match only to lose control. By Saturday night there would be eight left.

Mike Wilder sat with Paula Teal sipping a tall drink at one of the blue wicker tables in the Players' Tea Room. At Mike's feet rested a soft leather holdall like the ones used by the players for their equipment.

It was shortly before the traditional two o'clock starting time, and the tea room was even busier than usual. Players who were not involved in today's matches were eating the hot lunches served only to players. Reporters were crowded round the bar. Deals were in the making everywhere. Mike fancied he could hear the ringing of cash registers in the din.

'I've never seen anything like this,' Paula said, gazing around at the frenetic activity.

Mike said, 'It's a little like the floor of the Stock Exchange during a panic.'

'I didn't know you were interested in the market.'

'I'm not. I wandered into the place one day looking for an off-track betting office.'

'Hey, Mike! Mike, ol' buddy!'

Mike swivelled towards the voice calling his name and saw J. J. Kaiser coming towards the table. He was towing along a jut-jawed woman with massive forearms.

'This is luck, running into you,' J.J. enthused. 'Hi, Paula, good to see you again. Quite a crowd, isn't it, Mike?'

'Hello, J.J.,' Mike said.

Once again the little man performed his trick of producing a chair from nowhere. He deposited his female companion in it and squatted beside her on the floor. Mike glanced round looking for Geneva Sundstrum, but the big blonde was nowhere in sight.

'You people know Tina Gottschalk, of course,' J.J. said, indicating the woman he had brought with him. 'Tina's got a real shot this year at winning the women's singles. Tina, this is Mike Wilder, top sportswriter in the whole U.S. of A.'

'Hello, Miss Gottschalk,' Mike said. 'J.J. exaggerates.'

'About what?' Tina said, thrusting her jaw forward aggressively.

'About his ranking of the country's sportswriters.'

'For a minute I thought you were talking about my chances of winning.'

'I assure you that's not what I meant. I have no idea what kind of a tennis player you are.'

'I'll bet you haven't. Have you even watched a women's match yet?'

'A little here, a little there.'

'You'd never know it by reading your fucking column. There's never a word in it about women unless you've got some smart remark. You and your arsehole sportswriter buddies are all the same.'

Mike looked at the woman and blinked.

J.J. moved into the silence quickly. 'Ha ha, don't let Tina throw you, Mike, she likes to come on a little strong sometimes just to shock people. Tina's going to be using some of our Gilfillan equipment, aren't you, honey?'

'I told you I'd try it out in practice is all,' Tina said. 'I want to know if your shit's any good before I use it in a match. And don't ever call me honey again.'

'Yeah, yeah, right,' J.J. said hurriedly. 'Mike, how about working Tina into one of your columns, or maybe a *Sportsweek* piece? She'd make good copy.'

Mike rubbed his jaw and studied the scowling woman across the table. 'I might do something on her at that,' he said.

'You see, Tina,' said J.J., 'I told you he was a buddy of mine.'

Tina looked squarely into Mike's face. 'Don't do me any favours, bit shot,' she said.

'Don't worry, Miss Gottschalk,' he told her. 'I don't intend to.'

'I gotta go,' Tina said, standing up abruptly.

'Yeah, right,' said J.J. 'I'll see you after your match, okay hon—, uh, Tina?'

Tina Gottschalk turned her broad back on the table and walked away without further conversation.

'She's always tense before a match,' J.J. explained.

'Sure.'

J.J. dropped into the wicker chair vacated by Tina, and the bright smile slipped off his face as though it had come unglued.

Paula looked questioningly from one of the men to the other, then stood up. 'If you'll excuse me for a few minutes, I think I'll go and . . . "powder my nose" I believe is the expression.'

When he was alone with Mike, J.J. said, 'Who do I think I'm kidding?'

'About what?'

'That Gottschalk dame is a royal pain in the you-know-what. I'd like to tell her to go get fucked, but I think that'd be asking the impossible.'

'What are you saying, J.J., that you don't like your job?'

'Job? This is a job? I'm nothing but a frigging kissarse. My so-called job is sucking up to sonsofbitches like Yuri Zenger and foul-mouthed dykes like Gottschalk. Excuse me for laying all this on you, Mike, but sometimes this "job" drives me right up the wall.'

'If you feel that way, why don't you get out?'

'What else could I do? I've been hustling one thing or another since I was twelve years old. And I'm pretty good at it, if I do say so myself. Trouble is, hustling's the *only* thing I'm good at. I've got no talent, no skills, no education to speak of. I'm not crazy about the work I do, but it beats starving.'

'I never knew you felt that way,' Mike said.

'I never did before. I don't know what's come over me lately.'

'Well, you're not alone, J.J. Almost everybody has spells where he feels crummy about what he's doing for a living. Most of the time we get over it and realise we really haven't got it so bad after all.'

'Even sportswriters feel that way?'

'Even sportswriters.'

'I don't quite know how, but I think you've made me feel better. Thanks, Padre.'

'Bless you, my son.'

J.J. grinned at him, and Mike grinned back, surprised to find himself actually liking the little hustler.

There was a change in the tone of the conversations in the room, and Mike turned to look for the cause. It was not hard to spot. Geneva Sundstrum in a form-fitting pink dress was moving towards their table, her splendid blonde head well above the crowd. In her wake she left little eddies of admiring males.

'How did it go, J.J.?' she asked after greetings had been exchanged.

'So-so. Gottschalk wants to try out the stuff before she makes a commitment. If you ask me, all she's looking for is a load of free equipment.'

Geneva leaned across the table and spoke confidentially to Mike. 'J.J. thought he might do better with Tina if I wasn't around.'

Mike eyed the lush figure of the big blonde and made a mental comparison with the muscular lady tennis player. He said, 'I see his point.'

'We better buzz off, Mike,' said J.J. 'Zenger's got the opening match on the Centre Court, and I want to be sure he sees me cheering for him. Thanks for the sympathetic ear.'

'Don't mention it,' Mike said. He watched the tough little man walk away with the statuesque girl at his side. Silently Mike wished him luck.

Paula returned and sat down at the table. 'Did J.J. leave?' she asked.

'Yeah. Geneva showed up and they took off together.'

'I saw Geneva out in the ladies' room and we talked a little. She's a nice girl.'

'Seems to be.'

'And you know, I think she really loves the man.'

'I don't think J.J. is aware of it yet, but it looks to me like he's getting hung up on her too.'

'Isn't that fascinating? You could probably write a book about Wimbledon without ever mentioning the tennis.'

'Very likely. Here's another story coming in the door now.' Mike nodded towards the entrance where Jean-Pierre Leduc, young conqueror of the old champion, was coming in trailing a crowd of reporters and hangers-on. The French boy's command of English was small, but his answers to the reporters' questions were animated, and seemed to delight everyone within hearing.

'Today's hero,' Mike remarked.

'He's gorgeous,' Paula said. 'He's been in the papers and on television ever since he beat Ron Hopper on Tuesday.'

'The kid may develop into a top player,' Mike said, 'if the girls don't eat him alive first.'

'Yum. If only I were ten years younger. Better make that fifteen.'

'You're a lascivious old lady.'

'Isn't that true.'

'Fred Olney ought to be along soon,' Mike said. 'He said he'd meet me here by starting time.'

'Is he the little Australian? The one who's getting you a pass to the dressing-room?'

'Ssh, not so loud. If the other reporters find out I'm being smuggled inside they'll march on the American embassy. Here comes Fred now.'

The Aussie bounced over to the table and dropped into a chair opposite them. He winked at Paula by way of greeting, and said to Mike, 'I hope you appreciate all the trouble I've gone to for you. I'll be scalped if anybody finds out.'

'Torture won't drag your name out of me,' Mike said.

'I'll expect nothing less than a biographical article about me in that magazine of yours.'

'I'll see what I can do. I take it you got the pass.'

Fred glanced furtively over one shoulder, then the other. From a shirt pocket he produced a plastic-covered card which he slipped across the table to Mike. 'If you're captured,' he said, 'eat this.'

'Thanks, Fred, I appreciate it.'

'You'll have a chance to appreciate it properly tonight at the Bull and Crown over in Knightsbridge. Do you know the place?'

'I'll find it.'

'You did say I could bring along as many of my mates as I liked?'

'That was the deal.'

'Smashing. You'll be there too, miss?'

'You couldn't keep me away,' Paula said.

'All the better. I must pop off now and cheer on whoever's playing against Denny. First thing you know that bloke will start thinking he's a singles player and I'll have to get meself a new partner for the doubles.'

Watching Fred Olney swing off towards the door Mike said, 'I have a friend on the *Daily News* who always said tennis players were a pimple on the face of sports. He said they were arrogant, clannish crybabies, and were spoiled rotten. And I used to more or less agree with him.'

'And now you've changed your mind?'

'I've just learned once again what a bad practice it is to generalise. There are some bad people in tennis, no doubt about it, but there are baseball and football players I know who wouldn't carry that little Aussie's jock strap.'

'Does everyone you know play some sort of game?' Paula asked.

'We're all players at one game or another. Some of us win, some lose, some cheat, some are champions.'

'Goodness, aren't we philosophical?'

Mike grinned suddenly. 'Must be something I ate. Maybe those sausages you cooked for breakfast.'

'Not "sausages", Yank, "bangers". Do you want people to take you for a foreigner?'

'Sorry. Bangers, then. Hey, look at the time. I'd better get changed and assume my new identity, namely . . .' he paused to read the name on the card Fred Olney had provided, 'Henry Penny.'

'Henny Penny?'

'*Henry.*'

'Is that a real name, or is Freddie having you on?'

'If he's pulling a fast one, the Aussies are going to be drinking beer on their own money tonight, and I don't think he'd risk that. Let's go.'

They left the tea room and walked along a path through the hydrangeas to a public rest-room. While Paula waited outside Mike went in and changed into the tennis clothes he had brought along in the holdall. No T-shirt and gym shorts this time. Mike had outfitted himself in Adidas shoes, shorts by Fred Perry, and a shirt that bore the familiar alligator emblem of Réné Lacoste. Mike glanced at himself in the mirror and decided that if Wimbledon had a best-dressed division he would easily make the semi-finals.

He left the rest-room, rejoining Paula outside. He gave her the suit, shirt and shoes he had come in, tucking the dressing-room pass into the pocket of his tennis shorts.

'Now if you'll drop these clothes in the car,' he said, 'you can go on out and enjoy the matches. I'll meet you back here at, say, six o'clock.'

'Righto, Captain,' said Paula, giving him a snappy salute.

'I hope you don't mind too much watching the tennis alone,' he said. 'This is a chance I couldn't pass up.'

'Not at all,' Paula said. 'In fact I find this cloak-and-dagger business quite exciting. Rather like a James Bond plot.'

'I don't think it'll be all *that* exciting, but I do appreciate your help.'

Paula walked off in the direction of the car park carrying Mike's shoes in one hand with his suit folded over her arm. Watching her, Mike smiled, admiring the springy grace of her walk. He took a sun visor from the holdall and fitted it on his head, pulling the green plastic shade down to his eyebrows, and started for the dressing-room. He stopped again and took out his horn-rimmed glasses. With these on under the green eye shade, he decided he was sufficiently disguised. Not that his face was all that familiar, but a few of the players might know him. He would rely on the principle that nobody recognised his postman out of uniform, or his bartender sitting on the customers' side of the bar. Nobody would expect to see a sportswriter dressed like a tennis player, especially in an area where only players were allowed.

Mike swung into what he hoped was an athletic stride, and walked up to the dressing-room entrance where the two bobbies stood guard. He showed his pass to one of them. The policeman examined the card, glanced at Mike's face, and nodded an okay. With a silent sigh, Mike passed into the dressing-room. He was just a little pleased at being accepted so readily as a tennis player, even a senior.

The spacious locker room was a-swarm with activity as players in various stages of undress prepared for the afternoon's matches. In addition to the singles players still in competition, there were doubles players and men in the seniors competition. Mike sauntered through the room, concentrating on being inconspicuous.

He found a quiet spot on a bench along one wall and sat down. He took the old racket Fred Olney had given him from the pocket on the holdall and laid it across his lap. He fiddled with the strings, hoping it looked like he knew what he was doing.

The gabble of many languages filled the room, punctuated by laughter that was a little too loud to be spontaneous. The place smelled of sweat and rubbing alcohol.

As the players drifted out to their assigned courts Mike got up and wandered round. The dressing-room at Wimbledon was unique in the sports world. Just beyond the locker area were six private bathrooms. There the players could go after their matches and luxuriate in victory or soak away the pain of defeat. The baths were large enough for even the tallest players to stretch out, and were provided with long-handled back-brushes and sponges the size of footballs. In each bathroom there was a mirror and a shelf of grooming equipment to help the player prepare himself to re-enter the outside world.

Five trainer-masseurs were on duty in the dressing-room at

all times. As Mike walked past their tables all five were busy working on aching muscles and sore psyches. He sat down on the bench again and scribbled a few notes.

'Awright, Penny, you're due on court nine. Let's hop it!'

Mike started at the voice, and looked up to see Fred Olney grinning like a monkey.

'You look quite authentic in your new togs,' the Aussie said, 'except for one little detail.'

'What's that?'

'A sportswriter couldn't be expected to know this, but the jock goes *inside* the shorts.'

'Very funny. I thought you went out to watch Denny.'

'I couldn't stand it any more. The bloody fool's winning again. He'll probably drag it out the full five sets and have nothing left for our doubles match. We're supposed to play those two brothers from Nepal or some place like that.'

'That's tough,' Mike said, grinning. Despite Fred's complaining, he could see the little Aussie's pride in his friend's showing in the singles.

'Did you have any trouble getting in?'

'It went as smooth as butter.'

'Where'd you get the spectacles?'

'They're mine.'

'I've never seen you wearing them before.'

'I only need them for seeing.'

'They make you look a little like Clark Kent. A slightly overweight Clark Kent. In his underwear.'

'You're just being kind.'

'All the same, I'll bet there's been precious few unauthorised blokes got into this room. Security's even tighter for the women's locker. In a hundred years only two men have ever got in there. One was a blind masseur, and the other was the old French player, Jean Borotra. That was in 1925. Borotra lost his championship the same year. Don't know if there was any connection.'

Fred changed into his tennis clothes and headed out to check the condition of the court he and Denny would play their doubles match on. Looking after him, Mike saw that going out that way there were two directions a player could take. Off to the right a wide door led to the outer courts. To the left were the frosted glass doors to the Centre Court. On an arch over the doors was carved a quotation from Kipling: 'IF YOU CAN MEET WITH TRIUMPH AND DISASTER AND TREAT THOSE TWO IMPOSTERS JUST THE SAME.'

Mike went back and sat down, and after a while the players began drifting back in. The losers, generally, were in a hurry to get dressed and get out. The winners reacted differently, according to their personalities.

Milo Vasquez stormed in looking as angry as ever, and passed by the massage tables and bathrooms for a quick shower. He spoke to no one and left in a hurry, looking for all the world like a loser. However, Mike learned from the conversations around him that Milo had won again by playing a game of deadly precision most unlike his old blow-'em-off-the-court style. Mike wondered what devils were driving the Mexican on after his skills had eroded.

Tim Barrett came in looking exhausted after squeaking through in another tough, close match. As Tim headed for the baths Mike recognised the tell-tale smudges under the boy's eyes showing lack of sleep.

A Russian player named Kugarin seemed ill at ease in here without the two bulky 'trainers' who accompanied him everywhere outside. He smiled thinly to congratulations on his victory, but spoke no more than he had to.

Big Denny Urso had won his fourth straight match, and seemed as surprised as anybody else as he endured the good-natured needlings of Fred Olney and the other Aussies.

Brian White, the handsome 'gentleman player', was calm and gracious in victory, praising his opponent generously.

Yuri Zenger, as was his custom, came into the locker room as though he owned it. In case anyone had failed to get the news, Yuri described with gestures how thoroughly he had beaten down today's opponent, and how this was nothing compared to what he would do to whoever was unlucky enough to face him in the quarter-finals on Tuesday.

As Yuri well knew, his quarter-final opponent would be young Jean-Pierre Leduc, who had delighted the teenyboppers by winning again today. Jean-Pierre merely smiled at the

Hungarian's bombast, possibly because he understood very little of what was being said.

Alan Doughty, whose match had started later than some of the others, came in looking strangely subdued for a man who had just won his way into the quarter-finals. He spent a short time in one of the baths, then dressed and went quietly away.

Mike left the locker room before it emptied enough for him to be conspicuous. He still had a few minutes before it would be time to meet Paula, so he sought out the court where the doubles team of Olney and Urso was playing. A glance at the scoreboard told him the Aussies were having little trouble with the brothers from Nepal or wherever. Mike caught Freddie's eye and winked. Fred answered with a broad pantomime of downing a mug of beer, and Mike walked away chuckling.

Paula was waiting for him when he arrived at their meeting place.

'How did you do, champ?' she said, cocking her head at the tennis racket he still carried.

'Won in straight sets, of course,' he said with a bad attempt at a British accent. 'Surely you didn't expect less?'

'My hero!'

'We'd better go see about something to eat,' he said. 'I've got to buy beer for the male population of Australia tonight, and it promises to be a wet evening.'

Paula took his hand, and together they swung off along the path towards the car park.

33

Sunday morning arrived in Mike Wilder's world uninvited. His head throbbed and his mouth tasted as though it belonged to somebody else. Several seconds ticked by before he remembered where he was. In Paula Teal's flat in Chelsea. In her bed. Alone in her bed. He groaned aloud and his head felt worse.

From the direction of the kitchen came sounds of someone moving around. A radio played softly out there, and a woman was humming with the orchestra.

Mike lurched to his feet and stumbled into the bathroom. He brushed his teeth, rinsed his mouth, and ducked his head under the tap to let the cold water spill over it. When he felt he could risk a look in the mirror he winced at the bleary reflection and turned quickly away. When he went back into the bedroom Paula was standing at the foot of the bed wearing a neat quilted robe.

'What'll you give me if I refrain from commenting on the way you look?' she said.

'Name your price.'

'Are you ready for coffee?'

'Not yet. That was a helluva party last night. How come you look so healthy?'

'I didn't try to match the Australians beer for beer.'

Mike eased down to a sitting position on the bed. 'That was a bad mistake on my part,' he agreed.

'You kept telling everybody how you used to put it away at the old Phi Sig house.'

'I forgot how many years ago that was.'

'Here, I brought you something that might help.' She held out a glass of red-orange liquid.

'What is it?'

'Something my father used to take when he'd had a few too many at the local. Drink it down like a good lad.'

Mike accepted the glass and did as he was told. The concoction seemed to be mostly vegetable juices with some suspicious semi-solids that he preferred not to think about.

'It tastes awful,' he said.

'That's all right, it'll make you feel better.'

After a few seconds Mike said, 'By God, I think you're right. Could it be working already?'

'My father used barely to get the glass put down before he was ready for another party.'

'I'm not quite up to that, but I'm beginning to think I may live.'

'Glad to hear it. I wonder how the Australians are feeling today. Never in my life have I seen people drink so much beer so fast.'

'If I know the Aussies, they're already making plans for opening time at the pubs. There must be something in their diet – kangaroo maybe – that makes them immune to hangovers. They're probably feeling a lot better than some of the other players this morning, judging from my impressions in the locker room.'

'Who, for instance?'

'Tim Barrett, for one. He looks like he's not getting enough sleep.'

'That's not very surprising. Nobody who fools around with Christy Noone is going to do much sleeping.'

'I suppose not. Then there's Milo Vasquez.'

'The angry-looking Mexican chap?'

'Yeah. Something's really eating at him. I'd like to do a column on him, but he won't talk to the press or anybody else.'

'Heavens, there's certainly more going on at Wimbledon than one sees from the stands.'

'That's a fact. And maybe the strangest story of all is Alan Doughty. He's about to go into the quarter-finals – the best he's ever done at Wimbledon – the whole country's behind him, and he acts like he's on his way to an execution. I wonder how he feels this morning.'

Across the Thames in his Lambeth flat Alan Doughty came fully awake with a start. Hazel was not beside him in the bed. He pulled the covers back, stepped into his slippers, and went out to the kitchen. Hazel stood at the sink scouring out a saucepan.

'What's the trouble, love?' he said.

'Nothing. I woke up early and didn't want to disturb you, so I came out here.'

'Turn round and let's have a look at you.'

Hazel put down the saucepan and turned to face him.

'You've been crying,' he said.

'I can't help it, Alan.'

'I thought we'd settled this business.'

'When I saw you fall on the court the other day I couldn't think of anything but Aubrey Cooper falling that day at Southampton. He never got up again.'

'Hazel, you've seen me take a hundred tumbles on the court. Everybody falls now and again.'

'But everybody doesn't have . . . what you have.'

Alan pulled thoughtfully at his long jaw. After a moment he said, 'I want you to come for a jaunt with me today.'

'A jaunt? Where are we going?'

'To Craddock.'

'That's the village where your brothers live.'

'Yes, and the village where I was born, and where my mum and dad both died.'

'Are we going to visit your brothers?'

'Not this time. There's something there I want you to see. Something that may help you understand why I must play the game to the finish at Wimbledon.'

Hazel studied her husband's face for a moment, then dried her hands and went to change into something for the outing.

An hour later they were driving north through the gently rolling country of the English midlands. Unlike most of his countrymen, Alan kept the Rover at the new fifty-five-mile-per-hour speed limit while the few other cars there were on the road passed him doing sixty-five or seventy. A drizzle began, and worsened steadily the farther they got from London.

Alan spoke very little as he drove. Hazel stared out of the window on her side. The monotonous countryside was relieved occasionally by the ruins of a stone chapel, marking the spot where some eighteenth-century village had died. Several times they passed a gipsy caravan parked beside the road with a pile of rusted car parts waiting to be sold as scrap.

When they reached a point half-way between Sheffield and Leeds, some 180 miles from London, Alan turned off the motorway on to the decaying secondary road that led into Craddock. The first signs of the village were crumbling and abandoned cottages with weeds choking the little patches of ground that had once been gardens.

'When I was a lad people still lived as far out as this,' Alan said. 'All the mines were going then, and everybody working. After the war ended, most of the mines round Craddock were closed down. It would have cost more than it was worth to dig out what little coal was left. People died and people went away, and some moved into the village. There can't be more than three hundred left here now.'

They drove past more dead cottages and the angular skeletons of mine structures. The ground was scarred and scabrous where the coal had been ripped from the earth, and where nothing now would grow. In the grey steady rain the country looked drained of colour and life.

Alan turned on to a gravel drive that ran for a hundred yards alongside a chain-link fence. Behind the fence were a number of grey, faceless buildings. A path led between the buildings and beyond to where several tunnel mouths gaped in the hillside. Alan stopped the car at a locked gate with a wooden shed at one side. A painted metal sign over the gate read: 'Sheffield-Midlands Colliery.'

A man stepped from the shed, and Alan got out of the car and walked over to talk to him.

'The mine's closed today,' said the gate-keeper.

'I know,' Alan said. 'I wonder if we might walk in and look round a bit?'

218

The man eyed him suspiciously. 'Now what would you be wantin' to do that for?'

'I used to work here. My wife's never seen a coal mine.'

The face of the gate-keeper opened suddenly in recognition. 'Why, you're Alan Doughty, ain't you? I know your brothers well, I do. We're all hoping for you to win the Wimbledon.'

'Thank you,' Alan said. 'That's good to know.'

The man opened up a smaller gate set inside the large one. He said, 'You're welcome to go in and look round all you like, Mr Doughty, but if you don't mind my sayin' so, it's a queer place to be takin' your missus.'

Alan smiled his thanks. 'We shouldn't be too long.'

He went back to the car for Hazel. With the collars of their raincoats turned up, and a scarf to protect her hair, they walked through the gate. No live thing grew inside the fence. Everything – buildings, trucks, the path they walked on – wore a gritty film of coal dust.

'This is the last mine still operating in Craddock,' Alan said. 'They say it's good for two more years at the most.'

They walked past the buildings and headed up the hill to where the tunnels were. 'When my brothers climb this path every morning it's six o'clock and still dark in winter,' Alan said. 'They stop for a cup of hot tea there in the canteen, then put away their clean clothes in a locker and put on their dirty clothes to go into the pits.'

They came to the first and largest of the tunnels. A double-decker life-cage stood empty over a shaft that plunged down into darkness.

'Here's where they go down into the earth. I can't take you there, but I can tell you a little about what it's like. At seven o'clock you get into that cage and it drops you down two thousand feet below where we stand. They have to pump air down there, and it's cold. A lot of the boys go down with pneumonia, if the black lung doesn't get 'em first. Once you're down you walk maybe half a mile to the coal face where you're workin'. Sometimes the seam you're diggin' at narrows down to three feet or so. Then you crawl on your hands and knees, and you stay that way all day.'

Hazel said nothing, but hunched deeper into her raincoat and stayed close to Alan as they walked along the hillside. Some of the smaller tunnels they passed were boarded over with rotting timber. Others were choked with rocks.

'This was always a good mine,' Alan said, 'so it's usually dry down below. In some others the men have to work in water up to their boot-tops.

'At ten-forty you knock off for lunch. There's no time to leave, so you eat your sandwiches there where you work. And since there's no place to wash, you eat a lot of coal dust too.

'At two o'clock you come up from the pit and shower for twenty or thirty minutes to get as much of the coal as you can off your skin and out of your hair. It gets in all the openings of your body. Then you put on your clean clothes and go home.'

Alan started back down the hill and Hazel followed.

'It's a terrible life, isn't it?' she said.

Alan spoke without looking back. 'If it's the only thing you've ever known it's tolerable. But once you've got away, the thought of goin' back is worse than dyin'.'

The rain had slackened now to a chill grey mist. Alan talked briefly to the gate-keeper, thanking him for letting them in, and walked Hazel back to the car.

'You've seen my brothers and their families,' he said, 'so you know about the people who live here. The men have coughs, and there's black in their wrinkles and round their nails that will never come out. The women are pale and always look tired. Their faces are pinched together. The children are quieter than children should be.'

Alan said no more. He steered the Rover out of the gravel drive and headed away from Craddock. It was like leaving a house where someone was dying.

For nearly an hour they drove in silence. Then Hazel said, 'Alan, I'm so very sorry for the way I've behaved. I never really understood before why playing at Wimbledon this time meant so much to you.'

Alan let his left hand rest on her knee. 'You've nothing to be sorry for. No one can really know the mines who's not lived and worked in them. The way you've behaved has been out of love for me, and for that I count myself a lucky man.'

Hazel shivered although the heater was going and it was

warm inside the car. After a while she said, 'Tell me something, Alan.'

'Yes?'

'Who do you think you'll be playing in the finals on Saturday?'

Alan glanced at his wife in surprise, then a grin spread across his face. 'Oho, you've already got me past the Russian on Tuesday and whoever it may be in the semis on Thursday, have you?'

'Of course. Don't you think I know a winner when I see one?'

Alan relaxed and began to talk easily about the tournament and how he would play against each of his possible opponents. His eyes shone with the old excitement that had been missing for the past few days.

Hazel sat back with a soft smile and watched her husband talking. The dark shadow of fear had not gone, but she had put it away in a closed-off part of her mind.

34

Quarter-finals. Eight of the best tennis players in the world remained to contest the men's singles championship at Wimbledon. A full complement of reporters was on the scene now. Television coverage was beamed by satellite to all parts of the world. In the United States the events at Wimbledon were promoted from page three to page one of the sports section.

Shortly before two o'clock Mike Wilder sat in the Players' Tea Room talking with an earnest young man from the BBC who wore a tie that identified his school.

'Do I understand that you want *me* to appear on television tonight?' Mike said.

'That's right,' said the young man.

'I can't imagine why. Reporters interviewing each other always struck me as a waste of time.'

'It'll be just a short interview after we talk to today's winners. A view-from-across-the-Atlantic sort of thing. How an American journalist looks at Wimbledon and the English people.'

'I'm game if you are, but I'd better warn you I don't photograph well. I've got a dark beard that makes me look like a "Wanted" poster even when I've just shaved.'

'Not to worry, we can cover that with a touch of make-up. Oh, and wear something plain, will you? Stripes and plaids make too busy a picture. And a light blue shirt if you have one.'

'I have one,' Mike said.

'Splendid. Be at the studio at seven if you please.'

The BBC man flashed a set of perfect teeth and disappeared into the crowd. Mike looked after him, wishing he had got out of it somehow. The television thing would delay his dinner date with Paula, and he had come to resent anything that cut into their time together.

With a sigh he pushed himself up from the table and headed out to the courts where the quarter-final matches were about to begin.

On court one before seven thousand partisan fans, local boy Alan Doughty prepared to take on Ivan Kugarin, the Russian. Only a few years ago there were about as many tennis courts in the Soviet Union as there were polo fields. It was considered a game of decadent imperialism, unfit for the workers. However, when tennis began to attract international attention the Russians revised their thinking. They set out to master the game.

As with all their athletic undertakings, the Russians went into tennis with one goal – to be the best. The players were subsidised by the government twelve months a year. They stayed out of international competitions until the mid-1960s, when they felt they were good enough to win. A couple of years ago a Russian player got as far as the finals at Wimbledon, but that was the year the world's top players boycotted the tournament, so the achievement was tainted. Even worse, he was beaten in the championship by a Czech.

Ivan Kugarin was the best player yet to come out of the USSR. He had won several minor tournaments, and was seeded this year at Wimbledon for the first time. He played the typical Russian game – disciplined, dedicated and grim. His muscular 'trainers' were never far away. When he spoke to the press it was always through an interpreter assigned by the Soviet embassy, even though it was well known that he spoke excellent English.

Alan Doughty, playing at the very top of his form, soon found the Russian's weakness, and began to attack his second serve. Kugarin had a booming first service that was difficult to handle when it was in. However, he missed with it sixty per cent of the time, and his second serve lacked both speed and spin.

With the crowd cheering him on, Alan broke the Russian's serve early in the first set. The two watch-dogs stirred uneasily on the sidelines, and their player began to make errors. As they changed ends of the court there was a short, sharp exchange between Kugarin and his friends, and Alan knew he had him. He turned to wink at Hazel in the stands. She smiled back and gave him a thumbs-up. Alan went on to win in four sets without extending himself.

As he walked off the court Alan stopped suddenly, listening. That drumming in his ears – could it be . . .? Trying to camouflage the gesture, Alan felt his wrist to check the pulse there. Was it faster than usual after a match? He could not be sure. Seeing that people were looking at him, Alan smiled, waved and walked off the court. *Just two more matches,* he told his body. *Hold on for two more matches, and then we'll rest.*

On the Centre Court Tim Barrett was having a more difficult time with his match than was Alan Doughty. His opponent was the likeable American, Brian White. As he had all through the tournament, Tim was having trouble concentrating. He knew that as well as anyone, and he fought to keep his eye and his mind on the ball. However, he was acutely aware of the empty seat in the stands where Christy Noone should have been. She had promised to be there.

Also, there was the abrupt change that had come over his father. Jack Barrett, usually so free with advice and criticism for his son, had been strangely subdued ever since the dinner in their hotel room. After his match on Saturday Tim had apologised for walking out, but Jack had insisted on blaming himself for the argument. That too was most unlike him. Tim was sure his father was keeping something from him. But what?

Brian White, meanwhile, playing his usual controlled game, took advantage of Tim's mistakes and had him down two sets to one. Tim managed to wrench his mind back to the game long enough to win the next two sets and the match. He felt no joy when Brian congratulated him at the net. He knew if he did not get his thoughts together, next time he would lose.

The entire Australian contingent turned out to cheer for Denny Urso, the last of their countrymen still in the competition. There was a time when it was not uncommon to see two or three Aussies among the top four finishers. No more. The ageing of the old champions and the rise of tennis in the rest of the world had ended the dominance of Australia.

For Denny Urso, the whole thing was a lark. He cheerfully admitted he had come this far only by being lucky and playing well above his standard. Today that would not be enough. On this June afternoon Milo Vasquez reached into the past and came up with an echo of the devastating game that used to terrorise opponents before the drug did its work on the Mexican's body.

Milo's big serve exploded for one ace after another. At the net he was ten feet tall. Denny Urso went down in straight sets. To the gallery it looked easy. Only Milo Vasquez knew that he had drained the last drop of his vital juices in this victory. He was used up. After the final point was played he felt he could not have lifted the racket once more.

While Denny joked with players and reporters at the edge of the court, Milo brushed past them all on his way to the dressing-room. Although his body cried out in pain, he refused a massage and stood under an icy shower trying to freeze out the old hunger that was gnawing again at his guts.

The last of the day's quarter-finals pitted Yuri Zenger against the new darling of the teenyboppers, Jean-Pierre Leduc. From the time they began warming up it was evident that the crowd was cheering the French boy.

As though to show how little he cared for the cheers of the fans, Yuri began his act early – clowning, complaining, delaying, distracting. Jean-Pierre, who was used to playing according to the unwritten code of tennis etiquette, was unable to cope with the antics of the Hungarian. Before the end of the first set he was hopelessly confused and out of the match.

There was little doubt that Yuri could have beaten the French boy on sheer ability, but he chose to humiliate him, and at the same time show his contempt for the fans. His victory was received with cries of 'Shame!' Yuri's response, as he left the court, was to show the crowd an upraised finger.

The quarter-finals were over. And then there were four.

35

The quarter-finals at Wimbledon were of little concern to the people who lived in the big brick country house near Henley. They had other things to worry about. That evening the house was silent, except for the muted sound of a television set in an upstairs bedroom. Every minute or so Lady Teal would turn one of the big slick pages in *Country Life* magazine. Sir Oliver sat deep in his favourite armchair, a leather-bound book of prints unopened and ignored in his lap.

'It's been ten days now,' said Sir Oliver, as though to himself.

Lady Teal looked up from her magazine. 'What did you say, dear?'

'For ten days now Eric's lain up there in his room watching the bloody television, barely aware of what's going on round him.'

'He's had spells before.'

'Never one that lasted so long. I think we're doing him a disservice by keeping him here.'

'Oliver, you're not going to bring up the sanatorium again?'

'I don't know if he'd be better off there. Dr Ruick can provide professional help for him.'

'Dr Ruick can't provide a family. What's more, Miss Bellamy does an excellent job of looking after Eric's medical needs.'

'As far as I can see, all she does is give him vitamin pills in the morning, sleeping pills in the evening, and shove a thermometer into him several times a day.'

'She's just following the doctor's instructions.'

'But you remember Dr Ruick said it would be far better if Eric were to go to the sanatorium for a while.'

'Please don't let's discuss it any more. I want my son at home where he belongs. He's spent enough time in hospitals and sanatoria.'

Sir Oliver sighed and rubbed his eyes tiredly. 'I only hope he doesn't do anything violent – to himself or someone else.'

'Are you talking about that Wilder person who came to the house last week?'

'The man made some grave accusations.'

'The man talked rot.'

'Ann, you know better than that. Eric had no explanation of where he'd been. You saw the dents in his car.'

'Those could have happened in any number of ways.'

'Wilder had no reason to make up a story. It was we who lied to him, if you remember.'

'If it's true, then the man must have done something vile to Eric to cause him to react in that way.'

'Perhaps. Nevertheless, Wilder was quite decent about it all. He could have gone to the police instead of coming to us.'

'The police would have sent him packing in a hurry if he went to them with a story like that.'

'Yes, I dare say they would.' Sir Oliver opened his book, then closed it again and set it on a table beside his chair. 'I think I'll go up and see how he is.'

'I'll go with you.'

Sir Oliver and Lady Teal left the oak-panelled room where they had been sitting and climbed the broad staircase. They followed a passage on the first landing past the room where Miss Bellamy sat at a writing desk, and continued to the door at the end of the corridor. Behind the door they could hear the rich voice of a BBC announcer summarising the day's activity at Wimbledon.

Miss Bellamy came out of her room and joined them. 'Is there anything I can do?' she asked.

'No, thank you. Just thought we'd pop in and see how the boy is,' said Sir Oliver.

The nurse checked her wristwatch. 'It's almost time for his sleeping pill.'

'Does he *have* to take those?' asked Lady Teal.

'Yes, madam, until Dr Ruick decides otherwise. Without the sedative Mr Eric doesn't sleep at all.'

'Yes, well, if you'll wait for a few minutes before giving him his pill, we'd like to go in and talk to him first.'

'Of course, Sir Oliver.'

The old man knocked lightly on the door, then opened it. He and his wife walked into the bedroom. Eric lay in bed with several pillows propped behind his back. He watched the picture on the television screen without apparent interest. On the bed-table sat a tray of food, barely touched.

'Well, son, how's it going?' said Sir Oliver with false heartiness.

Eric rolled his head on the pillow to look at them. 'Hello, Father. Hello, Mother.'

'Anything of interest on television?' Sir Oliver asked.

'Just Wimbledon.'

'Ah, yes. I understand our chap Doughty won again today.'

'Yes.'

'Be good to see an Englishman get through to the finals for a change. Who does he play next?'

'Some Mexican.'

'Milo Vasquez, eh? It's rather a surprise to see him playing so well again. He's supposed to have contracted some mysterious illness after he won here ... what was it, three years ago? Seems longer.'

Eric turned back without answering to watch the screen again.

'Wasn't your dinner all right?' his mother asked. 'You haven't eaten much.'

'I wasn't hungry.'

'You should really try to eat more, you're getting quite thin.'

'Yes, Mother.'

Sir Oliver rubbed his hands together briskly. 'Well, then, is there anything we can do for you, old boy? Anything you'd like?'

'No, Father, there's nothing.'

Sir Oliver glanced at the television screen. A BBC commentator was interviewing a good-looking young American player who had won his match today, and would face Yuri

Zenger in the semi-finals. The player seemed distracted as he answered the questions.

'Very well, if you're sure there's nothing your mother and I can bring you . . .'

'No thank you.'

'We'll say good night, then.'

'Good night, Father.'

Lady Teal bent over the bed and kissed her son's cheek. 'Sleep well, dear. I'll come up and have breakfast with you in the morning.'

'That would be nice.'

His parents went out of the room, and Eric lay listlessly watching the people on the television screen.

How many days had he been lying here now trying to remember something? Surely it had been several days, but time was all out of focus. He knew there was something terribly important he had to do, and the time in which to do it was running out, but he could not think what it was. Every time he was about to grasp whatever it was, he was overcome with drowsiness. He did not want to sleep, he wanted to remember. The one feeling that kept returning was an overpowering sense of loss. Something had been stolen from him. Something very dear. If he could only think what it was. Or who had stolen it.

The television commentator had finished interviewing today's winners. Three of them, anyway. The Mexican fellow, it seemed, had been 'unavoidably detained'. Now the BBC man was talking into the camera.

'*For something just a bit different, we've asked a famous American journalist to come here this evening and give us his evaluation of the play so far, and perhaps add a few of his own impressions of Wimbledon and the British in general.*'

The camera pulled back to include a second man in the picture. The commentator went on smoothly:

'*It is my pleasure now to introduce Mr Michael Wilder.*'

The camera moved in for a close-up. The man's mouth moved and he spoke, but Eric Teal did not hear the words. Because suddenly he remembered.

Wilder. That was the name. And the face on the screen was

the one in the picture he had found in Paula's flat. Michael Wilder, stealer of other men's wives. Despoiler of marriages. Eric knew now what it was he had to do. Kill Michael Wilder.

He threw back the covers and got out of bed. He had to put out a hand to steady himself as a wave of dizziness went over him. Then he was all right. Thank God he had remembered in time. Wilder must not get away.

Eric found some clothes in a drawer and put them on quickly. He must lose no more time.

'Why, Mr Eric, what are you doing out of bed?'

Who was this large woman barging into his room asking questions? 'Get out of my way,' he snapped.

'You mustn't get yourself all upset, sir. Why have you got those clothes on?'

'Damn you, I said get out of my way!'

The woman stayed where she was, shaking her idiot head from side to side. When Eric started round her towards the door, she stepped in front of him. He thrust his hands out suddenly, hitting her in the chest. Taken by surprise, the woman stumbled backwards. Her heel caught in an electric flex and she fell heavily to the floor, thumping her head, and lay still.

Stupid cow, Eric thought. I told her to get out of the way.

Downstairs Eric's parents heard the noise. They exchanged a quick look, and Sir Oliver hurried out of the room, closely followed by his wife. They reached the foot of the stairs just as Eric started to come down.

'Eric, what are you doing?' said Sir Oliver.

'What day is it?' Eric demanded.

'Why, it's Tuesday.'

'Then I have four days left.'

'Four days for what?' Lady Teal asked, fluttering her hands helplessly.

'Four days to settle matters with the man who's stolen my wife.'

'Eric, that's nonsense,' said his father.

'Don't try to stop me,' Eric said. 'This is between him and me.'

Miss Bellamy appeared shakily at the top of the stairs, one

hand holding the back of her head. 'He's not rational, Sir Oliver,' she said. 'He knocked me down.'

Eric continued to descend the stairs.

'Son, come and sit down,' said his father in a calming tone. 'Let's talk about it.'

Eric reached the bottom of the stairs. Sir Oliver moved between him and the door.

'Stand out of my way, Father,' Eric said.

'Eric, don't do anything foolish.'

The butler appeared from the rear of the house. Behind him, looking uncomfortable, came the husky gardener. The butler spoke to Sir Oliver. 'Is everything all right, sir?'

'What the hell is this?' Eric snapped. 'Have you set the household staff against me?'

'I sent for no one,' said his father.

'I could not help overhearing, sir,' the butler said, 'and I took the liberty of summoning Haines.'

'Get out of my way, all of you!' Eric shouted.

'Eric, I can't let you do this,' said Sir Oliver.

Eric seized his father by the shoulders, and with surprising strength hurled him sideways against the wall.

As Eric started for the door, Sir Oliver signalled to the butler. 'Stop him, Davidson.'

The butler stepped forward and grasped Eric's wrist.

'Let go of me, you bloody fool,' Eric cried.

Davidson struggled to pin the young man's arms behind him while Eric thrashed about wildly. When it became clear that the butler could not hold him, Haines the gardener moved closer and looked questioningly at Sir Oliver. The old man hesitated only a moment, then nodded.

'I'm sorry, Mr Eric,' said Haines. He stepped forward and hit him with a short, crisp right-hand punch on the point of the chin. Eric grunted and went limp in the arms of the butler.

'Take him up to his room,' Sir Oliver said.

Haines picked him up like a sack of corn and carried him up the stairs.

'Davidson, pack a bag for my son.'

'Yes, sir.' Davidson followed the others up the stairs.

When they were alone, Lady Teal spoke to her husband. 'Why did you tell him to pack a bag?'

'Eric's got to go to the sanatorium, Ann. You must see that.'

'I suppose there's no other way.'

'The boy needs more help than we can give him here. For his own sake it's best that he's kept under close supervision, at least until this Wilder fellow is out of the country. I imagine he'll go back to America after Wimbledon.'

'I should have listened to you earlier,' said Lady Teal.

'It's all right, Ann. No permanent harm done. You run long upstairs and see how he is. I'll call Dr Ruick.'

36

On the evening following his quarter-final victory Tim Barrett
arrived at Christy's flat in Chelsea with his nerves jumping like
live wires. He raced up the stairs, taking two steps at a time,
and hammered on the door.

'For heaven's sake, wait a bit,' called Christy's voice
from within. 'I'm coming, you don't have to knock the door
down.' She opened the door and looked up at Tim in
surprise.

'You're a bit early, aren't you?' she said. 'I thought you were
coming at eight.'

'Where were you today?' Tim demanded.

'What do you mean where was I?'

'You weren't at Wimbledon. I looked for you.'

'I don't remember making any promises that I would be
there.'

'I gave you tickets for the entire tournament,' Tim said.
'Why didn't you come today?'

'Really, Tim, I don't see what difference it makes. After all,
I've seen you play three times already. What's so special about
today?'

'It was the quarter-finals.'

'Did you win?'

'Yes.'

'There, you see, you didn't miss me. I'll come out tomorrow,
probably.'

'The men don't play tomorrow. My next match is in the
semi-finals on Thursday.'

'Thursday, then. I don't see why it's important to you
whether I'm there or not with all those other people.'

'Christy, I thought we had something special together, you and I.'

Her voice softened. 'Of course we have, Timmy.' She reached up and touched his cheek, then turned and walked back into the sitting-room.

'I do like you a lot,' she said, 'but you must remember I have a life of my own.'

'I thought you'd want to be there today,' Tim said.

'There were some errands that I simply couldn't put off,' she said.

'Not even one day?'

Christy whirled to look him in the eye, and there was a flash of anger in her face that Tim had not seen before.

'No,' she said. 'Not even one day.'

Tim felt his control slipping away, but he couldn't stop the words. 'What happened, did your so-called "brother" come in from Brighton again?'

'What's that supposed to mean?'

'Take it any way you want.'

'All right, Tim,' she snapped, 'since you're so keen to know the truth, it happens I *do* have a brother in Brighton, but he hasn't been to London for six months.'

'Then last Friday . . .'

'I had a date with another fellow. Is that what you want to hear?'

'Is it true?'

'Yes.'

'How could you do that to me?'

'I didn't do anything to you except fib a little bit. And I only did that because I was afraid you'd act just the way you're acting now – like a jealous, possessive fool.'

'Goddammit, how do you expect me to act?'

'You needn't swear, you know.'

'Jesus H. Goddammit Christ, I'll swear if I want to!'

'Don't you think that's rather childish?'

'What the hell do you know about childish?'

'I know you could learn a few things about being a man from your father.'

234

Tim jumped on her words. 'What's my father got to do with this?'

Christy looked away. 'Nothing, really.'

'Yes, he has, or you wouldn't have brought it up.' Tim seized the girl's wrists and pulled her back around to face him. 'Now you tell me, what's this about my father?'

'He came to see me, that's all.'

'Here? My father came to see you here?'

'That's right, on Saturday morning. Now let go of me.'

Tim released his grip, and Christy stepped back, rubbing her wrists.

'What did he want?' Tim asked.

'He was worried about you. About your tennis.'

'I'll just bet he was,' Tim said with heavy sarcasm. 'What else?'

Christy's anger flared again. 'What else do you think? Do you think he made improper advances to me, is that what you think? Are you so bloody jealous that you suspect your own father?'

'No, I—'

'Well, if you want to know, it was the other way round.'

'What are you saying?'

'I propositioned him. Yes, I did. He's a good-looking, full-grown man, and I was attracted to him.'

'I don't want to hear this,' Tim said.

'You asked for it, mister, so you might as well hear it all. I propositioned your father about a roll in the hay, but he wasn't having any. More's the pity too, because of the two of you, I'd say he's the better man.'

Tim could only stand looking at Christy, the pain showing clearly on his face.

The anger passed, and her expression grew more gentle. She put out a hand towards him. 'Timmy, I'm sorry. I didn't mean . . .'

He did not wait to hear any more. He turned and fled from the flat, stumbling down the stairs and out into the street.

Blindly he walked through the streets as the night-time mist crept up from the Thames. Terrible brain-searing pictures flashed through his mind in spite of his efforts to keep them out. Faster and faster he walked, paying no attention to his direction, until he came to a park. He went a few yards down a path, round a corner, and found himself closed away from the city. He dropped on to a stone bench and put his head in his hands. He felt the tears run down through his fingers, and made no effort to stop them.

Tim had no idea how long he had been sitting there when he was startled upright by a gentle rapping of something wooden against the bench.

'Got some trouble, have you, lad?'

Tim looked up into the round, sympathetic face of a man who wore the uniform and helmet of the London police.

'I – it's nothing,' Tim said, fumbling for a handkerchief to wipe his face.

'I'm glad to hear that,' said the bobby. 'Seein' you all slumped over the way you were, I thought for a moment I had a victim of some foul deed here.'

'No, I was just . . . resting for a minute,' Tim said.

'Had a tiff with the girl-friend, I'll wager.'

'How did you . . .? How could you . . .?'

'My lad, after being a policeman as many years as I have, a man learns to read people just like readin' a newspaper. You've got all the signs of a young man with girl-friend problems.'

Tim looked down at his hands and didn't say anything.

'You needn't be afraid that I'm about to give you a load of advice on how to handle the lady,' said the policeman. 'If I was as bright as all that, I'd be in some other line o' work. I would say, though, that sittin' here in the park alone at this hour is not a good idea. We don't get too many bad people here in Kensington, but there's no use takin' chances now, is there?'

Tim stood up. 'You're right, officer, I'll be leaving now. Am I far from Beverley Court?'

'About half a mile, that's all. You walk back out by this path to Kensington Road, then go left past the Albert Hall. Take Exhibition Road down beyond Brompton Road, and the second turning after that will be Beverley Court.'

'Thanks, officer. Good night.'

Tim could feel the eyes of the policeman follow him back

down the path to Kensington Road. Now that he saw where he was, he knew how to get back to the hotel. He had explored the streets round here in the days just after he and Vic had arrived in the city. He must have walked up side streets from Christy's flat without paying any attention to his location.

Christy. The muscles of Tim's throat contracted as he thought of the trim blonde girl he had been so close to. What an ass he had made of himself tonight. He had no business at all getting possessive the way he had. Christy was right in calling him a child.

But damn it, why did she have to bring his father into it? No, that wasn't right. He went to see her. He must really think he had an idiot for a son.

But wait a minute. It had been three days ago that his father had gone to Christy's place. Tim had seen him several times since then, and there had been no hint of I-told-you-so in Jack Barrett's attitude. If anything, their relationship had been freer and more relaxed these past days.

What was it Christy had said? *'You could learn a few things about being a man from your father,'* Maybe he could, at that. Maybe it was time he did some growing up.

A new feeling of calm came over Tim as he walked. There was still a knot of pain in his chest over the scene with Christy, but it was small, and it would pass. Without his willing it, Tim's thoughts shifted gradually away from Christy Noone and his father. The face he saw now was that of Yuri Zenger. His concentration, like a slowly focusing beam of light, zoomed in on the Centre Court at Wimbledon and the man he would meet there in two days. For the first time in many days Tim Barrett was ready to play tennis.

37

Wednesday at Wimbledon was set aside for doubles play. Thursday would see the men's semi-finals, and Friday the women's. On Saturday the champions would be crowned in all divisions.

J. J. Kaiser spent Wednesday in the Players' Tea Room talking himself hoarse. He managed to get a few vague promises from some of the lesser players, but no contracts. His Wimbledon venture thus far had been a wash-out. Everything now depended on Yuri Zenger. Tomorrow the Hungarian would go into the semis against Tim Barrett. By that time J.J. had to have him signed, or the big boys from Wilson and Spalding would move in and Gilfillan would be out in the cold.

For that reason J.J. had not been as sharp today as he should have been. He could not keep his attention fixed on the players and the agents he talked to. He kept thinking about Yuri Zenger and Geneva Sundstrum. At J.J.'s insistence the big girl had not come with him today. He told her to take the afternoon off and go out shopping, buy herself some pretty things. J.J. did not think of it as any kind of an advance payment, even though this was the night Zenger was coming to the hotel to consummate their deal.

J.J. sat slumped now in their room as Geneva displayed the day's purchases for him.

'Yeah, yeah, nice,' he kept saying, without really seeing the things she had spread out on the bed. 'Very nice.'

'What do you think of this, J.J.?' she asked, holding up a filmy peach-coloured garment in front of her body. 'Sexy, huh?'

'Sure, sexy,' he said, not looking at it.

'Do you think I ought to wear it tonight when what's-his-name comes over?'

'What the hell do I care? Wear whatever you want.'

'Come on, honey, don't be grouchy with me.'

'I'm sorry, babe,' said J.J. 'I had a rough day. I shouldn't take it out on you.'

'Did you sign up any players?'

'No. All of them would be happy as hell to get a load of free Gilfillan samples, but they don't want to do anything for us in return.'

'It won't matter once we get the Rumanian signed up, will it?'

'Hungarian. No, it won't matter then.' J.J. shoved himself up out of the chair. 'I'll see you later.'

'Will you be in 803?'

'No, that room makes me itchy.'

'Where will you be, then?'

'I don't know. I'll be out. What difference does it make? You can handle things, can't you?'

'Sure, J.J. I just thought you might want me to call you after.'

'Don't call me, I'll call you.' It came out more harshly than he had intended, but he let it stand and banged out of the door.

What a shitty trip this one had been, J.J. thought as he rode down to the foyer. The whole thing had turned into a giant bummer. He should have known better than to bring the broad along. He had always worked alone before, and that's the way he should have kept it.

The door of the lift rattled open and J.J. stepped out into the foyer. He stood for a moment wondering what the hell to do with himself. Going to the bar was out. His attempt a week ago at dramatically drinking himself into a stupor ended abruptly with him being sick all over the front of his suit. Geneva had to come down and help him back up to the room. She mothered him back to a semblance of health, and they made love all night long and most of the following day, despite J.J.'s earlier vow of abstinence.

The rest of the week J.J. and Geneva had concentrated on

enjoying each other. The name of Yuri Zenger was not mentioned, yet the Hungarian was never far from J.J.'s mind.

He consoled himself now with the thought that after tonight it would all be over. He would have Zenger's name on an unbreakable contract and would never have to look at his ugly face again.

J.J. wandered over to the news-vendor's stand off to one side of the hall entrance. He picked idly through a rack of postcards with colour views of Buckingham Palace, the Tower Bridge, St Paul's Cathedral, Big Ben and all the other tourist attractions of London that he hadn't had time to see.

The revolving door from the street whooshed around then and Yuri Zenger strode into the hall. His silk shirt gaped open down to his navel, letting the curly black hair spill out in front. J.J. ground his teeth as he watched the Hungarian saunter over to the lift and jab the button with his thumb. He didn't wait to see any more, but pushed out through the door into the Strand and hurried away from the hotel.

As Yuri Zenger waited impatiently for the lift to arrive, a black anger boiled inside him. The cause of his anger was his friend and benefactor, Mrs Dorothy Keith. The woman had strung him along, he now saw, with promises she had no intention of making good. Yuri had made the discovery only this morning when, hearing that Lyle Coombes had returned to London, he had gone to the director's offices on Charing Cross Road. There a reluctant receptionist had been bullied into taking Yuri in to see Coombes.

With icy contempt Coombes had made it clear that he was not now, nor would he be in the foreseeable future, interested in casting non-professionals. As for the truck-driver and the barmaid, they were taken on early in his career, and luckily they had worked out. Now he had established stars waiting in line to work for him.

Yuri had raged at the man, called him a sonofabitching queer, and stormed out, his dreams of a film career in fragments. He intended then to confront Mrs Keith and tell her in plain language that from here on she could literally go fuck herself. However, going back to the house in Belgravia, Yuri cooled off as the practical side of his nature took over. He decided to say nothing to the old bag until after Wimbledon. At least he had a plush place to stay, with servants to wait on him and whatever he wanted in food and drink. Also, he figured the old bag ought to be good for a couple more of the expensive gifts she liked to thrust upon him.

So when he returned to the house Yuri merely mentioned as though in passing that he had been to see Coombes, and it looked as though they weren't going to be able to work out a deal. Mrs Keith had told Yuri how sorry she was to hear that, and had watched him carefully for some more violent reaction. However, Yuri kept his anger bottled up and pretended the whole thing was a closed issue. Mrs Keith was so relieved she did not object when Yuri told her he was going to see J. J. Kaiser this evening, and he might be out quite late.

Now, as he marched down the hall towards room 812, the suppressed anger seethed and bubbled like a capped volcano. The big golden body of Geneva Sundstrum would give him the outlet he needed for his emotions.

Yuri thumped on the door with the meat end of his fist and waited impatiently until Geneva opened it. He pushed past her into the room without bothering about a greeting. He went immediately to the telephone, yanked the instrument from its cradle and dropped it on the table.

'Nobody will interrupt us this time,' he said.

'You can't do that,' said Geneva, 'it'll just keep ringing down at the switchboard and they'll think something's wrong.'

Yuri snatched up the phone, listened for a moment, then barked into the mouthpiece, 'We want no calls to this room, do you understand? None!' He slammed the telephone back in place and spun around to face Geneva. 'Well, what are you waiting for? Get your clothes off.'

'Goodness, you're in a hurry, aren't you?'

'I've got no time for bullshit. We both know what we're here for, so let's get on with it.'

For an instant the big girl hesitated. A flicker of dislike shone in her eyes just before she reached for the buttons on her blouse. It excited Yuri all the more.

Geneva began slowly to undo the buttons. Yuri stepped

forward and batted her hands away. He grasped the material on each side and ripped it apart. Geneva wore nothing under the blouse.

'That's more like it,' Yuri said, stepping back to admire her. 'I like big tits.'

Geneva stood with her arms straight down at her sides, saying nothing.

Yuri reached out his two hands and cradled one of her breasts. 'Good and solid too,' he said. 'I like that. Now get that skirt off and let's see the rest of you.'

She unzipped the short skirt at the side and stepped out of it. This left her wearing only bikini panties of pale blue.

'Stop there,' Yuri ordered. 'I'll do the rest.' He ran his flattened hand down over the smooth, gentle mound of her belly, tracing one finger along the elastic at the top of her panties where wisps of gold curled out. He insinuated his fingers down under the flimsy material. He squeezed the soft flesh, softly at first, then harder. Geneva gasped.

'You like that, do you?' he said. 'Get over on that bed and I'll give you something to really like.'

Geneva walked across the room to the bed. She sat there with her back against the headboard. No emotion showed on her face. That was all right with Yuri. He'd have her begging for it before he was through.

Keeping his eyes on Geneva, Yuri peeled off the silk shirt. He ran a hand roughly over the matted black hair on his chest and stomach. With his other hand he slowly drew the heavy belt out of the loops of his pants. He doubled the belt and socked it against the side of his leg. He was pleased to see Geneva's eyes widen at the explosive sound it made. Some of them really liked the belt.

He walked slowly towards her, unzipping the front of his trousers. Still holding the belt, he pushed the trousers and a pair of jockey shorts down his legs with a single motion. He stepped out of them and straightened up to give Geneva a good look at his erection. It thrust upwards, angry and hard, the veins engorged with blood all along its length.

'How do you like it?' he said. 'This ought to be enough even for a big woman like you, eh?'

He waited for Geneva to say something. She didn't. That was all right, he knew she was impressed. Women always were.

He walked up to the side of the bed and stood with his standing organ inches from her face. 'Kiss it,' he told her. 'See how much you can get in your mouth.'

A sudden pounding on the door snapped Yuri's head around. He whirled and shouted, 'Whoever you are, go away and don't come back!'

The shouted answer came back through the panel. 'Open the door, you sonofabitch, or I'll kick it in!'

The voice was familiar, but the belligerent tone definitely was not. Yuri looked from the door to Geneva and back to the door. His erection drooped and died.

'I'd better open it,' Geneva said as the pounding grew louder. She got off the bed and took up a filmy robe from where it lay over the back of a chair. 'I'm coming,' she called as the door threatened to give way under the battering.

Yuri was fumbling into his pants as Geneva opened the door and J. J. Kaiser stalked into the room like an angry bantam rooster.

'Are you crazy?' Yuri said, still fumbling into his clothes.

'Get the fuck out of here,' said J.J.

'You're saying good-bye to a million-dollar deal, little man. You know that, don't you?'

'Get the fuck out of here before I break your face.'

For all his bluster on the tennis court and his loud threats against elderly linesmen and nervous ball boys, Yuri Zenger had no stomach for a fight. Besides, there was a crazy dangerous look in the eyes of J. J. Kaiser that he'd never seen before. Yuri pulled on his shirt, grabbed his belt, and edged around J.J. to get out of the door.

From the relative safety of the corridor he called back, 'You just made the biggest mistake of your life,' and hurried towards the lift.

When the Hungarian was gone, J.J. and Geneva stood for a long moment looking at each other. Then the anger drained out of J.J.'s face, and he turned to push the door shut.

'Go ahead and say it,' he told her. 'I blew the deal.'

'I guess you did, J.J.,' Geneva agreed quietly.

'That was really dumb. I mean, that act ought to win an Academy Award for dumb. J. J. Kaiser, the wise guy who knows all the angles, busting in here like some moon-struck pimply-faced high school kid. What do you think of that?'

'I think you're wonderful, J.J.,' said Geneva. 'I think you're the most wonderful, beautiful man I've ever known.'

'You're crazy, you know that?' he said. 'You're even crazier than I am.'

And then they were in each other's arms. Geneva let the robe fall open, and she enveloped J.J. in her warm, golden body.

Still locked together, they moved across the room and fell on to the bed. In moments their clothing lay in a tangle on the floor. For the first time since he was a teenager, J. J. Kaiser let himself go completely in his passion and his love. He did love this dumb golden hunk of woman. Damned if he didn't really love her.

'I love you, Geneva,' he heard his own voice say.

'Do you mean it, J.J.?'

'I mean it, Goddammit!'

'Oh, my man, my man, you're all I want in the world.'

There was no more talking then as their passion reached its peak and gushed over them in waves, then slowly subsided, leaving them spent and happy.

After they had lain together in silence for a long time Geneva said, 'What are you thinking about, J.J.?'

'I was thinking I just cost us both our jobs at Gilfillan.'

'It doesn't matter, honey,' Geneva said, nuzzling the top of his head. 'I never have any trouble finding a job, and we can live on what I make until you get into something else.'

'We?'

'Sure. You and me are going to be together from now on, aren't we?'

J. J. Kaiser thought that over. Until a couple of hours ago 'together' was a word that had been missing from his vocabulary. He decided his vocabulary, along with a few other things, could use a little upgrading.

'That's right, babe,' he said. 'Together. From now on.'

244

'And it won't bother you if we have to live on what I make for a while?'

J.J. gave her a playful swat on the rump. 'Are you kidding? Just because I make a chump of myself and fall in love doesn't mean I've turned into Joe Niceguy. I'm not about to turn down a big beautiful broad who wants to support me. There's a lot of the old J.J. in me yet.'

Geneva laughed. 'I'm glad of that.' She reached down and felt the reawakening of his desire. 'Yes, I'm really glad of that.'

38

In another, much smaller hotel room across the city, Milo Vasquez lay tense and sweaty on his narrow bed, trying in vain to
go to sleep. He had chosen this anonymous hotel east of the
Tower of London because it would be quiet, and no one would
intrude when he needed to be alone. Now the quiet screamed in
his ears like souls on fire.

With an angry motion Milo threw off the bedclothes and got
up. He snapped on the battered lamp at his bedside and pulled
on a pair of jeans and a loosely knit black sweater.

He left the room and went down the narrow flight of stairs to
the street. When he had moved in, the man at the hotel had told
him it was dangerous to walk the streets at night in this part of
London. It was not far from here, the man said, that Jack the
Ripper had done his bloody work. Milo was not impressed. He
had walked dangerous streets before.

The night mist formed pale balloons of light round the street
lamps. Milo wondered if you could ever see the stars in this
town. It was as though they hung a wet grey canvas across the
sky at night.

He walked the damp deserted streets without reading their
names. To occupy his mind he replayed, shot by shot, yesterday's match with Denny Urso. The Australian was, everybody knew, a doubles player, and had no business getting as far
as the quarter-finals in singles. Back in his glory days Milo
would have disposed of Denny as easily as swatting a fly. But in
winning yesterday he had burned up the last of his body's reserves. Every time his racket hit the ball it had sent a jolt of
pain through his body. The straight-set victory had wrung him
dry.

Tomorrow he had to play the Englishman, Alan Doughty, in the semi-finals. Milo had watched a little of Doughty's match with the Russian yesterday. He had seen enough to know it would take more than bluff and a scowl to beat the man. If Milo was to have any chance at all, he had to borrow strength from somewhere. But where?

The pub had no sign out in front. Only a dim electric bulb marked the entrance. Milo walked in without hesitating. It was as though he had an appointment there.

He ordered a beer and stood at the bar sipping it slowly, staring into the cracked mirror on the wall.

A brittle voice spoke close to his ear. 'Hello, dearie. Lonely tonight?'

Milo turned and looked into the face of a bony woman with faded brown hair and dark eye make-up. She smiled an invitation at him.

'No,' he said shortly. A woman was not what he needed.

'I could give you a good time. You'll not be sorry, I promise you.'

'Go away,' Milo said. He turned away from her and took another sip from his beer. The woman hesitated for a moment, then shrugged to show it made no difference to her, and wandered away.

In the mirror Milo let his eyes move over the faces of the people in the pub. Some smiled too much and talked too loudly, their eyes unnaturally bright. Others nodded in shadowy booths, muttering secrets to themselves. And there were the haunted ones who sweated and sniffled. Milo knew them all. He knew this place, though he'd not been here before. He'd seen it in Los Angeles, New York, Cleveland and Houston.

'Chill in the air tonight, ain't there?'

The man who spoke had been at the far end of the bar when Milo walked in. Now he was standing alongside. He was thin as a stick, and his eyes never stopped blinking.

Milo did not answer him.

'On a night like this a man wants something to fight off the chill,' the stranger continued. 'Sometimes it gets right down into your bones. Believe me, I know how bad it can be.'

'That's right,' Milo said. 'It can be bad.' He did not want to talk to this man, but he could not seem to help himself. It had been a long time since he had talked to someone who really knew what the chill was like. And the cramps. And the bloody retching when your guts turn over trying to vomit but nothing comes out because you haven't eaten for a couple of days. Nobody who hadn't been down that road could know what it was like.

'You're a South American, ain't you?' the man said.

'Mexican.'

'Same thing, almost.'

'No, it isn't.'

'I meant no offence, mate.'

'Forget it.'

The man with the blink moved a little closer. 'I hope you'll pardon my sayin' so, but you're lookin' a bit strung up tonight, as they say. Is there anythin' I could do to help?'

'I don't need anything,' Milo told him.

'Here, I wasn't meanin' to suggest that you did, mate. I could tell at a glance you wasn't sick or anythin'. The thought just come to me that you might like a little somethin' to put the roses back in your cheeks, so to speak.'

'No.'

'I've got a room just upstairs. It wouldn't take a minute.'

Milo looked down at the bar, and to his horror he saw his left fist clenching and relaxing rhythmically. The vein stood out like a blue worm. He slammed the fist down on the bar, spun away, and rushed out of the pub.

The insinuating voice of the man with the blink followed him. 'If you change your mind, mate, you know where to find me.'

Again Milo was in the streets. He walked with his head down, fists jammed in his pockets. The words of the man in the pub echoed in his mind: *I've got a room just upstairs . . . You know where to find me.*

Yes, Milo knew where to find him. He always knew where to find that kind. He thought he had rid himself of that demon, but it still lived somewhere inside him. And it was hungry.

Somewhere in the night a siren brayed. A scrawny cat fled out of a doorway as Milo passed. What the hell, he thought,

248

maybe the man in the pub had the answer. Maybe the strength he needed was waiting in that upstairs room. White powder in a spoon, held over a flame until it liquefied. Suck it up into a needle and shoot it into your blood.

Just as no one outside could know the hurt, no one could know the high. It was ten times better than being with a woman. It made you smart and strong and bigger than life. You could do anything. You were like a god. For a while.

Okay, so the feeling didn't last. Nothing lasts. Maybe one jolt now so he could sleep, another tomorrow so he could play. Then he could lay off again. That wouldn't be enough to make him sick. One jolt tonight, another tomorrow. Easy.

Milo looked up and was surprised to see he was standing again in front of the nameless pub. He must have turned round and walked back in this direction without being aware of it. Whatever it was that had pulled him here in the first place had pulled him back. Milo started towards the door. He was tired of fighting.

Before he could enter, something down the street caught his eye. A blur of colour, faint and undefined in the mist. The glow was too soft for it to be an electric sign; besides, there were none in this road. Curious, Milo began walking in that direction.

When he was half-way there Milo recognised what it was. A stained-glass window. A small window in a small church. He walked up to the plain entrance to the grey stone building and read the plaque there. 'St Xavier's.'

A name from Milo's childhood came back to him. Tía Louisa. Maybe she was not a real aunt, but he called her that. She used to take him to church on Sunday morning while his father slept off Saturday's wine. A woman with a great, gross body and arms like huge sausages, Tía Louisa had the most beautiful eyes Milo had ever seen.

'You must go to church, Milo,' she would tell him. 'Pray to the Blessed Virgin for the soul of your dear mother. Pray that you do not end up like your father, that *borracho*.'

Dimly Milo remembered the church in downtown Los Angeles with its great vaulted ceiling and the beautiful saints who looked out with compassion from their painted eyes. There was always the smell of varnish and of people freshly bathed. The musical, solemn language of the mass, the rich robes of the priest, the rituals of the altar – the boy Milo understood none of it. Yet sitting there next to Tía Louisa made him feel loved and protected, at least for a little while.

Milo entered the church. It was the first time since he was a boy. He touched his finger to the holy water and made the sign of the cross.

This church was much smaller than the one where he had gone with Tía Louisa. The wooden pews needed varnish, and the plaster of the saints was chipped. Still, the same feeling was there.

There were only a few scattered worshippers in the church, and none of them looked at him. Milo walked a little way down the aisle, knelt to the altar, and took a seat. He closed his eyes and tried to remember how to pray. It was no good. He had been away too long. A prayer from him now would be empty words.

He let his body relax and opened his mind to all the things he had locked out for so long. How he had been a champion and thrown it away. How he had betrayed the people who had believed in him. How he had spent his talent and quenched his fire in a thousand bars and bedrooms. How he had given himself to the needle.

And always there was Maria. Maria of the sad eyes. Maria crying. Maria pleading with him. Maria in pain. *Madre de Dios*, was there never a happy Maria?

Slowly Milo opened his eyes. He held on to the thought. He could not remember one single time when Maria had laughed. Not even in the first years when they were so very much in love. Always she had been sad. It was almost as though her last walk down the pier and into the sea was only the end of a journey she had begun long before.

It was not my fault alone, Milo thought. *I did not kill Maria!* He waited for the stab of guilt he always felt when he thought about Maria, but this time it did not come. And then he understood. For the part he had played in Maria's death, he had paid his debt. His penance was done.

Milo rose and walked down the aisle towards the altar. He

took a candle from the table and dropped a bank note into the cash box. He placed the candle in front of the Virgin and lighted it.

'For Maria,' he whispered. 'And for Tía Louisa. And for me.'

He knelt awkwardly and crossed himself. Then he left the church. He felt bone tired and cleansed, like after a long hard match, then a steam bath. He walked swiftly in the direction of his hotel. Tonight, at last, he would sleep. Forgotten for ever was the nameless pub and the man who blinked. Milo Vasquez had found his peace.

39

On Thursday afternoon the change in Milo Vasquez was quickly apparent to the fans who crowded the stands of the Centre Court for the semi-finals. In his previous matches the warm-up period had been a grim ritual for the Mexican player, as deadly serious as the game itself. Today he loped about the court with a casual grace most unlike the drum-tight Milo they had come to expect. Even the habitual black scowl had softened.

As play began the crowd marvelled at the new, relaxed Milo Vasquez. Not that the old power game had returned, but his strokes were picture smooth, his game steady and controlled. Once, when the crowd applauded a nice return, Milo startled everyone by raising his racket slightly in acknowledgment.

On the other side of the net Alan Doughty had to revise his own game to counter the change in Milo's. Alan's plan had been to hang back at the baseline and out-steady him, counting on the Mexican's nerves to tighten up and force him into errors. However, the new free-stroking Milo could not be handled that way. Alan was forced to go on the attack, rushing the net both on his own serve and on his return of Milo's.

Playing this slashing, aggressive game, Alan drew steadily ahead. He was leading two sets to one, and was up a service break in the fourth when the pain hit him.

It happened as he dug for the net to retrieve a well-placed drop volley. As he stretched for the ball a searing flame licked along his spine. The racket slipped from his hand, and Alan lurched into the net, grasping it instinctively to keep from falling.

The world went out of focus, and darkness rushed towards

his eyes. The sound of the crowd receded like a train down a tunnel. Alan fought to pull air into his lungs.

Dear God, he thought, not now. Not when I'm so close.

The pain eased and went away. The world swam back into view. He saw the brown face of Milo Vasquez close to his own. The coffee-coloured eyes were filled with concern.

'Hey, you all right, man?'

'I'm all right,' Alan said. 'Nice shot.'

He trotted back to his position at the baseline. He did not look up to the place in the stands where Hazel sat. There was only a faint ache now where the pain had been. A warning. The awful picture of a ruptured artery spilling blood pushed into his mind. He began to play too carefully, and he lost the set. The match was tied at two-all.

During the short break before the final set, Alan's eyes were drawn up into the stands. To his surprise, Hazel smiled at him brightly and gave him the familiar thumbs-up. Was it possible she hadn't seen what happened? No, she would not have missed his faltering step, the flash of pain that must have shown on his face. Yet she made herself smile to show she was with him. Alan saluted his wife and returned to the court.

When the fifth set began the fear left him, and Alan played his own game again. He hit out freely and ran for difficult shots without hesitation. He took charge early and won it 6–2.

When the players met at the net Milo shook Alan's hand and startled the spectators when he actually smiled.

'Nice going, man,' said the Mexican. 'It was a good win. You had me worried for a minute. I thought you were hurt.'

'Thanks,' Alan said. 'I was lucky to beat you. And, Milo, it's good to have you back.'

For a moment Milo gripped Alan's hand just a little harder. He said, 'It's good to be back.' Then he headed for the dressing-room to let the winner take his bows.

Tim Barrett took the court right on schedule for his semi-final match with Yuri Zenger. Zenger was nowhere to be seen. One of the Aussies came out to help Tim warm up. The crowd, aware of the ten-minute forfeit rule, grew restless.

Vic Goukas beckoned Tim over to the sidelines. 'Don't let

Zenger get to you,' he said. 'This is just one of his tricks – not showing up until the last minute.'

'He won't get to me,' Tim said.

'Good. Listen, everything's all right, isn't it?'

'Sure, Vic. Didn't you notice I was home early last night? I got nine hours sleep and ate a good breakfast. Believe me, I'm ready to play.'

The ageing coach stared up into the stands where Christy Noone's seat was empty again. When she didn't show up on Tuesday Tim's game fell apart and he almost got beaten. Today the boy hardly seemed to notice. He must have done some growing up in the last couple of days.

Two minutes before the match would have been forfeited, Yuri Zenger strutted on to the Centre Court. When the crowd muttered its disapproval he spread his arms and gave a mock bow. He started for the net with an exaggerated attitude of apology, but found Tim standing at the baseline with his back turned. That was Yuri's first hint that this time the young American might not be so easy to psyche out.

The Hungarian wasted no time going into his act. As Tim prepared to serve he would cough, shuffle his feet, bat invisible gnats from the air, or suddenly notice an untied shoe-lace. On his own serve he would bounce the ball ten, fifteen, twenty times while Tim waited in the knees-bent ready position. He argued on line calls, shouted at ball boys, glowered at the crowd, complained about the cameras.

None of it did him any good. Unlike Jean-Pierre Leduc, Tim had seen it all before. When Yuri went into a routine, Tim merely turned his back and waited him out. He never made the mistake of getting into a clowning contest with the master clown. By the time Yuri recognised that he could not rattle Tim, it was too late for him to get his own game together. Tim beat him decisively in four sets.

As the crowd applauded Tim's victory, hardly anyone noticed that Yuri stalked off the court without waiting for the traditional handshake. Tim only shrugged and continued to the sidelines where Vic Goukas waited, his battered face split in a grin.

'Nice going,' said the coach. 'You played like a champion today.'

'Thanks, Vic. Where's my father?'

'I don't know. He hasn't come down yet.'

Tim looked up to his parents' box and saw Jack Barrett still sitting there, making no move to come to the courtside as he usually did to share in his son's victory. He smiled at Tim and gave him a brief hands-clasped signal of the winner. Tim grinned back at his father, then turned away to talk to the reporters.

The defeat was a bitter one for Yuri Zenger. It was the first time he had lost to Tim Barrett. Always before Tim had succumbed to Yuri's psychological ploys. This time nothing worked. Coming on the heels of Yuri's fiasco with Geneva Sundstrum, the loss was particularly galling.

Yuri showered quickly and hurried out to where Mrs Keith's limousine would be waiting for him. To make matters worse, the car was not there. He vowed that the woman would pay for this slight. He would make her pay for a lot of things.

Angrily, he summoned a taxi and seethed inwardly all during the drive to Mrs Keith's house in Belgravia. As he started up the path towards the front door, the butler stepped out to meet him.

'Tell Mrs Keith I want to see her right now,' Yuri said.

The butler stood in his way. 'Mrs Keith has left the city,' he said.

'Left the city? That's not possible. She didn't say anything to me.'

'She instructed me to pack your effects, as you will be wanting to make other arrangements for the balance of your stay in London.'

The butler moved aside then, and in the entrance hall, ready to go, Yuri saw the matched set of calfskin luggage Mrs Keith had given him when he first moved in.

'Shall I call a cab for you, sir, or will there be friends picking you up?'

Yuri stared at the suitcases, then at the impassive face of the butler.

'No,' he said slowly. 'There will be no friends.'

40

The sanatorium operated by Dr Clifton Ruick was located outside Dunstable, about thirty miles from London. Set back from the road behind a tall cypress hedge, it looked like an innocent country estate. It had, in fact, once been precisely that. Dr Ruick had bought the house and grounds from a young peer who could not keep up the taxes. The doctor had converted it to a private hospital where his wealthy patients could be treated for mental problems in a genteel atmosphere.

In Eric Teal's room the television set remained tuned to Wimbledon all day on Friday. It was the women's semi-finals and selected doubles action. There were no surprises in the matches, and the tension built up for Saturday's meeting between Tim Barrett and Alan Doughty. None of this interested Eric in the least. He watched the screen only because they might swing to the press section and he could catch a glimpse of the man he hated, Mike Wilder.

Time was growing short, but Eric was nearly ready. Since he had been brought here three days ago, Eric had been a model patient. He saw at once that active resistance was useless. For all its rural charm, Dr Ruick's little hospital was quite secure, with multiple locks and white-coated attendants who looked as though they could look after themselves.

So Eric had seen to it that his behaviour was exemplary. Meanwhile, he used every opportunity to study the layout of the hospital and plan his escape. At night he would tuck the sleeping pill given him by the nurse under his tongue and only pretend to swallow it. He needed a clear, sharp mind to do what he had to do. Last night he got the last thing he needed – a roll of adhesive tape from the nurse's trolley.

In his supervised strolls about the house and grounds Eric had seen that all the entrances were closely watched or double-locked day and night. All, that is, except one – the back door into the kitchen where the staff came and went. That was his way out.

The best time would be in the very early morning, when a minimum of staff was on duty, and when watchfulness would be relaxed. As a part of his plan, Eric had got to know the night orderly, a muscular man named Hargreaves. To gain the man's confidence Eric pretended an interest in football and listened in feigned fascination as Hargreaves recounted the exploits of his beloved Manchester United.

On Friday night Eric hid the sleeping pill as usual, said good night to the nurse, and lay back to wait.

The hours crawled by. To fill the time Eric went over his plan. He would not go to Wilder's hotel this time – too many people there, too much activity on the day of Wimbledon finals. There was a much better place. A place where there would be only one witness.

Four o'clock. It was time to move. Eric got out of bed and dressed in the dark. He picked up the aluminium water bottle from the bedside table and tested it. Not satisfied, he took the bottle to the sink and filled it with water. Now it was heavy enough.

He jammed the stopper firmly into the bottle, and grasped it by the neck. Then he stepped to one side of the door and moaned softly. Nothing but silence from outside the locked door. He moaned again, louder. Footsteps this time, coming to a stop just outside. Eric groaned, ending in a convincing gasp of pain.

The lock clicked, the door opened, and Hargreaves stepped into the room. A pool of light spilled in behind him from the passage.

' 'Ere, now, what seems to be the—'

Eric hit him at the base of the skull with the filled water bottle. Hargreaves grunted and went to his knees. He toppled forward, his face smacking the hardwood floor.

Eric grasped the fallen man under the arms and hauled him over to the bed, lifting him on to it in sections. He stripped off the orderly's white jacket and laid it aside. He used the adhesive tape to bind Hargreaves's hands and feet and to gag his mouth. Eric put on the jacket and slipped out of the room.

He did not expect to be seen on the way out, but if he was, the white jacket would make him look from a distance like a member of the staff.

Eric descended to the ground floor and paused there in the hall. The only sound in the old house was the deep ticking of a grandfather clock.

Walking carefully, Eric went past the visiting rooms and the games room, through the deserted dining-room, and into the kitchen. He looked along the work-tops until he spied a thick wooden cutting board. In a drawer below this he found an array of knives. He tried several for feel, finally selecting a heavy French chopping knife with a nine-inch blade of carbon steel.

Tucking the knife carefully into his belt, Eric crossed to the door at the rear of the kitchen. He shot back the bolt of the single lock, opened the door and stepped outside. He ran across the dark lawn to the small space where the staff parked their cars. He chose a Triumph Stag driven by the young doctor on night emergency call. Knowing cars as he did, it took Eric only seconds to reach under the dash-panel and re-connect a pair of wires there, by-passing the ignition lock.

He belted himself into the driver's seat and drove out of the hospital grounds, heading south towards London. As soon as possible he would change cars to throw off any pursuit. It would never do to be caught now.

In the east the sky turned pink as dawn approached. This was going to be a beautiful day.

41

The buzz of the electric alarm clock in Paula Teal's bedroom died almost as soon as it began. Paula groaned and reached out her hand. It came to rest on the bare back of Mike Wilder.

'What time is it?' she said sleepily.

'Six o'clock.'

'It's barely dawn.'

'Sorry. I tried to catch the clock before it woke you. Go on back to sleep and I'll tiptoe out.'

'Do you often get up at dawn?'

'Hardly ever, but this is the last day of Wimbledon, and I've got a lot to do. I've been neglecting my work.'

Paula slipped an arm round him and massaged his chest. 'Playing hookey's been fun, though, hasn't it?'

He answered with a wicked laugh.

'And now you're going to leave me, are you?'

'Just for a few hours. I want to get today's column off early. Then I thought I'd go to Wimbledon and soak up some just-before-the-battle atmosphere. I'll come back here to pick you up at noon.'

'It's silly for you to drive all the way back here. I'll come and meet you at Wimbledon.'

'If you're sure you don't mind.'

'I don't mind. Now get out of here and let a girl get some sleep.'

Mike leaned over and kissed her. It began as a light, friendly kiss, but her enthusiastic response quickly turned it into something else.

'Hey, enough of that,' he said. 'I'll get no work done this way.'

'Lord, you're dedicated.'

'Go to sleep.' He dressed quickly and went out, blowing her a kiss from the bedroom door.

Paula stretched luxuriously and rolled over to the side of the bed that was still warm from Mike's body. Never had she felt so utterly content in mind and body. All the emotions she had kept locked in for so long had been released by Mike Wilder.

Then last night he had made the whole thing perfect. After making love they had sat together in bed, propped up with pillows behind them, Mike smoking and Paula drinking tea.

'Ever think of working in New York?' he had asked, a little too casually.

After a moment Paula had said, 'No, actually, I haven't. Why?'

'I was talking to the home office yesterday, and it seems Worldwide may be bringing out a new magazine. Light side of the news – features and interviews, that sort of thing. They're looking for an associate editor – somebody experienced but with a fresh outlook. I mentioned you to the boss, and he didn't say no.'

'Mike, I – I don't know what to say.'

'No hurry,' he had said. 'Think it over. I've got some vacation coming, so I'll be hanging around here for a week or so after Wimbledon. If you're interested, we could fly back together and you can talk to the people in charge.'

Interested! It was a dream come true. Not only would it be wonderful for her career, in New York she could be near Mike. Paula dozed happily for another hour or so, dreaming of the future, before she got up and took her shower.

She was drying her hair when she heard a faint sound from the other room. She snapped off the dryer to be sure. Yes, someone was out in the hall, tapping softly at the door. She belted on a robe and walked out to the sitting-room.

'Who is it?' she called.

No answer, just the continued tapping. Paula opened the door.

'Hello, Paula.'

'Eric! What do you want here?'

Eric, still wearing the orderly's white jacket, pushed his way into the room. He closed and locked the door behind him. 'You know who I want to see, Paula.'

'No. I don't know what you mean.'

'I want your lover. The American.'

Paula pulled the robe tighter and moved towards the door. 'I want you out of here, Eric, right now. Or I'll call the police.'

Eric's hand dived to his belt and came up gripping the heavy knife. 'Get away from the door, Paula. Sit down and be quiet, or I'll hurt you.'

Unable to keep her eyes off the knife, Paula backed away and sat down stiffly in a chair.

'What time is he coming for you?' Eric snapped.

'No one is coming for me.'

'Don't lie to me. Wilder has to be at Wimbledon every day. He wouldn't go to the finals without you.'

Paula shook her head, terror rising in her throat.

Eric glanced at a wall clock. 'Play starts at two this afternoon. It's just past eight now. We may have a long wait until he gets here, you and I. But that's all right, isn't it, Paula? We can find things to talk about.'

He smiled – a loose, lop-sided smile. Hatred smouldered in his eyes. He sat on the sofa, keeping the knife pointed at Paula's heart.

42

Mike finished writing his column in a little more than an hour. He read it over and decided it was the best he'd done in two weeks in London. Remarkable what a fulfilling sex life could do for a man.

He slipped the typed pages into an envelope and sent it off by messenger. Then he changed his clothes and went downstairs to have breakfast.

J. J. Kaiser and Geneva Sundstrum were sitting close together at a table near the door when Mike entered the hotel's restaurant. J.J. waved to him, and Mike walked over to say hello.

'How's it going, J.J.?'

'Great, Mike. Just great.'

'Glad to hear it. You must have signed up Yuri Zenger.'

'Nah, but who needs him. You'll never guess who called me last night wanting to sign a contract.'

'You're right, I'll never guess.'

'Tina Gottschalk.'

'No kidding.'

'I know what you're thinking. She's no Miss America, but right now I'd almost kiss her. If she'd let me.'

'That must be a helluva contract,' Mike laughed.

'It shocked the pants off me. Gottschalk tried out the Gilfillan rackets I gave her, and damned if she doesn't think they're the greatest thing in tennis since fuzzy balls. Starting at Forest Hills she'll use our stuff exclusively. Since she's going in the women's finals here today, we can't have worse than number two.'

'Nice going,' Mike said.

'He's a genius,' Geneva said.

'Baloney,' said J.J. 'I'm a lucky slob.'

Mike congratulated them both and went off to find a table, leaving the little man and the big blonde gazing happily into each other's eyes.

By ten o'clock Mike was out at Wimbledon. He stopped first at the Players' Tea Room. The usual background chatter had a desperate quality today. There was a new note of stridency in the voices. This was the last chance. Tournament organisers who had failed to sign up the stars scrambled for second-line players. Agents who hadn't made deals tried to explain to their clients. Players who had priced themselves too high offered to go for less.

Mike left the uproar of the tea room and walked down to the relative quiet of the Centre Court. The stands were just beginning to fill up. Paula was not yet in the box he had reserved for her, but it was still early.

Down at the end of the court where the trophies and the cheques would be awarded, the reporters had an impromptu press conference going with Tim Barrett's mother and father and Alan Doughty's wife Hazel. Mike walked over to listen.

There was not much going on worth writing about. Jack Barrett begged off on all questions about how he thought Tim would do today. 'You'll have to talk to my son,' he said. 'Tim's the player. I'm just here to enjoy the match.' Mrs Barrett smiled and agreed with her husband.

Hazel Doughty told them she was very proud of her husband. She was happy that the English people had taken Alan to their hearts. She knew he would do his best this afternoon.

Mike saw the flicker of anxiety that she tried to hide. His thoughts returned to the opening day when Hazel told him of her worry that something was troubling Alan. He wondered if she ever found out what it was.

Mike prowled round the grounds, watched the doubles players warm up, ate a dish of strawberries and wondered why Paula wasn't there yet. Maybe she was held up in the traffic. He should have picked her up.

When Tim Barrett and Alan Doughty came out to warm up

for their match on the Centre Court, Paula still had not arrived. Mike decided he might as well go on up to the press enclosure. He could see Paula's box from there, and when she came in he would go down and join her.

Both players looked in fine condition as they stroked the ball easily back and forth. The crowd stirred in anticipation of the battle to come. The warm-up ended and they spun a racket for service. Tim Barrett won and was given fresh balls from the green refrigerator behind the umpire's chair. The match was on.

At that moment an usher walked up to Mike's seat. 'Excuse me, Mr Wilder,' he said, 'there's a gentleman downstairs who wishes to speak to you.'

'What's the matter, doesn't he know I'm working?'

'He said it was urgent.'

Immediately Paula came to Mike's mind. An accident? He said, 'Who is the man?'

'Sir Oliver Teal.'

It took Mike a moment to shift mental gears. What could the father of Paula's ex-husband want with him? He left his seat and followed the man down under the stands.

Sir Oliver was standing just inside the entrance. He waited until the usher had gone before he spoke.

'I'm afraid there's been an unfortunate occurrence.'

'Yes?'

'First I should apologise to you for not being candid when you came to my house and asked about my son. You see, the story we told you—'

'Never mind that,' Mike cut in. 'I knew he was there. What's happened?'

'Last Tuesday Eric showed signs of violence, and we found it necessary to have him taken to a sanatorium run by a doctor friend. Early this morning Eric overpowered an orderly and escaped. Knowing the threats he has made against you, I came here to warn you.'

'You didn't call the police?'

'Eric has committed no crime.'

'But he's dangerous.'

'That's only an assumption.'

'It's a pretty damn good one. His former wife was supposed to meet me here this afternoon. She hasn't shown up.'

'Eric wouldn't harm the woman. I'm sure of it.'

'You've been wrong about him before, remember?'

Mike considered and immediately rejected calling the police himself. The old man was right; Eric had committed no crime. In the time it would take to convince somebody Paula was in danger he could be there himself. He started out of the grandstand at a run.

'Where are you going?' Sir Oliver called after him.

'To Paula's place to see if she's all right.'

'Why don't you telephone?'

'If Eric's there I don't want to alert him.'

'Let me come along. If my son *is* there I may be able to help.'

Mike had no time to argue. 'Come along, then.'

Showing surprising agility for a man of his age, Sir Oliver loped along behind Mike to where the Ford was parked. They jumped inside and Mike snapped the engine to life.

In the Centre Court a spatter of applause went up as Tim Barrett held his first serve. Outside the sound was lost in the squeal of rubber as the little car swerved out of the car park and headed for the city.

43

'You look tired, Eric. Wouldn't you like to lie down? Can I make you some tea?' Paula knew she was babbling, but she had to try to distract Eric somehow. As the morning slipped into afternoon he had grown increasingly nervous. His hands played constantly with the knife.

The action at Wimbledon flickered on Paula's television set. Barrett had just broken Doughty's serve, and led in the first set, 5–3. Eric pointed the knife blade at the screen. 'You don't suppose your lover went to Wimbledon without you?'

'I don't know, Eric. I told you he wasn't coming here.'

'You're lying to me, Paula. You've given him some signal that I'm here, haven't you?'

'How could I? I've been just here in this chair ever since you came in.'

For a moment Eric looked puzzled, then his eyes turned crafty. 'Oh, you're clever, I'll give you that. Clever enough to conceal your filthy affair as long as you did. Damned faithless wife!'

'Eric, I'm not your wife any more,' Paula said carefully. 'You've been ill. You should lie down.'

'Oh, yes, you'd like that, wouldn't you? Everybody wants me to lie down and take sleeping pills. If they get enough sleeping pills into me I may never wake up. Well, someone's going to die here today, but it won't be me.'

On the television screen, unwatched by captor or captive, Tim Barrett held his service to win the first set, 6–3.

Paula's eyes widened suddenly as Eric rose from the sofa and moved towards her.

'What are you going to do?'

'Part of the trouble is that you're too pretty. That's why you attract other men. That's why you get into trouble. I can stop that.'

'Eric, don't!' Paula jumped up and backed round the chair. She backed into the wall and was trapped.

'It will be best if you stand still,' Eric said. 'Otherwise I may cut deeper than I want to.'

As Eric reached for Paula's robe a fist hammered the door and Mike Wilder's voice shouted through the panel.

'Paula, are you in there? Are you all right?'

Eric seized Paula and spun her around in front of him. He pressed the knife blade against the pulse in her throat.

'Answer him,' he rasped in her ear. 'But be careful what you say.'

'I – I'm in here, Mike,' she called, her voice faltering.

'Can he get in?' Eric whispered.

Paula nodded.

'Tell him to come.'

Paula felt his right arm grow tense across her breast. She said, 'C-come in, Mike.'

A key scraped in the lock, the door swung open, and Mike Wilder took two steps into the room before he stopped short at the sight of Eric holding the knife to Paula's throat.

'Stay where you are or I'll kill her,' Eric said.

Mike froze and Eric eased round him towards the door, keeping Paula and the knife in front of him.

Sir Oliver Teal appeared in the doorway.

'Eric, what are you doing? Put down that knife!'

'Get out of here, Father. You shouldn't be here.'

'Let go of the girl, Eric.'

'I'm warning you, Father, get out or I'll cut her throat.'

'Do as he says,' Mike snapped. 'Out!'

Sir Oliver's eyes flickered from one of the men to the other, then he backed into the corridor.

Keeping Paula before him, Eric side-stepped the rest of the way to the door and slammed it shut. He shot the bolt into place

267

and flung the girl away from him. She stumbled and fell to the floor.

'Eric, you've got to stop this!' she cried.

'Stay where you are, Paula,' Mike ordered, keeping his eyes on Eric and the knife.

Eric held the weapon low, the blade angled upwards at Mike's mid-section. He moved it back and forth in a short arc, his free hand held away from his body for balance. Mike tensed for the attack.

Without warning Eric sprang at him, the point of the knife stabbing at his belly. Mike danced to one side and lashed out with his right hand to deflect the knife thrust. The blade caught his arm and sliced it from wrist to elbow. Eric stumbled off balance for an instant, and Mike stepped back, momentarily out of reach. There was no feeling in his right arm.

The sight of blood soaking through Mike's sleeve roused Eric to attack again. He forgot about the knife-fighter's stance, and charged in with the weapon held high for a downward strike. Mike leaped to the rear and the knife split the air an inch from his chest. He stepped forward again, and put all his weight behind a left hook to the kidney.

Eric gasped, and the sudden pain paralysed him for a second. It was all Mike needed. His first hook split Eric's mouth like a ripe tomato. The second broke his jaw. Eric collapsed as though his bones had dissolved.

As Mike retrieved the fallen knife, footsteps pounded up the stairs and something hard banged on the door.

'Are you all there?' called a man's voice.

Mike nodded to Paula, who had started towards him, and she went over and unlocked the door. Two uniformed policemen rushed in, followed by Sir Oliver Teal. Mike handed the knife to one of the policemen, then sat down on the sofa. Sir Oliver knelt beside his son, and Paula hurried to Mike.

'Darling, your arm . . .' she said.

Mike stripped off his shirt and took a look at the wound. It was long and clean, not too deep. The blood oozed out slowly. He clenched his fist and all the fingers worked. No veins were cut, no tendons severed.

'It's nothin', ma'am,' he said. 'Only a scratch.' Then he fainted.

On the unwatched television screen Alan Doughty won the second set, and the match was even at one–all.

44

'You're mad, you know,' Paula said as she and Mike ran from the Wimbledon car park to the Centre Court grandstand. 'You ought to be in hospital with that arm.'

Mike patted the fresh bandage gingerly. 'Nothing to it. They patched it up at the emergency station good as new. Anyway, I'm over here to cover Wimbledon. How would it look if I miss the finals? What's happening now?'

Paula put the transistor radio to her ear and slowed her step for a moment to listen. 'Sets are two–all, it's 6–5 in the fifth set, and . . . somebody's serving for the match.'

'Who? Who's serving for the match?'

'I couldn't hear, there was too much static.'

'Come on, let's get inside.'

Mike and Paula reached the courtside just in time to see the last point of the match – a booming overhead off a short lob that no mortal man could have returned.

In a gesture seldom seen in today's big-money tennis, the loser sprinted forward and leaped the net.

'Congratulations, Alan,' he said. 'You're the champion. You earned it.'

Alan Doughty took the young man's outstretched hand. 'Thank you, Tim,' he said. Then he added the sincere compliment of a fine player to a defeated opponent. 'I played well today.'

The players walked together to the side of the court where they shook hands with the umpire. Then Tim moved away to let Alan accept the applause of the crowd.

Tim walked over to the section of the stands where his parents sat.

Jack Barrett reached across the low wall and gripped his son's hand. 'I'm proud of you, Tim,' he said.

Tim looked deep into his father's eyes. He saw something there he had never recognised before. He saw love.

As the reporters clamoured for his attention, Alan Doughty held them off for a moment while he wrapped his arms round his wife.

'We did it, love,' he told her.

'Thank God it's over,' she said.

'Will you make a phone call for me after the ceremonies? I'll be tied up with the reporters for a bit.'

'Of course. Who do you want me to ring?'

'The doctor. Get him to book me in for surgery on Monday. You and I will have tomorrow to ourselves, then I'll go in and get that little job done I've been putting off.'

Hazel kissed her husband and watched with a swell of pride as he walked straight and tall towards the victory stand.

Mike Wilder watched Paula's face as they listened to Alan Doughty's short speech of acceptance.

'I want to thank all the people who have cheered for me, win or lose, over the years. We've come over a long road to be standing here today. This victory belongs to England.' When the cheers and applause finally subsided he added, 'This was my last game. Never was there a better way for a man to go out. Thank you all.'

Paula wiped tears from her eyes and turned to Mike. 'Why does he do that?' she asked. 'Why does he retire from the game when he's at the very top?'

'I'm not sure,' Mike said, 'but somehow I've got a feeling we're looking at one gutty Englishman.'

The reporters surrounded Alan Doughty then, and the television cameras moved in.

Paula said, 'What do you have to do now, interviews and things?'

'No, I'd just be in the way. Let's get out of here.'

As they walked arm in arm out to the car park Mike said, 'About that New York job ... there's one catch I probably should have mentioned.'

'Oh?'

'It includes a possible long-term arrangement with a heavy-smoking, near-sighted sportswriter. Will that have any effect on your decision?'

Paula brought Mike to a stop, stood on tiptoe, and kissed him on the mouth. 'It will,' she said. 'I'll take it.'